ATTEMPTED THEFT

As Leah rang Brandy up in stoic silence, I went and grabbed Theo from the back.

"Saw you talking to the bookstore chick," he said. "Get her number? She's hot."

"She's also a complete jerkwad," I replied. "Let's get out of here. It's burger o'clock."

Theo and I hung back as Leah bagged Brandy's book, and then we all filed out the door. Only once we were gone did Brandy ask me what had really happened in there with Leah.

"Nothing," I said. "Sheesh."

I mean, no wonder Aunt Holly and Grandma didn't like her. You did one tiny little thing that she wasn't into, and she became insta-bitch.

Brandy dropped it after that, but as we walked to the diner and ate dinner and hung out and then went home, I kept coming back to the scene in the bookstore. It worried me.

Not because Leah had caught me with her phone and I was probably on her shit list until the end of time. I couldn't care less about that. I was worried because, even after I'd stolen it away, that mole was still there, above the left corner of her lip.

OTHER BOOKS YOU MAY ENJOY

The Accident Season	Moïra Fowley-Doyle
The Alex Crow	Andrew Smith
The Art of Wishing	Lindsay Ribar
The Fourth Wish	Lindsay Ribar
Grasshopper Jungle	Andrew Smith
Half Bad	Sally Green
Legend	Marie Lu
Rebel Belle	Rachel Hawkins
Spontaneous	Aaron Starmer
Trouble Is a Friend of Mine	Stephanie Tromly
Wink Poppy Midnight	April Genevieve Tucholke
The Young Elites	Marie Lu

ROCKS FALL,
EVERYONE DIES

SPEAK
An imprint of Penguin Random House LLC
375 Hudson Street
New York, New York 10014

First published in the United States of America by Kathy Dawson Books,
an imprint of Penguin Random House LLC, 2016
Published by Speak, an imprint of Penguin Random House LLC, 2017

THE LIBRARY OF CONGRESS HAS CATALOGED THE KATHY DAWSON BOOKS EDITION AS FOLLOWS:
Names: Ribar, Lindsay, author.
Title: Rocks fall, everyone dies / Lindsay Ribar.
Description: New York, NY : Kathy Dawson Books, [2016]
Summary: "A paranormal suspense novel about a seventeen-year-old boy who
can reach inside people and steal their innermost things—fears, memories, scars, even
love—and his family's secret ritual that for centuries has kept the cliff above
their small town from collapsing"—Provided by publisher.

Identifiers: LCCN 2015030144 | ISBN 9780525428688 (hardback)
Subjects: | CYAC: Magic—Fiction. | Supernatural—Fiction. | Families—Fiction. |
Love—Fiction. | BISAC: JUVENILE FICTION / Fantasy & Magic. | JUVENILE FICTION /
Love & Romance. | JUVENILE FICTION / Social Issues / Values & Virtues.

Classification: LCC PZ7.R3485 Ro 2016 | DDC [Fic]—dc23
LC record available at http://lccn.loc.gov/2015030144

Speak ISBN 9780147517616

Printed in the United States of America

Design by Maya Tatsukawa

1 3 5 7 9 10 8 6 4 2

ROCKS FALL, EVERYONE DIES

LINDSAY RIBAR

speak

CHAPTER ONE

Brandy and Theo were about to break up. They just didn't know it yet.

They were fighting about this movie they'd seen last week, and Theo was going, "What's the point? The whole plot was just an excuse for explosions!"

Brandy responded with, "The explosions *are* the point," which I mentally added to the long list of reasons she was basically the hottest girl on the planet.

Me? I dipped yet another French fry in ketchup, shoved it into my mouth, and watched the action unfold.

Theo—poor, clueless Theo—just went, "Well, it was stupid," and took another giant bite of his burger. I'd already finished mine.

"You always think stuff I like is stupid," said Brandy. You could practically see the exact moment when she reached the end of her rope. "Always. God. You don't even *try* to like my stuff."

"I do so try," replied Theo. "I saw the movie with you, didn't I?"

"Yeah, because you wanted to grope me when the lights went down." Brandy tossed her hair, and I shoved a handful of fries in my mouth to keep myself from grinning.

Oh yes. Here it came.

"I swear, I don't know why I was ever into you."

"Wha . . . what?" Theo was so totally perplexed by now, I almost felt sorry for him. "You were plenty into me yesterday. Hell, you were into me five minutes ago."

It was four minutes ago. I'd been keeping track. But I didn't say anything, obviously. Just chewed my food in silence, trying not to let on how much I was enjoying this.

Unfortunately, Brandy's reply was interrupted by the sudden sound of a Black Keys song blasting into the quiet diner. My cell phone. Aunt Holly's ringtone.

"Hello?" I said. Beside me, Theo called Brandy a very rude name.

"Ma says there's a fault in the stone," said Aunt Holly in her usual curt voice. "How soon can you be home?"

Normally I would have pointed out that the house she shared with Grandma wasn't technically home for me—but there was no point in arguing semantics with people as easily provoked as her. So I just said, "Fifteen minutes if you make me walk. Five if you pick me up."

"God, you're lazy." She sighed. "All right, just meet us at the May Day field. Ten minutes." The line went dead.

"Guys, I have to go," I said, grabbing my jacket and easing out of the booth. "The relatives require my presence."

"See? That's another thing," said Brandy, without even missing a beat. "Look at the relationship Aspen has with his family. They call, he comes running. And vice versa, probably. That's how it should be! But all I ever hear from you is how much you hate your parents."

Brandy, on the other hand, called her father every single night after dinner. She pretended like it was her idea, as opposed to a product of her dad's all-encompassing paranoia about basically everything, but you could tell it was a pain in her ass.

Theo sputtered pathetic half words as he sank lower and lower into his seat. I couldn't blame him. Brandy always looked like a vengeful goddess when she got angry, and this was probably the angriest I'd ever seen her. I was kind of sorry I had to leave.

But up here, a call from Aunt Holly trumped everything—even something as potentially life-changing as this fight. I slipped a ten onto the table to cover my meal and headed for the door just as the waiter came over, probably to ask Brandy and Theo to lower their voices.

It was a gorgeous summer upstate New York night, the likes of which you never get down in the city. Instead of air conditioners spitting dirty water onto overheated sidewalks, Three Peaks was all cool mountain air tinged with the remnants of a hot day. Cool enough that I was comfortable in my long-sleeved thermal, warm enough that I didn't need another layer over it.

I made a left out of the diner and started walking down Main. Past the Bean Barn coffee shop, past the cutesy boutique clothing stores—closed for the night by this point—and past the single grocery store, which marked the point where the commercial section of town ended and the residential one began. A few minutes later, even the houses grew sparser, until there were only woods. To my left, at least.

To my right, lawns and well-groomed trees gave way to a wide, flat expanse of grass, so well-maintained that it could've been a soccer field, if not for the giant oak tree that stood right in the middle.

The May Day tree. This was where all the citizens of Three Peaks left little presents once a year, as some kind of . . . tribute? Payment? Something like that. I'd never been here for an actual May Day party, so I didn't know what all the gifts were supposed to mean. But I did know that they stayed under the tree until the Quick family—my family—came to get them.

I'd visited the tree several times over the past few years, always as a precursor to my family's triad ritual, but this was my first visit of the summer. Anticipation coursed through me.

When I reached the tree, I ducked under its branches and surveyed the trunk. Or rather, the giant pile of *stuff* surrounding the trunk. It looked more or less the same as it did every year: a collection of weird little odds and ends left by people who maybe were superstitious, or maybe liked tradition a little too much, or maybe both.

The first time I saw it, back when I was just a little kid, I thought it looked like a pile of magic.

Tonight, there was better magic happening at the diner I'd just left. I checked my phone, just to see if either of my friends had texted me—if the breakup had happened already, or if there was still fighting left to be done.

Nothing yet, though. Well, nothing except a text from Mom. Her second of the day; her tenth of the week. I deleted it without reading it, like I'd been doing for months.

Footsteps swished in the grass, steadily approaching. I looked up, and there was Aunt Holly coming my way, tall and straight-backed and dressed in what looked like a business suit. Her hair, the same dirty blond as Dad's, was pulled severely back from her face. I wondered if she'd come right from her office.

A few strides behind her was Grandma, a little bit shorter and rounder than Aunt Holly, her iron-gray curls making a halo around her smiling face. Hands in the pockets of her slacks, she ambled across the May Day field with the ease of someone forty years younger.

"Beat you here," I said as they approached.

"So you did," Grandma said, her voice as warm as always. "How was the lake?"

Theo and Brandy and I had spent every afternoon this past week at the big lake over in Elmview. Theo would play chauffeur in his fancy new car. We'd rent a canoe, paddleboat, something like that, or we'd chill out on the beach and pass around a bottle of whatever I'd picked up with my fake ID. After that, it was back to Three Peaks for burgers at the diner.

I shrugged. "It was whatever. Same as yesterday, same as the day before."

With a snort, Aunt Holly wandered over to the trunk of the May Day tree to inspect the pile, apparently eager to get the ritual started. Or maybe her eagerness was less about getting it started and more about getting it over with, so she could go back to hiding in her room and getting wasted.

Grandma, though, paid her no mind. She just patted my cheek with one warm hand and said, "It must be nice, having your friends here with you for the season."

"Yeah, it's cool," I said. It was true, too. I'd always liked spending time with Grandma, and Aunt Holly used to be okay back when my cousin Heather was still around—but this year, with everything so different, it was nice to have Theo and Brandy there as buffers. Even if it meant being a constant third wheel in their relationship.

Not that *that* would be a problem anymore. At least I hoped it wouldn't.

"You said two, right?" asked Aunt Holly impatiently. She was pacing around the tree, taking in the objects that lay there. A lopsided pottery bowl. A lanyard bracelet. A small plastic ring decorated with a large plastic ruby. A one-eyed teddy bear. Several action figures. A crapload of CDs. Books, pencils, envelopes, shoes, random pieces of paper. "What's the nature of the fault?"

Grandma glanced over at her. "Hm," she said, and closed

her eyes. Her hands began moving through the air like a spider's legs, like she could feel something there that we couldn't.

"One throwaway, one gift," she said at last. "One male, one female. Balance. That one."

Eyes still closed, she pointed into the pile, directly at a small plastic Batman that was missing its left arm. Aunt Holly bent and picked it up, cradling it to her chest like a baby.

"And that one," added Grandma, pointing to another place in the pile. To a book. This time, it was me who picked it up. *The Hound of the Baskervilles* by Sir Arthur Conan Doyle. I'd never read it.

Grandma looked back and forth between Aunt Holly and me for a second, then nodded, satisfied. "Come on," she said, and started across the field again, in the opposite direction from the diner.

I didn't ask why she'd chosen the Batman figure and the book. I'd given up asking about that stuff a while ago, because all Grandma would ever say was something like, "The Cliff wants what it wants. It's my job to find the closest energy match."

Which, yeah, made basically no sense at all. But that was fine. As long as the ritual kept working and the Cliff kept standing, I was good.

My grandmother's house was truly ridiculous. It had probably started as a shack or something, but since it was first built back in . . . whenever . . . so many extra floors and extra wings and other stuff had been added, now it was this crazy sprawling mansion that looked like it fell out of a Guillermo del Toro movie. There were turrets, for god's sake. Three of them.

Leaving our shoes by the front door, per Grandma's rule, the three of us headed for the den. Aunt Holly locked the sliding door behind us. She always did that for the ritual, but it was especially important now that Theo and Brandy could show up at any moment. Neither of them knew what my family did to keep the Cliff standing and the town safe, and I'd been expressly forbidden from telling them.

As if there was a chance in hell that I'd ever say anything. I mean, come on.

Grandma started the fire while, across the room, Aunt Holly slid a familiar wooden box out from underneath the love seat. I crept up behind her, ready to fish one of my leaves out.

"Do you mind?" she snapped, hugging the box closer to her chest, using the expanse of her back to block my view.

I was all ready to snap right back at her, but before I could, Grandma caught my eye and shook her head. I sighed, bit back my reply, and gave Aunt Holly her space. Normally I'd've ignored Grandma and told Aunt Holly not to be such an asshole—but it'd been less than five months since she'd lost Heather. She had the right to be a little bit of an asshole, probably. So I kept my cool. I went back to the fire and let my aunt do the leaf thing on her own.

In the fireplace, the flames danced like brightly colored ghosts, the logs beneath them crackling. For the first time, though, I noticed something else. Something buried under the logs, burning hotter and hotter as I watched. I squinted, trying to see what it was.

"Why's there a rock in there?" I asked.

Grandma came and stood beside me. "There's always been a rock in there."

"Oh," I said, feeling kind of dumb. "Huh. But why?"

"It's a piece of the Cliff," said Grandma. "When the flames touch it, they forge a connection with the stone and, through it, with the Cliff itself."

I nodded, rubbing my neck as the meaning of it sunk in. The rock was a conduit. Another link in the chain, just like me. Cool.

Finally, Aunt Holly finished her business with the box of leaves. She came back over to join us by the fire, holding three dry leaves in her hand. One long and thin, one small and spiky, one shaped like a fat teardrop.

"Oak, Ma?" she asked Grandma.

"Oh, yes, yes," said Grandma, and dug into her pocket. She, too, produced a leaf—only this one was green and freshly picked. An oak leaf from the May Day tree. Aunt Holly reached for it, but Grandma pulled it back. "Maybe our Aspen should go first. It being his first ritual of the year."

Shivers erupted in my stomach, but I didn't let on. I loved doing this. Being part of an ancient tradition. Using my magic for something bigger than myself. And, yeah, let's face it: showing off just how good I was at this stuff. Because I was *very* good.

"Yeah, let me," I said, reaching for the leaves.

Aunt Holly's lips tightened, but she handed over one of the dry leaves: the teardrop-shaped aspen.

Holding the leaf inches away from the fire, I repeated the words that my family had been taught since basically the beginning of time: "My name is my self, and I give them both freely." And I let my namesake fall into the fire. As it burned, I let myself imagine the flames connecting me to the stone beneath the logs, then to the Cliff, over a mile away.

"My name is my self, and I give them both freely," said Aunt Holly, and fed the spiky holly leaf into the fire. Grandma did the same with the willow leaf.

When all the leaves had crumbled to ash, Grandma silently gave the oak leaf to the fire, too—and that was when everything changed. The flames rose higher. They turned a thousand different colors at once, then finally settled into an eerie, unnatural shade of blue-green-turquoise. The flames stopped giving off heat, but kept flickering just like a real fire.

This

was

awesome.

"The toy first," said Grandma.

Aunt Holly held Batman out to me. "You do the reaching," she said. "I'll do the sending."

Grandma, who could do neither, nodded in agreement. That was fine. I preferred doing the reaching anyway. Sending was boring.

I took Batman from her and closed my eyes. I always felt things better when I didn't rely on sight.

Running my hands over Batman's torso, legs, and pointy-eared head, feeling the fabric cape between my fingernails, I looked for a place to reach in, beyond the physicality of the object and into the invisible something that would point me in the right direction. Toward the person who'd owned it, and then given it to the May Day tree.

Only when my finger touched the empty left arm socket did I find the place. I wasn't just holding an action figure anymore. I was holding a well-loved thing that was most at home in the hands of one specific boy. The figure remembered the boy as he was now, a confident teenager who'd recently convinced himself that he no longer needed his broken childhood toys—and as he'd been years ago, a reckless grade-schooler who knew in his heart that when it came to toys in general, and action figures specifically, *broken* was just another way of saying *favorite*. Which was why he hadn't minded when, during a particularly vicious battle against Wonder Woman, Batman had lost his left arm.

A sense of lost attachment to his toys? Maybe that was something I could take.

"Not enough," said Grandma, startling me a little. "Aspen, this fault will need something stronger—something *brighter*—in order to heal. Even though the things we take are all just energy by the time they reach the Cliff, that energy comes in different flavors, different strengths—"

"I know, I know," I interrupted, but without annoyance. Grandma did that sometimes. Slipped into teacher mode during the triad ritual. I guess it came with the territory of having to teach the ritual's ins and outs to whoever had time to come visit and help her out.

"I know you know," she teased. "So get on with it."

I reached further into the boy who'd owned Batman. There was a persistent lack of caring about his grades, even though he had a solid B average. A fierce, protective love of his family, even when he hated them. A strong, slow-burning love for a particular girl, who he'd first noticed in fifth grade, when she'd beaten him in a field day race. Tendrils of friendship stretching outward in many directions, immovable and important. A confidence in his ability to play football, basketball, soccer, table tennis, regular tennis, god this was a lot of sports . . .

Ah. A competitive streak.

Maybe that was what I needed. Something bright, as Grandma had said—but still something he wouldn't necessarily miss when it was gone.

Got it, I thought—and then realized I'd said the words aloud. I opened my eyes to see Grandma nodding thoughtfully at me.

"An inclination toward competition," said Grandma, squinting again as she regarded me. "Toward winning.

That's good work, boy. Subtle, strong, definitely bright. Good. Take it out."

That was the cue I'd been waiting for. Closing my eyes again, I hooked my will into the boy's competitive streak like it was a physical thing. It took a moment to pry loose, which wasn't surprising since it was so deeply rooted in his personality—but I managed it.

Ritual reaching wasn't the same as everyday reaching. When I reached into people and took stuff away, I usually did one of three things with it: absorbed it into myself, gave it to someone else, or released it. The ritual, though, required pushing my talents in a slightly different direction.

Concentrating hard, I guided the energy of the kid's competitive streak toward the fireplace . . . and there it sat, a glowing orb of orange-yellow-purple, actually visible where before it had just been a very solid idea.

Grandma put her hand on my shoulder, looking so very proud. "Good work, Aspen. Very good. As always. Now, Holly, your turn."

"I *know*, Ma," she said irritably.

Grandma raised her eyebrows, but didn't reply.

I stepped back from the fireplace, my knees like jelly, my body suspended between drunk and hungover, my mind suspended between my own consciousness and that of the person I'd just stolen from. Not terrible, as far as reaching hangovers went, but still incredibly disorienting. To say the least.

That was why this ritual needed three people. The thing

in the fireplace was already beginning to flicker and fade, and soon it would disappear completely if someone didn't step in and point it in the right direction. And in my current state, there was no way that someone could be me.

Aunt Holly moved toward the fire, sleeves rolled up, and took the orange-yellow-purple thing into her hands. She didn't do anything. Just stared at it. And stared. And stared. And as she kept staring, her hands started moving together, slowly, shrinking the glowing ball into a tinier, more compact version of itself.

I smiled. This was part of why I loved the triad ritual. Normally, the reaching stuff that my family did was totally invisible. But when we were linked to the fire like this, I could see everything. The results of my reaching were right there in front of me, glowing and pulsing. And I could watch as Aunt Holly sent it, converted by the fire into pure energy, to the Cliff—the giant wall of rock that loomed over the town of Three Peaks—mending the fault in its stones, making it whole again.

The whole thing was undeniably badass.

"Did it work?" said Aunt Holly, turning toward Grandma.

Grandma's eyelids fluttered closed, and she did that spider-legs thing with her hands again. After a moment, she said, "We've made progress. Now, the book. Take something different this time, Aspen. Something a little less bold. A little smaller, perhaps. A little more personal. Whenever you're ready."

By now, my head was clear enough. Setting the Batman figure down in front of the fire, I picked up the battered little paperback instead. Closed my eyes. Ran my hands over it, looking for a place to reach in.

I found it when I brought the book up to my nose and breathed in its dusty, musty, old-paper smell. A person came into focus in my head. A girl, seventeen, like me. Quiet about some things, loud and opinionated about other things. The book had traveled in her backpack, slept under her pillow, gone away to friends' houses and come back missing her. Or maybe she'd missed the book, not the other way around. It was hard to separate the two, with the smell of paper in my nose and the feel of rounded page corners against my fingers.

Reaching further into the book's memory of her, I dug around for something I could take. Her lingering guilt over a friendship she'd lost? Her loyalty to her boss at—where was it—ah, a local bookstore? The crush she had on one of her friends? Maybe that would do the trick.

"Not enough," said Aunt Holly in a harsh voice that jolted my eyes right open. She was staring at me. Glaring. Yeah, that was the other thing about the ritual. Normally, when I reached, I didn't have an audience. Even the person I was reaching into couldn't tell I was doing it. But during the ritual, everything and everyone was connected. Which meant Aunt Holly and Grandma could watch me as I worked.

"Ma said something personal," Aunt Holly went on. "Weren't you listening?"

I thought a crush was plenty personal, but Grandma didn't contradict her, so I just nodded and closed my eyes again. Reached.

"Is that who I think it is?" I heard Aunt Holly whisper. "That girl, *again*? Didn't we just deal with her?"

Grandma huffed. "A few months ago. Yes."

This girl loved books. She liked most animals, but didn't trust birds. Her favorite foods were Buffalo wings and vegetable dumplings. She liked thrift-shopping, and had made a point of cultivating a strange sense of fashion. She liked being alone.

"That," Grandma breathed. "You're on the right track. Just go deeper."

I didn't know what she was getting at, but I focused on the aloneness thing and went deeper. This girl spent entire afternoons in the woods, reading in the shade of trees. In warmer weather, she often pitched a tent and spent the night the same way. Or she would rent a canoe from . . . Was that the same lake Theo and Brandy and I had been going to? Yes. It was.

She'd rent a canoe, paddle out to the middle of the lake, create a cocoon for herself with a beach towel—and read. For hours. Alone, separate from the entire rest of the world.

Grandma's hand landed on my arm, gripping it so hard, I could feel her nails in my skin. "Good," she said. "Perfect. Thinks she can just run away from real life, does she? Thinks there won't be consequences? *Well*."

I didn't know what that was about, but I wasn't gonna ask. Not in the middle of the freaking ritual. For now, all I asked was, "The boat thing?"

"The boat thing," she confirmed.

So I latched on to the girl's affection for boats, and for the peaceful solitude they provided. I dug my will into the places where it melted into the rest of her personality.

"Good," said Grandma again. "Good work. Keep going."

I did keep going, even though the girl was proving weirdly difficult to latch on to. Clutching the book harder, I increased my focus and tried to tune out the rapt attention of my grandmother and my aunt as they watched me. I pulled.

I pulled.

I *pulled*.

Something came loose—but it didn't feel the same as last time. With Batman's former owner, it had been easy. Smooth, like sliding a block out from the side of a Jenga tower. This time, though, I had to pull so hard that I felt something sliding out of place within *myself*. I could feel the echo of the girl's loss within my own body. Weird, especially since the thing I'd just taken wasn't very big.

But I still managed to hold on to it. I still managed to nudge it toward the fire, where it hung suspended, a bigger orb than the first one, orange-yellow-purple with flickers of red around the edges.

As Aunt Holly began to work her magic, I braced myself for a reaching hangover even worse than the first one. It made sense, given how much effort the stealing had taken.

But the usual hangover feeling didn't come.

Weird.

I looked down at the book, sitting harmlessly in my hands. *The Hound of the Baskervilles*. Nothing unusual about it at all.

Aunt Holly finished her magic. The orb disappeared. She turned toward Grandma and asked, "How's the Cliff?"

"Good," said Grandma, after taking a sip of her tea. "Solid. The fault is gone."

As she spoke, the fire's flames turned normal again. Shades of orange instead of shades of blue. I lifted the cover of the book, just to see; there was a *My Name Is* stamp inside, under which a name had been written in textbook-perfect cursive.

Leah Ramsey-Wolfe.

"Good," said Aunt Holly curtly. "Then I'm going to bed."

Without so much as a *good night,* she unlocked the door again and left. Grandma and I both watched her go.

When the silence between us started to grow uncomfortable, it was me who finally said the obvious: "She's still depressed."

Grandma's eyebrows lifted. "Can you blame her? It's only been a few months."

I nodded. I knew that. Hell, I'd even been to the funeral. But it wasn't like Heather and I had been close or anything. We'd seen each other like once a year. Maybe twice, tops. And yeah, we used to have fun hanging out, and obviously

I was sad when she'd died—but was grief really supposed to last this long?

"Heather was her only daughter," Grandma went on, her voice all soft. "I know you don't have any idea what it's like to lose a child—and I hope you never do—but try to give her the space she needs, all right?"

I nodded again, even though I'd barely seen Aunt Holly since my friends and I had arrived. When she wasn't at her office, she only came out of her room for meals. Sometimes not even then.

I rubbed my neck, which had gone tense at the thought of Heather and the funeral and Aunt Holly. Talking about awkward stuff always did that to me.

"Anyway," I muttered, basically dying for a change of subject.

"Anyway," Grandma echoed, her voice a gentle mockery of mine. It made me loosen up a little. "You did good work tonight, Aspen. You always do, of course. But your talents are even stronger than the last time I saw you. Even more precise—and that's saying something. I'm proud of you."

This was a much easier thing to talk about. Especially since I knew she was right. I *had* gotten better at reaching since last summer. I was glad she'd noticed.

"Thanks," I said. "Oh, hey, so, what's your deal with Leah Ramsey-Wolfe?"

"Leah?" said Grandma, looking suddenly suspicious. I pointed at the handwritten name in *The Hound of the*

Baskervilles, so she could see where I'd learned it, and her expression turned into one of understanding. "Ah. Yes. Well."

"I mean, you clearly can't stand her. Either of you. So . . . ?"

Grandma sighed, shaking her head. "It's nothing. Old scores. Bad blood. Nothing you need to worry about."

That sounded interesting. "Come on. Tell me."

"Aspen," said Grandma, sounding almost as sharp as Aunt Holly. "Leave it alone."

"Whatever," I said. If she didn't want to tell me, I could just as easily find Leah Ramsey-Wolfe myself, and get my own damn answers.

"Whatever indeed," said Grandma. "Shouldn't you see if your friends have returned yet?"

Brandy and Theo. I'd almost forgotten.

"Yes," I said. "Yes, I should."

I darted around her, out the door that Aunt Holly had left open, and into the foyer. I recognized Brandy's sparkly sandals among the shoes arranged neatly by the door. But Theo's shoes weren't there. A quick glance up the stairs told me that none of the lights were on. Huh.

Next, I checked my phone—and there they were. Five texts. One from Brandy, four from Theo. I read Brandy's text first:

Going 2 bed. CU 2mrw. Ughhh worst day evr.

Worst day ever? I smothered a grin and clicked over to Theo's texts.

Ummm Brandy just broke up with me?????

I'm gonna go for a drive.

Don't wait up.

And don't ever get broken up with, man. It blows.

I turned my phone off, slid it back into my pocket, and let out a long sigh of relief. Back at the diner, when I'd decided to reach into Brandy and take away her love of Theo and put an end to their stupidly cutesy let's-make-out-in-public-all-the-goddamn-time relationship, I hadn't really been thinking ahead, and—

Well, okay, that was kind of a lie. I'd thought about breaking them up for months now. Planned out various ways that I could do it, planned out what I'd do afterward. But there'd always been something in the way. The thought of people asking questions, the thought of repercussions at school. Stupid shit like that, keeping me firmly on the fence about whether or not I should actually do something.

But then, earlier this evening, Theo had stolen one of my fries—*my* fries—and hand-fed it to his girlfriend, complete with ridiculous airplane noises. Brandy had looked totally embarrassed, but also totally charmed, and she'd eaten the fry. She'd *eaten* the damn thing, and just like that, I was off the fence.

Without even giving it a second thought, I'd reached into Brandy and removed her love for Theo. And apparently, it had worked out in the best possible way. Which was to say, with a breakup.

"Aspen, honey?" said Grandma, making me jump. And

making me realize that I'd been standing stock-still in the foyer, grinning at my phone like a total creep. "Is everything all right?"

"Oh, totally," I said. "Everything's awesome."

Because a breakup didn't just mean I'd never have to hear those stupid-ass airplane noises ever again.

It also meant Brandy was single.

△ BEFORE △

February always sucks. This is a scientific fact. But at the time, I remember thinking that this was objectively the worst February that had ever happened to anyone, ever, in the history of the entire world. There were three reasons for that.

First there was Heather. Aunt Holly called Dad, and then Dad told Mom and me. It was something with her lungs. Some fast-acting disease that I never found out the name of. There was a lot of hugging, in which I participated, and a lot of crying, in which I did not.

We went upstate for the funeral, and it was just me and Mom and Dad and Grandma and Aunt Holly and a couple of distant relatives who'd flown in to help scatter her ashes. None of Heather's friends came, which kind of surprised me. But then, Heather had been kind of a giant nerd. Maybe she just hadn't had any friends.

The second reason February sucked was Brandy. I'd had a raging crush on her for almost two years, but never worked up the nerve to ask her out—and then, on February tenth, I caught her making out with Theo on his front stoop during a party. Brandy admitted that they'd been going out for a week or so. They just hadn't told anyone yet.

Then there was the third reason. The one I couldn't have

23

seen coming even if I'd been a goddamn clairvoyant.

My mom left us on Valentine's Day, of all days. She'd always told me it was a greeting-card holiday that didn't mean anything, so it shouldn't have mattered, but there was something extra wrenching about sitting in my room that night, knowing Mom was on a train to Long Island *at the same time* that Brandy and Theo were probably out at some romantic dinner-and-movie thing, being all coupley.

The sitting-in-my-room part happened after my fight with Dad, which was after Mom had taken me by the shoulders, looked me in the eye, and given me a speech that she'd clearly practiced: "Aspen, if you ever want to leave, too, you just call me, okay? I'll come get you, no matter when it is. Even if it's ten years from now, if you want to change—if you want to get out of all this—you just call. Okay?"

I'd asked her, of course, what the hell she was even talking about.

"You'll figure it out," she'd said, her eyes going all wet. "God, I hope you will. Just remember this: You're a good person. If you want to get out, just call. I can help you."

Then she'd taken a single suitcase, and she'd left.

As soon as I'd recovered from the shock of her absence, I'd gone into their bedroom, where my suspicions were immediately confirmed: Mom had left so abruptly, she hadn't packed much of anything at all into that suitcase of hers. Her side of the closet was still mostly full. Her slippers were on the floor. Her night table was still cluttered with stuff.

I picked something at random—the tiny book of Chinese

poetry that her father had sent her from Hong Kong—and brought it out to Dad, who was slumped at the kitchen table. He looked like he was trying not to cry.

"Okay, I don't know what the hell's going on with you two, but you need to make her come back," I said, slamming the book down in front of him. He looked up at me, uncomprehending, so I said it again, in much simpler terms: "Make. Her. Come. Back."

He blinked a few times. Looked at the book, then at me. "Aspen, I can't do that."

"Hello," I said. "Obviously you can."

He sighed.

A newer, uglier thought occurred to me: "You don't *want* her back?"

Dad rubbed his hands over his face. "Of course I do," he said in this tiny, delicate voice that made my skin crawl.

"So what's the problem?" I said. "Do it."

"No," he said.

I slammed my palm down on the book's cover. "Do it. Reach. Or I'll do it myself."

He sprang to his feet. It was like I'd flipped a switch that turned Dad from a rag doll into the goddamn Terminator. Looming over me, he said, "You absolutely will not."

But I stood my ground. This was *Mom* we were talking about. "Yes. I will."

"All right. You listen to me, and you listen carefully. You will not alter your mother in any way. You know the rule."

"Oh, come on, just this once—"

"Absolutely not." Dad's eyes were hard. "Do you understand me, Jeremy?"

That shut me up. Dad never used my first name. Neither of them did. I'd switched over to my middle name, Aspen, when I was eight, and I hadn't looked back since. My parents only called me Jeremy when they were seriously pissed off at me.

So I nodded.

I could have fixed everything. Reached into Mom and taken away whatever had made her want to leave. Reached into Dad and taken away whatever it was that made him not want me to fix her. Reached into both of them, found the thing that had split them apart, and gotten rid of it.

But we have one unbreakable rule in the Quick family. We don't steal from one another. We just don't. And Dad was right about one thing: Mom was still part of the family, whether she wanted to be or not. So unless I wanted to admit that she *wasn't* part of my family anymore, I couldn't reach into her.

Which meant I couldn't bring her back.

CHAPTER TWO

My morning wake-up call in Three Peaks was the smell of coffee and bacon wafting up from the kitchen. And it wasn't even intended as an alarm clock substitute, really; Grandma figured if I wanted to get up, I'd get up. If not, that wasn't her problem. As long as I was there when the Cliff needed me, she didn't really care what else I did with my time. But I always got up when Grandma cooked breakfast. I mean, come on. Bacon.

That morning, though, the bacon-coffee smell came with a new addition: the sound of yelling, over in the east wing.

Usually, I stayed in the east wing when I came to visit. That was where both guest rooms were, so it only made sense. But this summer, Brandy and Theo had taken those rooms. One room each, if you asked Aunt Holly or Grandma. Me? I knew they were really both staying in Theo's room.

I, meanwhile, was staying in Heather's old room in the west wing. Not nearly as creepy as it sounds, since it'd been basically stripped bare after the funeral. There were still some clothes in the closet, and some random stuff in the drawers, but nothing out in the open. Nothing you could see without digging a little.

The yelling didn't contain words I could make out—it wasn't loud enough for that—but there was a degree of urgency that told me I should maybe go check it out before I headed downstairs. So I felt around for my glasses, paused in front of Heather's full-length mirror to make sure my hair wasn't doing anything too stupid, and headed over to the east wing.

"You're being a baby." Brandy's voice, coming from Theo's room.

I got to the door just in time to hear his response: "No, I'm not. You wanted space, right? That's what you said. Space. So that's what you get." He said all this while pulling clothes out of drawers and shoving them into his open suitcase.

This was not good.

"Oh, I get it," said Brandy, who was standing over him, arms crossed. Even scowling, she was the hottest girl ever. "You're being noble. How sweet of you. How *chivalrous*."

"Noble?" said Theo, shoving his phone charger into a corner of the suitcase. "Please."

"Please," mimicked Brandy. "That's right, go running home. What about Aspen, idiot? You're just gonna abandon your best friend at a time like this?"

A time like this, meaning while I was still dealing with

my feelings about Heather's death. But really, I mostly had feelings about Aunt Holly's feelings about Heather's death. Which was to say, I had a serious lack of desire to be any-where near Aunt Holly while she was still going through her anger-depression-drinking-et-cetera thing.

That was it, honestly—but Brandy kept insinuating that I should be sadder than I was, or I should have issues to work through, or whatever. And since there was no way of correcting her without coming across as a callous douche bag, I just kind of didn't bother.

"One of us has to go," said Theo. "I sure as hell don't feel like spending the rest of the month in the room next to you. Not after yesterday."

"Then I should be the one who leaves," said Brandy.

I tensed up. She couldn't leave. Not when my chance was finally here.

"You?" said Theo.

"Obviously," said Brandy. "You're his best friend, not me. He only invited me because I'm dating you. *Was* dating you."

Well, that was untrue.

Theo paused, a bunch of T-shirts clutched in his fist. "Oh. So *you* want to be the noble one."

"Oh my god, you are such a baby!" said Brandy again. "Ugh. I'm gonna go pack."

That was when she turned toward the door, saw me standing there, and stopped cold.

"Aspen," she said.

Theo looked over at me, startled. "Oh. Hey, man."

"Hey," I replied, and for a second we all just sort of stared at one another. I had to figure out how to smooth this thing over, stat.

"Okay, your choice," said Brandy, who'd recovered fastest from the awkwardness. "There's a one o'clock bus back to the city. Which of us should be on it?"

"Neither of you," I said. "Come on. I'll switch rooms with Theo if it'll make it less weird. But don't leave, okay?"

They glanced at each other and had one of those two-second-long silent conversations that only couples ever seem to have. And recently-ex-couples, I guess.

"Just pick one," said Brandy, sounding suddenly exhausted. "We won't be offended. Promise."

Theo's face went tight, and I could tell he'd be very offended indeed if I chose Brandy to stay.

"Come on, guys," I said with an exaggerated sigh. "Can we at least eat breakfast first? Like, have some coffee and actually talk about this?" There would be no talking, of course, because that meant there'd be a chance I wouldn't get my way. But I needed time. Just a few minutes, so I could figure out what to do.

Another silent conversation. Then Theo said, "Yeah, I guess."

Brandy nodded sharply and marched past me, out of the room, and downstairs. Theo looked after her, his face creasing with hurt. Hurt from the breakup. Or hurt at the thought that I might choose Brandy and send him home, when he'd finally, after years of bugging me to bring him along, gotten to come upstate for the summer. Whatever the reason, I knew I had to get rid of what he was feeling. Especially since I'd caused all that hurt in the first place.

"You got my texts?" His voice was even more gruff than usual. I nodded. "Man, what the hell, right? Just. Out of nowhere. Bam. I said something that set her off, and then she's like . . . done with me. Forever."

I made a sympathetic face. "That sucks. It really does."

"You don't even know," said Theo. He was still holding those T-shirts.

I totally did know, was the thing. Well, not exactly. But I still remembered how I'd felt the night I'd found out they were dating, and I couldn't imagine this was any worse.

"Sucks," he said one more time. Then sighed. Then said, "Breakfast?"

"You go ahead," I said. "I just wanna put in my contacts first."

Theo threw the T-shirts onto his suitcase, then headed for the stairs. I went slowly toward the bathroom—but as soon as he was out of sight, I doubled back. I grabbed a shirt off Theo's suitcase, then went into the blue room, where Brandy was staying, and grabbed one of her hair clips off the dresser.

I reached into the hair clip first. Immediately apparent was the empty space where, only yesterday, I'd stolen her love for Theo. It hadn't healed just yet, and in the jagged spaces around it, there were tendrils of resentment and an-

31

noyance that her former love had been keeping at bay.

I took hold of her negative feelings and pulled them away. Then I took away her very small, but very present, desire to leave me and Theo and Three Peaks behind.

Inside Theo's shirt, the desire to leave town was a little stronger, a little more difficult to wrap my will around. But I stole that, too, along with the desire he felt to get back at Brandy for breaking up with him so suddenly, not to mention so publicly. And then, finally, I stole his desire to try and get back *with* Brandy.

It was a lot of effort. By the time I was done, I had to sit down and shut my eyes. Just for a second. Just long enough that the reaching hangover faded away, and I couldn't feel their minds inside my own anymore.

By the time I got downstairs, where Theo was spooning eggs onto four plates, Brandy was already murmuring apologies from her seat at the table. Apologies for breaking things off without any warning. Apologies for the name-calling. Apologies for no longer having the feelings she thought she had.

Grandma stayed silent through it all, but as I sat down at the table, she caught my eye and smiled. She knew what I'd done. Oh, yeah. She definitely knew. I gave her a slight nod, even though it wasn't really necessary.

Theo, oblivious to our silent exchange, just listened to Brandy's apologies and went, "It's fine. Seriously. Don't worry about it."

⚠

We decided, as usual, to go to the lake. Personally, I was kind of ready to change it up a little, but in the interest of keeping things as normal as possible among the three of us, I gave in.

It was maybe a twenty-minute drive, and the car was super quiet the whole way. But the good kind of quiet, not the kind where everyone's silently plotting everyone else's death. I played DJ from the passenger seat. Theo played steering wheel drums to every song. And in the backseat, Brandy doodled on her bare arms, like she always did.

When we arrived at the lake, I grabbed the pile of beach towels that hid the remaining three-quarters of yesterday's bottle of vodka, Brandy grabbed the bottle itself, and we headed down the well-worn sand path to the beach.

It was kind of overcast, not to mention a weekday, so aside from us, there weren't that many people around. We dropped our stuff in a random spot, and Theo and I went over to the boathouse while Brandy put sunscreen on.

"Kayaks today?" asked Theo. "We haven't done kayaks yet."

I remembered wanting to try a kayak yesterday, but today, for some reason, my stomach twisted just thinking about it.

"Nah," I said.

Theo shrugged. "Canoe again?"

We'd done a canoe yesterday. My stomach lurched at the memory. Ugh, maybe going out on the lake wasn't a good idea today. All those waves, all that rocking . . .

"Or a paddleboat? Come on, man, pick one."

I put a hand on my gut, willing it still, and shook my head. "You pick. I might sit this one out."

Theo peered at me. "You okay?"

Was I? I wasn't sure. I hadn't woken up feeling like this, but maybe it had started at breakfast. Maybe the bacon had been undercooked.

Except Brandy and Theo had eaten the bacon, too, and they both looked fine.

"My stomach's just doing something weird," I said. "I dunno. Maybe I shouldn't get out on the water today."

Theo looked dubiously at the lake. Then shrugged. "That's cool. We'll just chill on the sand."

"I mean, you guys can still get a boat if you want."

"Hm," he said. "Maybe."

Ha. Here he was, ready to rent a boat with Brandy, when just this morning he'd been packing to go back home, just to avoid being near her. I was so good at my job. Ha-*ha*.

We made our way back to Brandy, who'd spread all three of our towels in a neat row. She was sitting on the far left one, but she got up as we approached. "Is there a wait?" she asked, looking pointedly at the lack of crowd around us.

"I thought maybe kayaks today," said Theo. "But Aspen's sick."

"I'm not sick," I said. "My stomach's just doing a thing."

"Aw," said Brandy. "Well, hey, how about this. My arms are still kind of tired from rowing yesterday. So why don't you get a kayak, and I'll keep Aspen company?"

This couldn't have turned out better if I'd planned it. And I honestly hadn't. But damn, if I'd known a stomach bug, or whatever this was, would result in alone time with Brandy, I'd've faked it a lot sooner.

"That cool, Aspen?" asked Theo.

"Go for it," I said.

And off he went, back to the boathouse. Brandy and I watched as he strapped an ugly orange life jacket over his T-shirt, then dragged a bright yellow kayak all the way to the water's edge. "Whoosh," said Brandy, as Theo pushed off from the shore and began paddling. His rhythm was even, and the boat moved fast. He could probably win races or something.

"So," I said, settling on the middle towel. "You dumped him, huh?"

Brandy blew out a long breath and flopped back onto her own towel. "Is it too early for vodka?"

"It's never too early for vodka," I replied, and dug out the bottle. It was actually an empty Sprite bottle that we'd filled with vodka, because there were cops on this beach sometimes, and keeping up appearances was often easier than reaching into people to fix whatever mistake you'd just made. I took a sip, then Brandy took a sip, then I asked, "What happened?"

"Ugh, I don't even know," she said, passing the bottle back to me. I put it aside. "Look, I'm really sorry it happened while we were up here. I didn't want to have all that drama on your family's turf, but, like . . . I just had this moment of clarity, you know? At the diner last night."

"Clarity?"

"Yeah. Like here's this perfectly nice guy that I've been seeing for five months—six months?—and he's a great person and stuff, but we have nothing in common. Nothing. Like zero things. We can't even see movies together, because every time I go see one of his ridiculous sports-underdog-makes-good movies, I want to stab myself in the eye, and every time he sees one of *my* movies—"

"Where someone literally gets stabbed in the eye," I said. I was very familiar with Brandy's taste in movies. It was more or less the same as mine.

"With any luck, yes," she said, shooting a grin at me. "But yeah, he can't stand it. My movies either gross him out or bore him to death. And it's music, too. And video games. And books and school and, just, the way we live life, you know?"

I nodded. I did know, because I'd been thinking the same thing for basically the entire time they'd been dating. Theo was a good dude, but he was also kind of a nerd sometimes, and Brandy deserved someone better. Someone who liked to read real books instead of comics, for instance. Someone who liked movies that were actually fun instead of just award-baity.

"Ooh, I forgot to ask," I said, "have you seen *Blood of Jupiter* yet?"

Brandy perked up immediately. "Dude. Twice. You saw it?"

"The day it came out," I said. "Wasn't it great? I actually thought of you when they blew up Mars—oh, and when the thing with the fingers happened."

"The thing with the fingers!" She sat up a little straighter. "Right? The alien, and the guy's *fingers,* and I can't even *deal,* that was so gross and awesome and awful and *aaaahhhh,* I want to see it again!"

"I'd see it again with you," I said.

She grinned, pushing her sunglasses up her nose. "Aw. But Theo wouldn't want to come, and I'd feel bad ditching him."

"Theo didn't like it, huh?"

"God, no. Afterward he just kept going on about how, like, spaceships couldn't really be shaped like that, or there isn't really life on Jupiter—"

"I mean, there *isn't* life on Jupiter," I said. "But that's hardly the point of the movie."

"See?" she said, and I could see excitement spreading across her face again. "That's exactly it. The point isn't science. The point is that stuff blows up and the baddies die at the end and some guy's fingers get chopped off, tiny slice by tiny slice, until—"

"Ugh, stop it," I said, giving a shudder, only slightly exaggerated, at the memory.

Brandy laughed. "You know you loved it."

"Ugh," I said again.

"Ooh," said Brandy, leaning back on her hands. "Finger Slices. That's a good one."

I paused, trying to figure out if I'd missed something. "Wait, a good what?"

"Sorry. Band name." She gave me a secretive kind of look—the kind that made me wish she weren't wearing sunglasses, so I could see her eyes. "I have this dream where I'm suddenly super talented, and I start a band. So I kind of keep a list of band names I could use, in case it ever happens."

"Finger Slices," I said, nodding. "Yeah, that's a good one."

She thought for a second. "And our first album could be called *Rivulets of Blood*."

I laughed. "Lead single: 'I Can See Your Tendons.'"

"See?" she said excitedly. "You get it. I should have known you'd get it."

Well, obviously I got it. And Theo was a moron if he didn't.

That was when Brandy's phone chimed. She rummaged in her purse, pulled it out, and made a face.

"Your dad?" I guessed.

"Right in one," she said, then cleared her throat and read the text aloud. "'Hey honey. Tornado on the news today. Just making sure you're all right.' Then three smiley faces. *Three*."

"Tornado?" I said. "We don't get those here."

Brandy rolled her eyes. "It was probably in the Midwest. Doesn't matter. Hurricane in Florida? Dad texts me during English class. Tsunami in Japan? Dad's suddenly sure I'm dead."

"He's just overprotective," I said, but she didn't answer, because we both knew that wasn't true. Ever since Brandy's parents had split in junior high, her dad had become certain that Brandy would disappear, too. And there was a very fine line between wanting to make sure your kid is safe and, say, pulling her out of school for two days because there'd been a news story about a school shooting two time zones away.

Basically, it was a goddamn miracle that he'd let her come upstate with me and Theo for an entire month. Well, a miracle shaped like my dad telling her dad that it would be good practice for when she went away to college—but still. Miracle nonetheless.

"Here, this'll help," I said, passing her the bottle again. "Good thing Theo's the designated driver, huh?"

Brandy took a swig, wiped her lips, and laughed. "Sucks to be him."

△ BEFORE △

My crush on Brandy McAllister began somewhere in the haze of ninth grade, when the first-week jitters had started wearing off and we'd begun to venture outside the comfort of our junior high cliques. I'd started wearing hats, thinking they made me look older; I attracted other hat-wearers and people who liked people who wore hats. And theater kids.

Brandy wore giant necklaces and a leather jacket and drew pen tattoos all up and down her arms; she attracted the kids who smoked weed and talked about getting real tattoos as soon as they were old enough to score fake IDs.

There was more overlap between these two groups than you might think.

Even so, Brandy and I didn't actually say anything meaningful to each other until early October, when we landed in detention on the same day. It was her, me, and this group of three nerdy guys who sat in the back, complaining loudly about the unfairness of the high school justice system. The teacher sat at his desk, headphones in his ears, ignoring us all.

Brandy sat at the desk right next to mine, reading the

Charles Dickens thing we'd been assigned for English class.

"What're you in for?" I asked, lowering my voice just enough that I might be able to pass for an old-timey gangster.

She threw me a crooked little smile. "Texting."

"Really? That's it?"

"During gym class," she said, bright blue eyes lighting up as she spoke. "I wasn't paying attention, and a volleyball hit me in the arm. We lost the game because of me. Everyone was so pissed."

She said this last part with a snicker, almost like she was proud.

"Still," I said. "That must've hurt."

"Oh, totally." She hiked up the short sleeve of her shirt, looking positively gleeful. "Check out this bruise. Give it a couple days and it'll be so gross. All green and yellow. Zombie skin. I can't wait."

I examined the bruise, then I examined her forearm, which was covered in black, purple, and blue ink. A colorful drawing of a mermaid stretched from her elbow almost down to her wrist. She wore a seashell bra and was looking wistfully into the distance, hair billowing behind her in the water.

"That's really good," I said, pointing at the mermaid.

"Thanks. I don't think her fins are really right, but maybe next time. Her name's Shelly," she added with a smirk. "Get it?"

I groaned, but then laughed it off and checked out the fins. They looked fine to me. Something else caught my eye, though: a patch of skin, half disguised by Shelly's torso, that was slightly shinier than the skin around it.

"What's that thing?" I asked, pointing again.

"Oh, just a burn," she said. "I dropped my hair curler and—*ssssss*."

Hair curler. My eyes traveled up to her mostly straight blond hair, the ends of which curled in and brushed against the fabric of her shirt, below her shoulders. I'd always assumed that happened on its own. Hearing her say *hair curler* felt like being allowed into a secret part of her life—into the place where Brandy became Brandy. Before that moment, Brandy had been Just Another Girl. One of the many mythical beings with soft-looking skin, interesting curves, and touchable hair that populated my school and my neighborhood and my incredibly vague fantasies. But now, thanks to the Shelly-tattoo-*hair-curler*-burn-scar, Brandy was different. Brandy was real.

(Brandy was also, incidentally, the catalyst for my vague fantasies starting to become very, very specific.)

". . . just kinda wish I could get rid of it, you know?" she was saying. "I mean, it was cool for a few days, but it's been almost a year now, and I'm just sick of it."

She rubbed the little patch of skin, lightly enough that she didn't smudge Shelly's ink, and I resisted the urge to reach over and do the same. I wanted to feel the difference between Brandy's regular skin and Brandy's scarred skin.

Instead, I asked, "Do you draw stuff on your arm to cover it up?"

She gave me a funny look. "No. I draw stuff because I like drawing stuff."

So if her scar magically went away one day, she would still use her skin as a canvas for her art. That was good to know.

"Can I borrow a pen?" I asked.

She fished one out of her bag and handed it to me. I spent the rest of detention using it to do my social studies homework; when we were finally dismissed, I conveniently forgot to return it.

That night, I reached into Brandy's pen, heart racing as I looked, for the first time, not for a personality trait or an emotion or some other intangible thing, but for a concrete piece of Brandy's physical self: the burn scar on her forearm.

I found it and, with not much effort at all, I pulled it away. I held it for a moment in my mind, savoring the sensation of having part of Brandy so close to me . . . and then I paused. I could have more of her this close to me, if I wanted. This pen probably held so many secrets about her. I could see what she wrote in her diary, assuming she kept one. I could see every single thing she'd ever drawn on her arm. I could maybe even see her naked.

I shivered at the thought.

But for whatever reason, I didn't reach any further. If she wanted to show me more of herself, she could do it in her own time, of her own free will. I could wait. Brandy—newly special, newly real—was worth waiting for. I put down the pen and let the burn scar go.

I wondered when she would notice it missing.

I wondered how she would explain its absence to herself.

I wondered what she would draw on her arm tomorrow.

CHAPTER THREE

We didn't stay at the lake too long, mainly because Theo got bored without Brandy and me kayaking with him, but also because it was cold. That happened up here sometimes, even in summer. Not only were we north of the city by five solid hours, but we were also in the middle of the mountains. So before Brandy and I had even put a dent in the remaining vodka, Theo was dragging his kayak back onto the shore and wondering aloud what else there was to do up here.

The answer: Not much. Especially if you weren't into hiking, which I wasn't. Theo was, and so was Brandy, but neither of them was wearing good hiking shoes, so we just decided to head back to Three Peaks and explore Main Street in daylight, when the stores were open. We hadn't actually done that yet.

That was its real name, by the way. Main Street. Like we were in some boy-and-his-dog fifties sitcom or something. It was a three-block stretch of stores, bookended by a grocery store and a bookstore. In between were a bunch of cutesy retail places, the diner with the really good burgers, and the Bean Barn, where they actually made a decent cappuccino.

At Brandy's request, we started at the Bean Barn so she could get herself a chai latte. Then, despite Theo's vague protests, she led us into one of the cutesy stores—and immediately back out again, when she discovered that all the *locally made* clothes cost, like, four hundred dollars per shirt. That was Three Peaks for you.

After that, the only thing left to check out was the bookstore, Waterlemon Books. A little bell jingled above my head as I pushed the door open. The air conditioner was blasting, despite the cool afternoon, and "Sympathy for the Devil" was playing faintly on the overhead system.

It was far from busy inside. A couple people were examining books together in the almost-hidden back corner of the store, and a stuffy-looking old guy was straightening some stuff on a shelf labeled *Local Interest*.

"Ooh, local legends!" said Brandy, and headed over to join the old guy. Theo went straight for the graphic novel section. My attention, though, was caught by three people talking loudly right at the front of the store: a guy and a girl who both looked about my age, and an older woman who was hovering over them like a mom.

The boy was all baggy pants and oversized hoodie and I-don't-want-to-be-here attitude. The girl was tall and stately, with dark hair that fell messily around her shoulders. She wore one of those hippie skirts, running shoes with no socks, and a giant bulky cardigan cinched at the waist with a striped necktie. Keen-eyed and unsmiling, she looked like the world's scariest—and possibly youngest—English teacher.

Brandy had a couple outfits that were pretty similar. I looked over at her, wondering if she'd noticed the girl, but she was already absorbed in a book that had a faceless man in a suit on the cover. So I didn't bug her. I just perused the best sellers display and eavesdropped.

"I never was much of a reader myself, if we're being honest," the mom was saying. She held a sheet of paper out to Necktie Girl, almost like a shield. "The only one I've read on this list is the Hemingway, and . . . well, the thing is, I didn't even like it."

Ah. Summer reading list. I still had to read *Gulliver's Travels* and *Frankenstein* before September. I'd get to them eventually. Maybe.

Necktie perused the list. After a moment her lips quirked into a wry smile. "Oh, yeah. *A Farewell to Arms*. I didn't like it much, either. What about *The Handmaid's Tale*?"

The boy's eyes widened in horror. "But that's a girl book!"

"Yes, it is," Necktie Girl said smoothly, her smile going tight. "Which means you might just be the only boy in your class who reads it. You're John, right? You go to Three Peaks High?"

47

He nodded, looking more and more wary by the second. "Starting tenth grade in the fall?"

He nodded again.

"Thought so," she said. "I had this list two years ago. Mr. Smythe broke us up into study groups based on what book we'd read, and we had to do group projects for a week. I read *The Handmaid's Tale,* and so did five other girls. And one boy. Just one. Which meant that he spent an entire week surrounded by six girls who, let me tell you, were *very* impressed that he'd read a feminist classic."

The boy was starting to look interested, but his mom eyed Necktie suspiciously. "I'm not sure that's the best reason to choose a book. . . ."

"It's also not the worst," said Necktie.

The mom hesitated. Licked her lips. "Maybe there's something in the list with more . . . well . . . boy appeal?"

Necktie's eyes narrowed; I could almost feel the air in the room growing thinner. "Boy appeal," she echoed flatly. "When you say that, do you mean books written by men? About men? With no women in them except one-dimensional characters who only exist because the men need love interests? Is that what you mean?"

Over by the Local Interest shelf, Brandy had her eyes on Necktie instead of her book. She caught me watching her, and we exchanged a raised-eyebrow look whose meaning was very clear: Necktie Girl was awesome.

The woman's jaw dropped, and for a moment I wondered if she'd accuse Necktie of being rude, or maybe ask to speak to her manager. But she didn't get the chance, because before she could say anything, the boy said, "Um. Maybe I'll read *The Handmaid's Tale*."

Necktie's aggressive stance vanished like a mirage, and she grinned at the boy. "Good choice." She picked a book up off the summer reading display. The boy took it. Necktie checked the list again. "So that's modern classics done. What's next? Ah, the good old European classics list. Come with me."

She turned and headed deeper into the store. The boy followed like a trained puppy. His mother scowled after them, but the expression quickly softened into a shake of her head and something that almost approached a smile. She turned toward the best sellers table—and caught me watching.

"I guess I should've seen that coming," she said, kind of wryly. "Leah's got strong opinions about books. I just . . . don't read that way, I guess."

"Leah?" I repeated. The name rang an alarm bell in my brain, but it took me a second to realize why. Last night's ritual, and Grandma's dislike of the girl who'd once owned *The Hound of the Baskervilles*. "As in Leah Ramsey-Wolfe?"

The woman nodded. "My Robert was in her older sister's class. Rachel. They graduated a few years back. Rachel was the same way. Smart as a whip, but opinionated to the point of rudeness."

Shaking her head again, she wandered away—just in time for Brandy to come back over to me.

"You know her?" she asked, gazing after Leah. The tone of her voice wasn't unlike the tone you might use to ask, say, *You know Lady Gaga?*

I didn't know Leah, obviously, but if I said that to Brandy, then I'd have to explain why I knew her full name—and, just, nope. So I opted for changing the subject instead. Picking up a best seller at random, I said, "Hey, have you read this?"

"*The Hunger Games?*" Brandy rolled her eyes. "Well, yeah, hasn't everyone and their mom read that?"

"I only saw the movie," I said, and began reading the first page.

Brandy took the hint and went back to the Local Interest shelf.

Leah led the boy to the register, where his mother paid for a small mountain of books. As they left, a smug look crept over her face. It was a nice face, actually, if a bit severe. She had an unusually *solid* sort of look. Like everyone else in the world was a little less real than she was. Even Theo and me. Even Brandy.

And there was a small mole above the left corner of her lip, like an old-fashioned movie star might have. Sexy.

Leah went behind the register, opened a blue notebook, and started writing something inside, grinning to herself the whole time. I moved closer, closer, closer, until I could see what she was writing.

> *Got a H.S. boy to buy Atwood. Am best feminist ever, y/n?–LRW*

Curious, I read the line above what she'd just written:

Hand-sold 5 copies of American Gods in 2
hours. Go me.–JH

A quick scan up the page showed more of the same: Leah and someone else, exchanging notes about what they'd sold and to whom. I wondered who the second person was.

"This one's not for sale," said Leah. It took a moment for me to realize she was talking to me—and another for me to see that she was pointing at the blue notebook.

"Oh," I said, stepping back with my hands up. "Sorry, I wasn't—"

"Spying on me? Sure you were," she said with a little laugh. "No big deal, though. What can I help you with?" She gave me a two-second once-over and said, "Allen Ginsberg? Jack Kerouac? We've got a great collection of beat-type stuff just over there."

I blinked at her, kind of stunned. I looked down, just to make absolutely sure I hadn't put on my *On the Road* shirt this morning and then forgotten about it.

I hadn't.

But before I could answer, Leah added, "Hey, haven't I seen you before?"

"Um, I don't think so."

"No, I totally have." A moment passed, then her face brightened. "Up at Elmview Lake! Earlier this week. You and your friends were renting boats. That was you guys, right?" This last with a head-tilt in Brandy's direction.

"Oh, yeah, we've been up there a couple times," I said

as the image clicked. I'd seen it during the triad ritual: Leah cocooning herself in a canoe so she could read without anyone else around. I'd also seen that she worked in a bookstore. Right.

"I get up there whenever I can," she said. "It's so nice. I love being on the water."

My brain skidded to a halt. That was wrong. Hadn't I just stolen that very thing from her last night? A love of boats and water and all that?

"You do?" I asked cautiously.

"Oh yeah. I'd go every day, but, you know. Job." She spread her arms wide, indicating the store.

Okay, had I messed up the ritual somehow? Was Leah still intact? Maybe she meant all this stuff in the past tense. It didn't seem like it, though. . . .

"Speaking of your job, I was actually wondering if I could see that," I said, nodding at the notebook. "It's just, I had a summer job at a bookstore down in the city last year, and they wouldn't let us take notes on sales like you're doing. Big chain politics. You know."

Total lie, of course. I'd never had a summer job, nor would I have aimed for a bookstore if I'd needed to get one.

"It's not that exciting," she said, handing the notebook over. "Just me and my friend Jesse snarking at each other, mostly."

I moved my eyes up the page, as if skimming the notes in reverse—all the while prodding the paper for a way to reach in. I found it soon enough. Turning the page as an ex-

52

cuse to adjust my hands, I reached. But what I found inside wasn't just Leah. It was Leah and several other people, all tangled up so tightly that I couldn't even tell them apart, much less pull anything out.

Public property. I should have known it'd be useless. I needed something that belonged only, or at least primarily, to Leah.

Trying not to let my disappointment show, I focused on one of the notes as I pulled my will out of the notebook. I smiled up at Leah and offered it back to her. "You dared him to recommend Anaïs Nin to someone? That's just cruel."

Her eyebrows shot up. "You know who that *is*?"

Only because Brandy had told me. But still. I shrugged and said, "Maybe. Anyway, I'm looking for . . ." I cast a quick glance around the store, just to see which sections were farthest away from the register. Romance. Children's. Graphic novels, where Theo was leaning against a shelf and reading. "Actually, my friend over there was looking for recommendations. He's into, like, manga and stuff, and he's been talking about wanting to find a new series."

This was actually not a lie. Theo didn't read often, but when he did, he preferred his books to contain pictures. Brandy was convinced that didn't count as real reading, but whatever.

"Ooh, hmm," said Leah. "Yeah, I'll go talk to him. Be right back!"

As soon as she was out of sight, I beelined for the counter, pausing only to make sure neither the old guy nor Brandy was about to start paying attention to me. I ducked behind the register. A cup full of pens. A stack of notebooks. Register tape, bookmarks, random tchotchkes—and a smartphone in a glittery purple case. Jackpot.

It took me less than a second to find a way in, and less than a second after that to confirm that it belonged to Leah. I reached in, sorting through the phone's memories, looking for something I could take. Not something big—that was hardly necessary—but definitely something where I'd be able to see the difference immediately.

Which was to say: not her personality, but her physicality. I shifted my perception just a little bit, pressing my will into the phone until it gave me a clear picture of the Leah I'd just been talking to, and that's when I saw it: the little mole, just above her lip. Perfect.

I pulled, and away it came, easily as pulling the wrapper off a candy.

"Hey! That's mine!"

I jumped. I thought about putting the phone back, but it was too late.

"Sorry, I—"

"Wanted to steal my phone?" she said, snatching it out of my hand. "Was that it?"

But as I looked at her face, my response got stuck somewhere in my throat. "Uh," I managed, trying and failing not to stare at the spot above her lip. My neck tensed up as I looked at it.

"What else did you steal?" she demanded.

The old guy was squinting at us from across the store—and Brandy was rushing over, striding between display tables and even knocking some stuff over in her haste to get to us.

"He wasn't stealing anything!" Brandy hesitated, then looked at me. "You weren't, right?"

"Of course not!" I said, because stealing someone's mole does not count. "I just . . . wanted to know the time, and there were no clocks, and . . ."

Leah pointed to the wall above the register. There was a clock hanging there, twice as big as my head, the second hand ticking away.

"Oh," I said. "Duh."

"Are you guys buying anything?" said Leah. "Because if not, I think you should probably leave."

"Actually, yeah," said Brandy, and held up the book she'd been reading.

As Leah rang her up in stoic silence, I went and grabbed Theo from the back.

"Saw you talking to the bookstore chick," he said. "Get her number? She's hot."

"She's also a complete jerkwad," I replied. "Let's get out of here. It's burger o'clock."

Theo and I hung back as Leah bagged Brandy's book, and then we all filed out the door. Only once we were gone did Brandy ask me what had really happened in there with Leah.

"Nothing," I said. "Sheesh."

I mean, no wonder Aunt Holly and Grandma didn't like her. You did one tiny little thing that she wasn't into, and she became insta-bitch.

Brandy dropped it after that, but as we walked to the diner and ate dinner and hung out and then went home, I kept coming back to the scene in the bookstore. It worried me.

Not because Leah had caught me with her phone and I was probably on her shit list until the end of time. I couldn't care less about that. I was worried because, even after I'd stolen it away, that mole was still there, above the left corner of her lip.

△ BEFORE △

I don't remember learning how to reach any more than I remember learning how to walk. It was just always something I could do. What I do remember is the exact moment I learned why we had the rule about not telling anyone outside the family about what we could do.

It was a snowy Friday afternoon about ten years ago, and Theo Valdez had come over to my apartment after school. Theo was terrified of snow because, a couple years back, his dad had gotten into a car accident during a blizzard and landed in the hospital for almost a week. So when the doorman let us up, the first thing he did was tromp straight to the living room in search of the phone. "I have to call Daddy," he said, frantic.

(We were in second grade. I still called my dad "Daddy," too.)

I followed, dodging the wet spots Theo's boots had left behind, and caught up with him just as he finished dialing. Seconds passed. Then more seconds. Theo's face fell. Finally he said, "He's not at the office. I'm gonna call his cell phone."

His dad didn't pick up the second time, either, so Theo

left a message and hung up. He was breathing hard, prob-ably holding back tears, shaking his head and looking at me like I needed to fix this somehow. He had two older brothers; he was used to other people fixing things for him.

So I dashed over to the couch, fished the TV remote out from between the cushions, and handed it to Theo. "Hold this."

Despite his obvious confusion, he did what I said. Held the remote in both hands, like a waiter holding a tray. Stared at it. Then at me. "Just hold it? Should I turn the TV on?"

"No, reach into it," I said eagerly. "There's calm in there. My mom always gets calm when she's changing channels. I don't even think she likes to watch anything. She just likes seeing what's on every channel. It's weird. But it makes her calm. Try it."

I'd been stealing Mom's calm for a couple months by then. Shortly after the snowstorm incident, Dad found out what I was doing and made me stop—which, incidentally, led to Mom not needing her anxiety meds anymore.

(That was my first lesson in why we had the No Stealing From Family rule.)

Theo misunderstood me. He turned the TV on and started changing channels as fast as he could. Soon he was gritting his teeth, like he couldn't make it go fast enough. He was the opposite of calm.

"No, no, no," I said, stepping between him and the screen, blocking the signal. "I mean the remote, not the TV. *Reach*. Till you find the calm. Then take it out and keep some for yourself."

He sort of squinted at me. "You sound like a loony."

A loony. The word hit me harder than it should—not because it was an insult, but because I suddenly understood, with a clarity I'd never felt before, how different we were from each other. He couldn't reach. I could.

Fortunately, my seven-year-old brain managed to come up with a retort that both deflected his sudden suspicion of me and distracted him from his missing father:

"I know you are, but what am I?"

Theo grinned, instantly ready to play. "A *moron*!"

"I know you are, but what am I?"

"A *douche-nozzle*!"

(Like I said: two older brothers.)

"I know you are, but what am I?"

"A *fart-monster*!"

(Like I said: second grade.)

This went on and on for a while, until it devolved into a very intense game of Why Are You Hitting Yourself?—during which Theo's dad called back and confirmed that he was not, in fact, dead.

But when I went into the kitchen a little while later to get sodas for us, I came back to find Theo pulling the remote apart, like maybe he could understand what I'd meant if he only took the batteries out and looked inside.

"Whatcha doing?" I asked, even though I was pretty sure I already knew.

He shoved the batteries back in and clicked the little compartment closed. "Nothing. Let's play video games."

CHAPTER FOUR

The weird thing was, my magic was totally intact. After the Leah incident, I tried stealing other physical stuff—a freckle off the back of Theo's arm, a patch of sunburn off Brandy's back—and it worked. All of it. So I figured the mole had just been one of those fluke things. Maybe I hadn't been concentrating. Maybe I'd been off my game or something. Either way, it wasn't a big deal, right? It was just a mole.

Despite Brandy being the one to drag us into the expensive Three Peaks boutique scene, it was Theo who actually went back for a second visit. Now that he didn't have a girlfriend to tether him to our little trio, he wanted some Alone-in-the-Woods Man Time. His words. So he went into one of those stores, got himself some hardcore hiking boots and a compass, and started disappearing into the woods behind Grandma's house every morning after breakfast. He came back every night in time to hit the diner, with stories about wading through creeks and climbing boulders and other stuff that I had zero interest in ever doing.

I was totally fine with this. I liked Theo plenty, but I liked having Brandy to myself even better.

"One of these days, Theo's gonna come back with a bear pelt over his shoulders," said Brandy, as we lounged on the sand up by the lake. We'd stopped renting canoes and stuff—it'd always been Theo who was the most enthusiastic about that—but it was still a good place to chill out and drink and whatever.

"Or a lion," I said. "He'll be wearing its head as a hat or something."

"Do they even have lions here?" asked Brandy. "Or, like, anywhere on this continent?"

"I think only in zoos," I replied. "Unless you mean mountain lions."

"Theo could definitely slay a mountain lion," said Brandy, grinning up at the sky. "He's ever so manly."

She had this way of saying *manly* where it was obviously not a compliment.

"I wonder how you'd even catch a mountain lion," I said, unscrewing the cap on the Sprite bottle.

"Me personally?" said Brandy. "Feminine wiles. Obviously."

"Har-har," I said, even though, yeah, my heart maybe sped up a little at the phrase. Brandy could use her wiles on me whenever she wanted.

"I know," she said. "But Theo? Theo would never have to resort to such tawdry things. I'm sure he has a variety of nefarious mountain lion skills up his manly, manly sleeve."

"I wonder what these various nefarious skills entail," I said.

Her expression suddenly went dead serious. "Various Nefarious. Good band name. *Great* band name, actually."

"It's all yours," I said proudly. "Ooh, hey. Album title: *Squeaky Sneaky*."

Brandy nodded solemnly. "Lead single . . ."

"'Previous Devious'?" I suggested.

"You," she said, poking me in the arm with her index finger, "are very good at this. You should be in my fake band, too. Can you play anything?"

"I play a mean air guitar," I replied.

"Excellent, excellent. So, so far we've got you on air guitar, Lauren on imaginary drums, and me on silent vocals. We'll be the new Beatles in no time flat." She made a grabby-hand in my direction. "Vodka, please."

I began to pass it to her, but stopped myself just in time. "Actually, we don't have Theo today. And I've already been drinking. Which means you're the DD—unless you want to take the blame for wrecking Theo's car."

Brandy made a face. "Fine. But you're DD tomorrow."

"Deal," I replied, and did another shot.

Truth was, I could easily reach into Brandy, steal her sobriety for myself, and be totally fine to drive. It was a neat trick that I'd used many times, and it wouldn't even affect her, since when you steal sobriety from a sober person, all that's left underneath is more sobriety. But it would be pretty hard to explain, at least without revealing a few more things about myself than I wanted to.

So I kept drinking, and Brandy kept watching me wistfully, and we both kept coming up with names for her fake band that I, apparently, was now part of. And when we got back to town and found Theo already waiting for us at the diner, the first thing Brandy did was tell him today's list of band names. All fourteen of them.

"Aspen came up with half of those," she added, sliding into the booth beside me. "The best one was mine, though."

"Which one was the best?" said Theo, looking completely disinterested. Seriously, how had Brandy ever dated a guy who wasn't even interested when she talked?

"Frenemesis. Obviously." Brandy smiled proudly. "You know, like frenemies. Except more so."

I added the bits I'd come up with: "Album title: *You're Awesome and I Hate You*. Lead single: 'Those Spiders in Your Pillow Are Totally Not From Me.'"

"Aspen's gonna be my air guitarist," she said.

"Uh-huh," said Theo, raising an eyebrow at me. For a second I was sure I saw jealousy on his face, but no, it was just a regular Theo look. I'd taken care of any potential for jealousy on the morning after the breakup. I'd basically fast-forwarded to the part where they were totally over each other and fine with just being friends.

"So how was your hike?" asked Brandy, after we'd put in our usual orders. "Meet any mountain lions?"

I cracked right up. So did Brandy. She leaned into me and

there was this great moment where I was hyper-aware of this joke that only she and I shared. Only Brandy and me, out of all the people in the entire world.

"Uh, no," said Theo, who obviously didn't get it. "I did meet a girl, though."

That shut me up.

"A girl!" Brandy leaned forward, elbows on the table. "Pretty?"

"I guess," said Theo, who suddenly seemed to find the table very interesting. He traced one finger along a line in the wood, following it with his eyes. "Kinda pretty, yeah. Into hiking. And she showed me this cool waterfall. Her name's Natalie."

"Niiiiice," said Brandy. "You, my friend, should totally hit that."

Yup. The fast-forwarding was working out very, very well.

"Gonna see this Natalie again?" I said.

Theo shrugged. "Maybe."

Brandy shot me an exasperated look. "Only maybe?"

"Well," said Theo, "she kinda invited me to a party . . . ?"

"Only kinda?" said Brandy, her patience clearly wearing thin. This had always been a Brandy-and-Theo issue, even back when they'd just started dating and everything between them was sunshine and puppies and unicorns that farted rainbows or whatever. Brandy was a talker. Theo was the exact opposite, and it bugged the hell out of her.

Just one of many reasons I'd done them a favor by breaking them up.

Theo shrugged. "It was one of those 'if you're free, this is going on' things. She said I could bring you guys, too."

"Dude, that's not a 'kinda' invitation," I said. "That's an actual invitation."

Beside me, Brandy nodded. "Details. Now."

"Fourth of July," he said. "After the fireworks. Guess they have fireworks here?"

"They have fireworks everywhere," I said, because Theo was one of those kids who'd never lived anywhere but Brooklyn, and didn't completely believe in the existence of places that weren't part of New York City.

"Huh," he said. "Anyway, here's the address."

He pulled a crumpled piece of notebook paper from his pocket and spread it on the table. I peered at the address. Cherry Street. I knew where that was.

"So we're going to this, right?" said Brandy.

I thought for a second. On the one hand, I'd never really been into the idea of mingling with the locals up here. On the other hand, I still remembered how devastated Theo had been after the breakup—before I'd stolen his negative feelings away, at least. He deserved to have a cute new girl to flirt with.

"Apparently the girl whose house it is? She does this every year." Theo let himself grin for the first time since mentioning the mysterious Natalie. "And her parents are never home."

Just like that, we had plans for the Fourth of July.

⚠

Three Peaks was so named for the most obvious reason in the world: It was a valley town, hemmed in by land that sloped gently upward, except for three points that weren't very gentle at all. There was the Slope to the north, where even in summer you could see the purposeful lines of ski trails striping through the trees. To the southwest was the Hill, a weird lump of land that looked like it had once wanted to grow up and be a real mountain, but had forgotten to eat its vegetables along the way. Then there was the Cliff. The same Cliff that I'd helped repair only a few nights ago. The same Cliff that the Quick family had been repairing for . . . well, I didn't know how long. According to Grandma, if we ever stopped performing the triad ritual, the wall of rock would crumble, sending an avalanche down the incline, through our house and through the May Day field and straight into town, crushing everything in its path.

To be honest, when I'd first learned about the ritual's purpose, back when I was a little kid, I was skeptical. After all, the Cliff wasn't really that high, and there were more than enough trees to stop the falling rocks before they reached the town. But Grandma had insisted that it was true, and Dad agreed with her, so who was I to argue? It wasn't like I was an expert on nature. The closest we came to nature in Brooklyn was Prospect Park.

If I ever needed absolute proof that nobody in Three Peaks knew what my family did for them, or how dangerous the Cliff actually was, it was this: Every Fourth of July, at the foot of the Cliff, the town's fire department shot fireworks into the air—and the rest of the town gathered on the Cliff's edge to watch.

That night, Brandy, Theo, and I spread out a blanket and observed said sparkly lights from a point not too close to the edge, but not too far away, either, all of us going "Ooh" along with the kids and parents and grandparents around us.

At one point, Brandy said, "Look at how the fireworks are lighting up the treetops. I feel like we're in *Harry Potter* or something."

Theo's reply was, "My roof is still better."

"Shut up, it is not," I said. Brandy gave me a smile. The kind of smile that lingered. The kind of smile that shone brighter than fireworks, even though I was the only one who could see it.

When the show was over and everyone started packing up their stuff, Theo said, "Come on. Let's beat the traffic."

We raced away from the crowd, toward the lot where everyone had left their cars—and Theo started down the mountain, driving faster than I'd ever seen him drive. Although, to be fair, I'd never seen him drive toward a potential hookup before. I guess that changed things.

Eventually, we reached a street clogged with parked cars, and Theo slid in behind a bright red thing. And then, before I could even unbuckle my seat belt, he was out the door and bolting toward the house.

I raced after him, up the street and across a fancy lawn—the rural kind of fancy, which included symmetrical flowering bushes framing the porch. Every light in the house was on, and I could already hear the faint sounds of people laughing and screeching and generally having a good time.

Brandy sprinted after me, and we caught up with Theo just in time to see him giving the door a surly look.

"Um, try knocking?" said Brandy.

He threw a glare at her. "Already did. But nobody's—"

That was when the door flew open, revealing a petite redheaded girl on the other side. She stopped short, like she hadn't been expecting to see us. "Oh! Theo!" she said.

Theo's face broke into a giant, doofy smile, the likes of which I hadn't seen since he'd first started dating Brandy. "Hey, Natalie."

"I told you, call me Natty," she said. "And this must be Brandy and Ashton."

"Aspen." She looked over at me when I spoke—and instantly I could see why Theo was into her. She had these bright blue eyes that reminded me of . . . well, of Brandy, actually. "Aspen Quick."

"That's a weird name," she said, nodding, like she approved.

"I know, right?" I said. This was why I'd ditched my real first name, Jeremy, back in third grade. I liked being the guy with the weird name.

She smiled. "Quick, though. Any relation to Heather?"

"You knew her?" I asked.

Natalie tilted her head a little. "The population of Three Peaks is, like, eight people. Everyone knows everyone. Of course I know Heather." Present tense. Which was weird, but before I could comment on it, she continued: "Anyway, I'm so glad you guys could make it! We always need fresh blood at these things. But I was gonna go meet someone out front, so I'll see you by the pool?"

"Pool pool pool," Brandy murmured under her breath, bouncing a little on her toes. It was so cute.

"See you then!" said Theo, waving with this sort of glassy-eyed expression on his face.

Natalie pushed past us—but as soon as her feet hit the lawn, she turned back. "Oh, and here's a tip, since you're all newbies. Don't drink the Red."

"The what?" I said.

"You heard me."

"But what does that even mean?" asked Brandy.

"You'll see," said Natalie, and started across the lawn, toward a car that was pulling in behind Theo's.

The house was empty. Lights on but nobody home— which probably meant everyone was in the backyard. So the three of us added our shoes to the giant pile by the front door, and followed the faint noise of the party through a hallway and a kitchen and out through another door—and that was when the volume cranked up to eleven. I let out a low whistle as I took it all in.

The pool, packed with kids splashing around and dunking each other and trying their best to hold their cups aloft. The massive deck that surrounded it. The hot tub. I mean, there was a *hot tub*.

"Still think your roof is better?" said Brandy, smirking at Theo. She was already stripping her dress off, revealing . . . ah-ha. She was wearing a bikini underneath. A neon-blue one.

Brandy

in

a

bikini.

Seriously.

Apparently oblivious to the fact that my eyeballs were trying to pop right out of their sockets and attach themselves to her skin, she rolled the dress into a ball, tossed it off to the side, where it landed on a pile of purses, and ran for the pool.

And . . . cannonball.

A few people shrieked with glee as a wave of water cascaded outward from the epicenter of Brandy's cannonball, and then she resurfaced, blond hair dark with water, mascara already staining the tops of her cheeks, lips curled up in a grin. She waved at us. Theo waved back. A couple seconds passed before it occurred to me that I had muscles in my arms, and I could use those muscles to make my hand wave, too.

I made my hand wave, and I made my face smile, and oh god, Brandy in a bikini. Up at the lake she always wore this old black one-piece thing. But *this*. This was . . .

"You okay, man?" said Theo. "You look like you're about to keel over."

I tried to make my smile look a little more natural. "Um. She, um."

Theo glanced back at Brandy, whose top half—oh, what a top half—was still visible above the water. Then he looked back at me. "Ah."

"Your roof," I said firmly, "is definitely not better than this."

He side-eyed me. "You're into her, huh?"

Like he hadn't noticed me ogling her for the past two goddamn years.

"Would you be cool if I were?" I asked, trying to sound more chill than I felt.

Theo took a moment to think about this. Then he shrugged. "Not like we're ever gonna get together again. But listen, man. If you hurt her? I will break your face. You get that?"

If I hurt Brandy, I'd gladly break my own face.

"Got it."

"Cool," said Theo, and clapped me on the shoulder. "I'm gonna go find Natalie."

When he was gone, I took a moment to scan the party around me. The air buzzed with energy, the whole place smelled like alcohol, and almost everyone, whether in the pool or not, wore nothing but a bathing suit.

It was one thing to strip down to my shorts at the lake, where it was just my friends and some old people and little kids and we were all in our separate boats, minding our own business—but something about the closeness of this crowd made me want to keep my shirt exactly where it was. So instead of diving in after Brandy, I looked around for the booze—and immediately spotted a group of people clustered together in one corner of the deck.

I moved closer, until I saw a long bench containing not bottles or cans, but four ugly orange coolers with handwritten labels: *Blue. Green. Yellow. Red.*

A girl in a long skirt and a fringed suede vest was bent low over the Yellow cooler, filling a cup. She handed it up to a waiting guy, who tipped it back and downed half its contents in one gulp. "Top me off?" he said.

"Back of the line, Kendrick," said the girl. Her voice was familiar, even though I was pretty sure I hadn't met her before. But then it clicked—just as she turned toward me and said, "What's your poison?"

Leah.

Her hair wasn't down, like it had been when I'd met her a few days ago. It was up in a series of messy knots—at least eight of them. Between that, the dark lipstick, and the vest that she wore over her T-shirt, she looked like she belonged at Woodstock. Or an eighties Goth club. Or both at the same time.

Either way, the whole look was kind of unnervingly hot. But then, of course, we had the thing where she probably still hated me.

"Oh," I said.

"Oh," she said back, narrowing her eyes as she recognized me. "Who invited you?"

Yup. Definitely still hated me.

"Um. Natalie. I mean, she invited my friend Theo. You met him the other day and—"

"Does Natty know you're a thief?" said Leah.

"Look, I swear I'm not," I said. "I was just . . ."

She pushed herself to her feet, letting her multi-layered peasant skirt swirl around her as she stared me down with black-rimmed eyes. "You were just what?"

I had to think of something, fast. Something that, however stupid, would at least get me off the hook for attempted thievery.

"I wanted to put my number in your phone," I lied, trying my best to look contrite. "I thought you were cute and, um . . ."

She blinked at me—and then, to my surprise, she actually laughed. "So you're not a thief? You're just kind of a moron?"

Well, I was definitely more thief than moron, though not in the way that she thought. But since I obviously couldn't say so, I just rubbed absently at my neck, which had tensed up yet again, and shrugged.

Without waiting for a real reply, she rolled her eyes. "Well, make no mistake about this: If I catch you stealing my stuff again, or anyone else's stuff for that matter, I will cut off one of your extremities and I will make you eat it. And you don't get to pick which one. Got that?"

"Which one would *you* pick?" I asked, raising an eyebrow.

"Oh my god, please don't tell me you came over here to flirt. It's not doing you any favors."

Ouch. But also, fair point. That had been weak. "Well, I actually came over for a drink. Are you the lady I should be speaking to?"

"That I am," she said, and took a cup from the stack between the Green and Yellow coolers. "Color of preference?"

"I'm not sure yet," I said. "What's in them?"

Leah laughed. "That's the one question I can't answer. You're looking at tonight's Sadie Ellis Specials. They come in a variety of colors, and each one contains whatever ingredients Sadie found necessary to achieve exactly the right hue. Behold," she said, lifting the lid off the Blue container. Sure enough, the liquid inside was the kind of blue usually found in crayon boxes and artificially flavored ice pops.

I considered my options. "Well, Natty said not to drink the Red. So, anything but that."

Leah's lips curled into a wry grin. "That's because Natty Frain has the tolerance of a chipmunk. According to Sadie, Red's the cream of the crop."

Ah. So it was a question of tolerance, not taste. Well, I had the tolerance of a two-hundred-pound linebacker. Mostly because I'd reached into a two-hundred-pound linebacker one time and stolen his tolerance. So, yeah, Red would not be a problem.

"Are you drinking the Red, too?" I asked.

"I'm drinking Sprite," she replied. "I'm Sadie and Jesse's designated driver."

That was when a wet, towel-clad girl ran up to us, feet slapping on the deck. "Fill me up, Wolfe!" she said.

Leah took her cup and held it under the Red spigot until it was full.

"Hey," said the boy beside me—Kendrick—who'd drained his Yellow entirely by now. Behind him, a few more people frowned, too.

"Hey nothing," said Towel Girl. "I made these, so I get to cut the line. Artist's privilege."

"You're Sadie Ellis?" I asked, as Leah handed her cup back.

"The one and only," she replied, and took a long sip of Red. "And you are . . . ?"

"Aspen Quick," I said. "I was just about to get some . . . Red, I guess."

"Wait, *Quick*?" said Leah.

"Good choice," said Sadie. "Red's the shit. Hey, Leah, have you seen Jesse yet?"

"Quick, as in related to Heather?" Leah continued.

"As in yeah," I said . . . and took in her expression, which had gone instantly sour. "Why?"

"Nothing," she said curtly, then turned back to Sadie. "Nope. No Jesse yet."

"Dude, are you getting a drink or not?" said Kendrick, poking my shoulder.

Below me, Leah was already kneeling and pouring a drink for me. "Here you go," she said, and turned away from me as soon as I'd taken my cup from her. "Give it here, Kendrick."

I knew she was just making sure the kid got his drink before he went ballistic, but I got the distinct impression that I'd just been dismissed. That I was back on her shit list, this time for a reason I couldn't figure out.

"Try it," said Sadie, who'd skirted around Kendrick to stand beside me. She nodded at the drink in my hand.

I sipped. It tasted bitter and sour and sweet all at once— and very, very alcoholic. "Damn," I murmured, eyeing the cup. It was almost full. I wasn't actually sure I could make it through the whole thing.

"I know, right?" said Sadie gleefully. "Best one I've ever made. I'm on my third. Isn't it so good? I just wish Jesse were here to try it. He'd be on the *roof* by now!"

"Why's Leah . . . I mean, wait, who's Jesse? And, like, literally on the roof?"

"Wait, I'll show you," said Sadie, and reached below the drinks bench, where a couple purses were stashed. She withdrew a phone, punched in a password, and scrolled through her photos until she found the set she was looking for.

"That's Jesse," she said, holding up a shot of a guy crossing his eyes for the camera. It was a weird face he was making, but even weirder was the fact that I could've sworn I'd seen him somewhere before. I squinted a little, but before I could process the details of his face, Sadie scrolled to another photo. Jesse and a girl, leaning shyly together on the same bench that currently held the drink coolers.

Not just any girl, though. It was Leah. Had I seriously thought *shy* in reference to Leah? But I looked closer, and sure enough, that was how she looked. Shy. Young. Oddly hopeful.

Sadie scrolled again, and this time I saw what she'd been talking about before. The guy from the photos, no longer cross-eyed, was standing on the roof of this same house, arms aloft, weird streaks of light all around him.

"Glow-stick hula hoops," explained Sadie, using her fingers to zoom in. "He strung a bunch of them together to make hoops, and it didn't really work, but who cares? Still awesome."

That was when it hit me. The face in the picture was the same face I'd seen during the triad ritual the other night. This was the guy who'd once owned the one-armed Batman. I'd taken away his inclination toward being competitive.

I wondered if my magic had worked better on him than it had on Leah.

Realizing she was waiting for an answer, I said, "Yeah, awesome. So . . . he's not here?"

"Apparently not," she said, and paused to put her phone away again. "He's been MIA for a couple days now. He does that sometimes. We figured he'd be back for the party, but . . ." She trailed off with a shrug.

Jesse'd been missing for a couple days? That was weird . . . but it had to be a coincidence. My magic couldn't make people disappear. Parts of people, sure, but not *whole* people.

"Hey!" Sadie shouted. "Why're you still dressed in *clothes*? You should come swimming!"

I eyed the pool, all splashes and shrieks and bikinis and guys with pecs and muscled arms. Seriously, every single guy in that pool looked totally built. How was that possible?

"I'd better not," I said. "I, ah, forgot my bathing suit."

"Just swim in your boxers," said Sadie, tugging at one of my belt loops in a way that probably would've been hot if she weren't slurring so badly. "Unless you're a tighty-whities guy. Oh my god, you're totally a tighty-whities guy, aren't you!"

"Yeah," I lied. "And you, lovely lady, are drunk."

"Yes I am!" she said. "Now get your butt into that pool."

Sadie tugged at my belt loop again, this time with way more force. So I put my hand on her shoulder, where her towel had fallen away to reveal the black strap of her bathing suit. I reached into the suit, found her desire to swim with me—more a whim than an actual desire, and not very big at all—and took it away.

Then I said, "Nah, I'm good."

"Okay!" she replied, and let her towel fall to the deck. She tipped her drink back, finishing it off with one gulp—then, with a running start, she cannonballed back into the pool, just like Brandy had done.

On the other side of the pool, I spotted Theo, talking to red-haired Natalie. It looked like a good conversation, all smiles and wide gestures on her part, lots of fervent nodding on his. I'd have pegged it for a hookup about to happen, except that they weren't alone. There was another girl—a tall pasty-white brunette—smiling and gesturing right alongside Natalie.

Whatever. Maybe eventually the other girl would get the hint and leave them alone.

I rolled my shoulders and sipped more of my Red.

"Hey, Aspen," came a voice from right below me. A few feet away, Brandy propped her elbows on the pool's edge, water glistening in her eyelashes as she smiled up at me. "Is that for me?"

"What do you—oh!" I said, remembering the Red. "It's mine, but you can have some." I knelt down on the deck to hand her my cup. As she took it, I considered how much closer I was to her, now that I wasn't standing. The deck was wet, but I suddenly didn't care. I sat cross-legged right at the edge of the pool, watching as Brandy took a long drink of my Red. "How's the water?"

"So nice." She tilted her head a little. "You should come in."

"Nah, I didn't bring anything to swim in."

Brandy grinned. "And that, my friend, is how skinny-dipping was invented."

"Umphthlgg," I said. Or something like that.

"Come on," she said, touching my knee with two wet fingers. "You be the trend-setter. I'll be the second-in-command. Everyone else will totally follow. Let's be those weird out-of-towners who turned a good party into a *great* party."

Or, at least, that's what I thought she said. Honestly, I

didn't hear much of anything after *I'll be the second-in-command*. Meaning if I stripped off all my clothes, so would Brandy.

I took a long, deep drink of my Red, and willed the rest of my body not to notice what my brain was thinking.

"Come onnnnnn," she said, her hand still on my knee.

If I'd been absolutely sure she was kidding, I'd've played along, no question. But there was this shadowed look in her blue eyes, this mischievous party-after-dark look, that made me hesitate. Made me kind of afraid that if I agreed to anything, she'd actually hold me to it.

Which was why I said, "Rain check? For when there aren't a zillion people around?"

"Is that a promise?" she asked.

This time, I was absolutely sure she wasn't kidding. Her smile was hungry, her wet shoulders rigid and waiting. This was it. This was the moment I'd been waiting for. The next move was up to me.

I leaned down, and Brandy pushed herself a little farther out of the pool, arching her neck to bring her lips up to mine, like she was a mermaid and I was a sailor. We kissed, and we kissed, and holy epic everything, I was finally kissing Brandy, *finally*. Her lips tasted like chlorine and warmth, nothing like I'd imagined, everything like I'd imagined.

She parted her lips, tilting her head to the side for a better fit, and someone went "Oo-*oo*-ooh!" behind us, and I was just wondering how much tongue she liked, when my god-damn neck did a stupid spasm thing and I had to pull back.

"Aspen?" said Brandy, her expression caught between worried and offended.

Wincing, I rubbed at my neck. Rolled my shoulders. Waited for the pain to subside to its usual dull background noise. "Sorry," I said.

"Oh, your neck again?" she said, all sympathetic.

"Yeah. Weird angle, I guess."

She paused. "Just the angle, though, right? Everything else was . . ."

"Not weird at all," I replied. No, that wasn't anywhere close to the whole truth. "The exact opposite of weird. It was great."

"Great is not the opposite of weird," said Brandy, but she was smiling.

Smiling in a way that was weirdly shy, considering that not even five minutes ago she'd basically ordered me to take off all my clothes.

I sipped my Red. Then gulped. Then chugged, because Brandy was still giving me that shy smile, and chugging my drink seemed like the appropriate response to that. Then I set my cup aside, which meant that there was no longer anything between my eyes and Brandy's chest. Gah. Her hand was touching my knee again. *Gahhh.*

"You broke your drink," she said, nodding at my empty cup. "How about you fix it, and get one for me while you're at it?"

"I am thy knight in armor," I replied. "I shall do as thou commandeth."

The mission was more Red. And more Red was so close! Leah Ramsey-Wolfe was right there, still holding cups under spigots and giving colors to people who were not me. I had to get over there.

Step one was standing up.

I did that.

I stumbled, and heard Brandy giggle behind me.

Then I righted myself and aimed for Leah and started walking and held out my cup when I reached her. "More Red, iffen you please."

She glanced at the cup, and then at me. "Looks like Natty's not the only one with a chipmunk tolerance. Go chug some water, then we'll talk."

I looked at her lipstick, which was smudged, and her multi-knotted hair, which should not have looked good but did, and her vest, which was just a seriously cool thing to wear.

"Where's water?" I asked, because I really did want to talk. Not to her, though. I wanted to talk to Brandy. Actually, no, I didn't, because in order to talk, you had to not be kissing. Kissing was definitely the main thing I wanted to do with Brandy.

"Kitchen," she said, pointing. I followed her finger with my eyes. The house was so far away, and suddenly, more than anything ever, I needed to sit down. So I sat down. "Jesus," said Leah, squatting beside me. "You okay, newbie?"

"Aspen," I said.

"Aspen Quick," she said. "Yeah, don't remind me. Stay

where you are, okay? Hey, Sadie! Get out of there and get this boy some water!"

There was a shout of protest from the pool, which set Leah grumbling. I couldn't tell what they were saying, but I knew that the result wasn't going to be water.

"Get Brandy instead," I said. "Or that other one. Theo!"

"Who?" said Leah.

"Sprite!" I said. "You said you had Sprite. Can I have some?"

She hesitated for a moment, then got up and got her cup and handed it to me. "Drink slowly. If you need to barf, trash can's over there."

I drank slowly. I did not need to barf.

"Not much of a drinker, huh?" she said.

"I've had a few drinks in my time," I replied loftily.

"Uh-huh," she replied. "What about food? Did you eat today?"

I thought about that. I'd had a sandwich for lunch, and then . . .

My stomach growled. Yeah, I'd forgotten to eat dinner.

I sipped some more of her Sprite. Leah's Sprite . . . in Leah's cup. She'd been holding it, drinking out of it, for at least as long as I'd been here. Maybe for hours.

"You," I said, focusing on Leah. "You have not been drinking. At all. Correcto?"

Someone snickered, but Leah just raised her eyebrows. "Not even a drop since I got here."

I felt around the cup for a place where I could reach in

and find her sobriety. I just wanted a piece of it. A little, tiny piece. She wouldn't miss it, because there'd just be more sobriety left in its place. She wouldn't miss it, and it would help me so very much.

I reached. I found. I pulled a piece away, maybe not a little piece, maybe something more like a medium-sized piece—and I directed it inward, letting it settle inside me.

There was a moment of peace.

Then my stomach heaved, and my vision blurred, and the whole world

went

black.

△ BEFORE △

I remember the exact moment the idea hit me. It was the Monday of spring break, or maybe the Tuesday, and it was just about midnight. Brandy and her friend Lauren had already gone home, thanks to their parents' rigid ideas about curfews, but Theo was still out, because *his* parents were out of town on yet another business trip. Me? I was out because I didn't give a shit what my dad thought.

It was Theo who'd suggested going to Wowza, this East Village club that was supposed to be super awesome despite its incredibly stupid name. It was also Theo who remembered that we'd tried to get into Wowza a few weeks ago, but the bouncer had been able to tell that our IDs were fake.

But it was me who had the most genius idea ever, and insisted on trying again.

When we got to the front of the line, the bouncer gave me this look, like he could already tell he'd have to turn us away. But when he beckoned us forward and asked for ID, I pretended to trip, and used his thick arm to keep myself upright. His arm, which was covered in a suit jacket. I reached in and stripped away his memory of how to tell a fake ID from a real one. Thirty seconds later, Theo and I were inside.

My phone vibrated over and over again in my pocket, just like it did every time I stayed out late. I wondered if Dad had called Mom this obsessively, when she'd left. I wondered what would happen if I didn't go home tonight. I wondered if he'd find something of mine and reach into it and bring me back, and then I could point out that if he was willing to break the No Stealing From Family rule once, he might as well break it again to bring Mom back—

"Hottie alert," said Theo, pointing at a group of girls on the dance floor, all wearing stilettos and slinky dresses.

I switched my phone from vibrate to silent, and I danced and danced until I couldn't stand up anymore.

The next morning, Dad woke me up early, looming in my doorway dressed in a suit and tie.

"Spring break, 'member?" I mumbled. "No school. Leavemealone."

"What time did you get home last night?" asked Dad.

"Dunno. Like one? Two?"

"Son, you can't do that."

Yes, I could. I pulled my pillow over my face and stayed quiet.

"And if you do," Dad went on, "you have to pick up when I call. Or text me and tell me you're alive. If I hadn't known you were out with that Valdez kid, I'd've . . ."

I listened closely. He'd've what? Brought me back?

He sighed. "I almost went to the police."

Sure, but only almost. He hadn't gone to the police, and he hadn't reached into me and brought me back. I left the pillow on top of my face, and willed him to go away.

"Aspen, this past month, you've been . . . acting out. I've gotten calls from your teachers about missed classes. Complaints about your behavior when you do bother showing up. Is this still to do with your mother leaving?"

That was such a dumb question, I couldn't help laughing. The pillow muffled the sound, but Dad definitely heard it.

"Son, you know you can talk to me, right?"

Ugh, that was it.

I removed the pillow. I sat up. I talked: "Bring Mom back, and I'll stop staying out late."

"Aspen, this isn't about—"

"Yes, it is."

Silence fell. In the darkness of my bedroom, Dad stared at me. I stared back.

Finally, he reached up to his neck and adjusted his tie. "I have to go to work."

"So go," I said.

From then on, I stayed out as late as I wanted.

CHAPTER FIVE

Something was slapping my face. Someone was saying my name. Someone had replaced my tongue with a dead mouse.

"Did I throw up?" asked someone with my voice. I could feel the dead mouse moving.

"Nope," said a guy. "You just blacked out. What the hell'd you give him, Leah?"

"Red. One cup. And some Sprite. The Sprite's what made him pass out, which, *what*?"

I pried my eyes open. Some guy was kneeling in front of me, palm open, ready to smack my face again. I recognized him: Kendrick, the one who'd been drinking the Yellow. Behind him was Leah Ramsey-Wolfe, arms folded crossly over her chest.

"You spiked the Spike," I said. Then corrected myself: "You sprite the Spike. Ugh. YouknowwhatImean."

"I did no such thing, you idiot," said Leah, although she

was starting to smile. "Come on. Get on your feet. Did you drive here?"

"No, Theo drove. He was with Natty Natalie. Where's she?"

Leah scanned the crowd, then pointed across the pool. There indeed was Natalie, and she was kissing . . . not Theo. That definitely, definitely wasn't Theo. That was the tall brunette girl who'd been talking with them before.

"Ooh," I said, because come on, that was super sexy.

That was when I spotted Theo, a little ways away from Natalie and her ladyfriend. He was chugging something out of a cup, chugging, chugging, then tossing the cup away, then running for the pool, then jumping in. More of a belly-flop than a jump, really. And he was still wearing all his clothes.

"So much for that guy," said Leah. "Kendrick, who else here is even close to sober?"

"Not I," he replied. "I'm on Yellow number, like, four billion."

"How about Corey?" asked Leah, sounding increasingly desperate.

"How about *you*?" said Kendrick.

Leah made a face. "I said I'd drive Sadie and Jesse home, not everyone. Well, just Sadie now, I guess, but . . ."

"You," I said, "have an excellent vest on. You should drive me."

"What's going on?" came the nicest voice in the universe, from right out of nowhere. Brandy, pretty beautiful lovely

Brandy, was coming toward us with a towel draped over her shoulders. She was dripping pool water everywhere. She looked like a mermaid with legs.

"You look like a mermaid with legs," I told her.

"He's drunk," explained Leah.

Brandy's lips twitched. "So I see." She knelt in front of me and put her palm on my forehead. I leaned into her. Her hand was wet and warm, just like her lips. "Theo's, um, slightly indisposed. But, want me to drive you home?"

"Please, please do," said Leah. "You been drinking?"

"Like one sip," said Brandy. "What are you, the sobriety police?"

"Basically yes," said Leah. "But if you're good to go, then please, be my guest."

Brandy held out a hand to help me up, and I thought fast. She was about to drive me home, which meant we'd be alone in a car together, and that was the kind of thing you want to be sober for. But I was drunk. Really drunk. And that needed fixing. So when I grabbed her hand and heaved myself to my feet, I made sure my other hand brushed her hip, right where her bikini was. I left it there just long enough to reach into the fabric, pull out some of *her* sobriety, and pull it into myself.

My head cleared instantly.

Holy *hell* had that been bad.

"Let me just find out where Theo put his keys," said Brandy. "Don't go anywhere."

She headed for the pool, in which Theo had joined a

bunch of the shirtless guys. There seemed to be a wave war going on, guys versus girls, and Theo looked like he was having a good time. I wondered if he'd already forgotten about Natty.

I turned back to Leah, who'd started taking drink orders again.

"Sorry I passed out," I said.

She handed a cup of Blue to some girl, then turned a sour expression on me. "Well, look at who's suddenly capable of saying words again."

"Heh," I said, more than a little mortified. Instinct was telling me to brush against her, reach into her, and steal her memory of the past few minutes—but I wasn't actually sure I *could* steal the memory from her.

Plus, that look she was giving me? That definitely wasn't just because I'd passed out. She'd been giving me the same look since before I'd even started drinking.

"Hey," I said. "Why'd you act like that when I told you my name?"

"Like what?" she said. "I didn't act like anything."

"Like a snot, kind of," I said. "Were you and Heather enemies or something? Or frenemies? Or frenemeses?"

She let out a huff of laughter. "Nobody says 'frenemies' anymore, newbie."

I smiled. "Nobody says 'newbie' anymore, frenemy."

"I do," she said, and did not smile back.

Well then.

A few minutes of awkward silence later, Brandy came

back, dress once again covering her bikini, key ring around her index finger. Her hair was still dripping pool water onto her shoulders, but she didn't seem to care.

"Ready?" she asked.

I glanced over at Leah, who'd apparently lost interest in me. "Yeah. Ready."

Brandy drove in silence down the quiet street, then another, then onto Main Street, which was also quiet except for a small crowd of smokers outside the town's only pub. Main Street grew smaller and smaller as it sloped upward, into the mountains, toward the Cliff. Just over the bridge that spanned the tiny creek, then past the second S-curve, marked by a sign that had long since been hidden by creeping vines and drooping tree branches, was the left turn that would take us to Grandma's house.

Brandy took the bumpy driveway slowly until Aunt Holly's car came into view. Then she parked and killed the engine. Then she . . . didn't say anything. For the space of three full breaths, she didn't say anything. Then:

"Aspen, do you wanna date me?"

I turned sharply toward her—so sharply that my neck tensed up again. Brandy had this way of saying things where you sometimes weren't sure if it was just a plain question, or if there was an accusation in there, too. Her eyes usually tilted the balance in favor of one or the other, but it was dark in Theo's car. I couldn't see her eyes at all.

Either way, though, the answer was the same.

"Um, yes? As in *hell* yes?"

She smiled. "Yeah, I thought so."

My stomach curdled a little. It was a warm *thought so,* but it wouldn't be the first time Brandy had let me down easy.

"Yeah?" I said.

She nodded. "It's funny, because I just broke up with Theo, what, twenty seconds ago? We were together for months. I should still be getting over it. I shouldn't be sitting here, wanting to . . ."

"Wanting to what?" I asked, trying not to sound too eager.

"You know." She laughed, light and airy. A cotton-candy laugh. "Make out with my ex's best friend. In his car, no less."

Yup. That was my cue. I leaned over, craning my head carefully to the left, and our lips met again. She tasted the same as before. She kissed the same, too. But the rest was different. Instead of shouting, splashing partygoers around us, there was the closed-in quiet of the car, and the soft, uneven sounds of breathing—which started to grow deeper, heavier—

"But isn't it weird?" she said, pulling away abruptly.

"Huh?" I said dizzily.

"This," she said, gesturing from me to her to me to her. "This should feel like . . . too soon, or something. It doesn't. That's messed up."

So, wait, I'd fast-forwarded both of them through the post-breakup process, and Brandy was *still* finding a reason to second-guess hooking up with me? This was so not fair.

"No it's not," I said. "Every breakup's different, right?"

"Like you would know," she said, in this voice that was half teasing, but also half not.

She had a point. I'd been so hung up on Brandy for so long that I'd never bothered finding anyone else to date. The closest I'd come was this girl Keisha Sullivan, but that was a one-night stand after junior prom, followed by a solid two weeks of being unable to look each other in the eye. That wasn't dating.

"Still," I said, and put my hand on her shoulder. And reached in. If I could just find the doubt that was keeping her away from me, I could pull it away, and—

She shrugged my hand off. "Just go inside, okay? I should get back to the party. Theo said he scored crash space, but I should still check on him. . . ." She took a deep, audible breath, and let it out again. "And I'll think about this."

"This," I repeated. "As in you and me?"

"As in yeah," she said. "I like you, Aspen. But Theo's still my friend. I kind of want to, you know . . . see if he's cool with this."

Well, in that case, everything was fine. Theo wasn't looking to get back together with Brandy. I'd made sure of that.

"That's a good idea," I said, and unbuckled my seat belt. "Don't stay out too late."

"You're not the boss of me."

I laughed and got out of the car. "Drive safe. And stay away from the Red." ♥

"Bet your ass I will," she said, and started the engine again so the headlights could light my way to the front door.

"You were out late," said Grandma, from the living room.

I shed my shoes and meandered in to see her. The overhead light was off, and there was a fire burning low in the hearth. The regular kind of fire, not the turquoise triad-ritual kind. Grandma was curled up in her armchair, a knitted blanket draped over her knees, a thick book propped up on the pillow in her lap.

"Not as late as everyone else," I said. "I was the first person to leave. I . . . wasn't feeling too great. Brandy drove me home."

Grandma squinted past me, as if trying to see into the hall. "Where is she, then?"

"Oh, she went back to the party. Theo's still there, and it's his car."

She eyed me. After a moment, she put the book carefully on the table beside her, next to a mug and a pair of glasses. "Have you been drinking, Aspen? I know everyone drinks at those get-togethers."

"I am one hundred percent sober," I said. "Want me to walk in a straight line? Or, here: Z, Y, X, W, V, U, T—"

"More to the point," she interrupted, a sly smile curving her lips, "whose sobriety did you steal?"

"Oh," I said, and found that I was too surprised by the question to give her anything but the truth. "Brandy's. How did you know?"

Grandma waved a dismissive hand at me. "My Holly's been doing it for months. Drinking herself stupid and then stealing sobriety so she can drive herself home. Or else drinking herself stupid in her bedroom, so she doesn't have to bother with thievery. She keeps Scotch in her closet, like she thinks I don't know." She sighed, rolling her shoulders as her eyes turned sad. "I always know."

"From her breath?" I asked.

"From her eyes," she said. "Aspen . . . you do understand that there's a difference between drinking at a party with your friends, and drinking alone in your bedroom. Don't you?"

I'd never actually thought about that before. And why would I? As far as I was concerned, the entire point of alcohol was to make hanging out more fun. Social lubricant, Brandy liked to call it.

But I was pretty sure I knew what Grandma was getting at. I nodded.

"Good," she said. "Remember that difference, my boy. You'll have a much greater chance at being happy if you do."

I nodded again . . . and then noticed something.

"Are those leaves in your hair?" I asked.

"Hm? Where?"

I leaned forward and plucked them out: two leaves, both small, tangled in Grandma's steel-gray hair.

"Goodness." With a little laugh, she patted her head with one hand, like she was checking for more. "I didn't even think to look."

I grinned. "Did you go to the fireworks? I didn't see you there."

"No. Lord, no. Too many people. I took a walk, but not until afterward. I wasn't going to venture out in a crowd without you or Holly there to steal memories for me."

"Steal memories?"

She raised an eyebrow. "Remember the favor you did for me, the night you first arrived?"

I did remember. The night Theo and Brandy and I had driven up from the city, Grandma had taken us out for pasta. Not particularly good pasta, at least by Brooklyn standards, but still. She'd pulled me aside afterward to tell me something—something about the triad ritual, or else she'd've just said it in front of my friends—and one of the servers had overheard. Grandma had asked me, shortly after that, to steal not just the guy's memory of our conversation, but his memory of having met her at all.

"You do that all the time?" I asked.

"It's easier to move through the world when you have a degree of anonymity on your side, Aspen."

Was that supposed to be profound? I couldn't tell.

"So Aunt Holly didn't go on your walk with you?"

"She's staying the night at her office," replied Grandma. "Very busy right now."

Aunt Holly was a lawyer. If television was to be believed, lawyers were *always* busy. But still: "It's the Fourth of July. And it's almost midnight."

Grandma laughed. "Well past midnight, you'll find."

Well past midnight, and there was nobody to hang out with except Grandma. Not that Grandma wasn't cool, but . . .

"I guess I should go to bed," I said.

She nodded. "A fine idea. Sleep well. The Cliff is weakening again, and I expect there'll be another fault by tomorrow. A small one, probably, but you'll need your strength."

"We could fix it now," I said, trying not to sound too eager.

"Tomorrow," she said, firmly but kindly. "You don't fix a thing before it's broken. And you know this isn't a job for fewer than three of us."

I did know that. It was part of the reason I'd come up in June this year, instead of August, like I usually did. Grandma and Aunt Holly had been hosting a slew of relatives since Heather's death, all of whom had helped with the ritual in her absence, and I'd been next on the list.

"Speaking of that," I said, "any word on Aunt Calla moving out here permanently?"

Grandma made a face. My aunt Calla was the frontrunner for replacing Heather as the ritual's permanent third—except she was old and cranky, and she and Grandma got along about as well as Batman and the Joker. Still, she was retired, so moving to Three Peaks would be easier for her than for most of my other relatives.

"Holly's still asking. Calla's still saying no." Grandma sighed. "For the sake of the Cliff, I hope she changes her mind. But the thought of that woman staying under my roof for more than a week's time . . . Well. It's hardly your problem, is it. Good night, Aspen."

There was a weird edge to her voice, like she might be implying exactly the opposite of what she was saying. But Aunt Calla *wasn't* my problem—I mean, I'd only ever met her twice—so I didn't think too much about it. I just said good night and went upstairs to my room. Well, Heather's room, technically.

I flipped on the light—and practically jumped out of my skin. "What the . . ."

Brandy smiled up at me from where she sat on the bed. "Hi, Aspen."

"But you," I began, gesturing vaguely toward the drive-way downstairs. Hadn't she gone back to the party? She'd started the car again, for sure. But had I actually heard her drive away?

"Theo has crash space," said Brandy. "He said so. Plus he was already wasted when we left. Even if I go back, he'll hardly be able to have a coherent conversation tonight."

Her bare feet swung idly against the sky-blue carpet. Her toenails glittered silver. I took a few cautious steps into the room.

"You, on the other hand, seem weirdly sober for a guy who passed out like an hour ago."

I grinned. "And they say Asians have no tolerance."

"Maybe that only applies if you're a hundred percent," she said.

"Or maybe I'm just a superhero."

Brandy's smile widened. "So that'd make me, what?" She leaned back on her hands, her chest sticking out in a way that was absolutely on purpose. "Lois Lane?"

"Superman?" I said, trying to focus on her face, not on anything below it. "Seriously? I say superhero, and you pick the worst one?"

"Way to miss the point completely, Quick."

Her voice was low. Husky. The sound of it made my mouth go dry. "And what point would that be?"

"Shut the door," she said.

I did.

"We'll have to be quiet," she continued, beckoning me closer to the bed. I moved toward her like a marionette, guided by her hands. This was really happening. Brandy was on my bed, and she wanted me there, too, and she wanted to do things where being quiet might not be easy.

"I can if you can," I said, sitting beside her, resting a hand on her knee. "Except. Shit. I don't have any—"

"I do," she said, holding up a little foil packet. "Come here."

Then we were kissing again, hungrier than before, messier, because the kissing wasn't the endgame anymore. Soon her hands were under my shirt, lifting it up and over my head, and I was easing her dress off, and it was so *fast,* two hours ago we'd never even *kissed,* and wasn't this supposed to go slower?

But Brandy wasn't my first, and I knew I wasn't hers, either. Maybe the slow stuff was just for first-timers.

Or maybe we were both just really, really into it, and there weren't any rules about how fast or slow it had to be, and I should just stop overthinking and—

and—

△ BEFORE △

Mom didn't call Dad after she left. Ever. At least, not as far as I knew. She only ever called me, and it was always on my cell—never the landline—and it was always during the week, always between three thirty and six, after school got out but before Dad came home from work.

At first, I let it go to voicemail. She'd leave messages that all meant the same thing: "I miss you" and "I just want to make sure you're okay" and "I love you" and "Call me back." I did not call her back.

Until Dad announced, a week later, totally out of the blue, that we were moving. Not permanently. Just for a few days. We were moving into a hotel so that Mom could come over with the movers she'd hired, and get her stuff in peace.

"Not just her stuff, but all the stuff we shared, too." I remember his eyes going kind of vague. "We'll have to get new furniture."

I didn't get it. Mom was the one who'd left. Surely she wasn't allowed to keep stuff like furniture if she was the one who'd left.

But when I told this to Dad, he said, "It's not about being allowed. She doesn't want me to have anything of hers. Even couches she sat on, wineglasses she used, things like that."

I should have understood then. Maybe there was a part of me that did, but I didn't let myself think it. Not yet.

The next day, when Mom called, I actually picked up. She was so relieved that she ended up doing most of the talking. All those pent-up things she wanted to say to me, gushing out at once.

"I miss seeing your face every day, Aspen, you have no idea how much," she said.

"How is your father holding up?"

"I hope you'll forgive me."

"It wasn't because of you."

"Are you dating anyone? Do they know about your abilities?"

I said, "Me too." And I said, "Fine" and "Sure, whatever" and "Okay" and "No," until she finally got to the one question I couldn't answer:

"Will you come and visit me? You remember how to get to Aunt Mona's, right? You just take the Long Island Rail Road from Atlantic and—"

"You don't have your own place?" I cut in.

"Not yet, honey. I'm still getting all my finances in order. It could take a while."

"In other words, you're taking all our furniture and you don't even have anywhere to put it?"

She didn't reply right away. The silence went on long enough that I checked to see if my phone had dropped the connection. It hadn't.

"It isn't about the furniture," she said. "And anyway,

your father's well-off. They're just things. He can afford new things."

"Then what's it about?" I asked. "Just screwing up our lives as much as possible?"

"Aspen, sweetheart, no," she said. "I'm only trying to look out for myself. That's all."

"What's that supposed to mean?"

Another silence, this one briefer than the last.

"The ability that you share with your father." Mom's voice went a little bit fragile, as it often did when she talked about our magic. Which was rarely. "I know he would never use it against me. But I would feel much safer if he *couldn't*."

That was when I let myself understand. Our furniture had to go because she'd used it, too. Because Dad and I could still reach into it and get to her.

"You don't trust us," I said, and immediately felt dumb. Obviously she didn't trust us. She'd *left* us.

"I trust *you*," was her only reply. "Come visit me, will you?"

"Why did you really leave?" I asked. "Was it because of our magic?"

A third pause. The longest one yet.

"Not because of the magic itself," she said.

"Then what?"

"Aspen . . ." I heard her taking a deep breath. "Do you miss your cousin?"

"What do you . . . wait, you mean Heather?"

The funeral had been weeks ago. We were all back to our normal lives by now.

"I do mean Heather," said Mom.

"I don't . . . I mean . . . I barely even knew her. It's sad she died, obviously, but it's not like we ever really bonded or anything."

"You cried at the funeral, though," said Mom gently.

"Um, no I didn't," I said. "Maybe you're confusing me with Aunt Holly?"

"You did," said Mom, totally ignoring my joke. "Ask your father. He was there, too."

"Yeah, whatever," I said, and let her go back to convincing me to visit, even as I silently swore I never would.

Later that night, I asked Dad about the funeral. I asked if he remembered me crying. He thought about it for a second, then shook his head. "I could be wrong," he said. "But I really don't think so. Why do you ask?"

"No reason," I said. And that was the end of it.

CHAPTER SIX

I slept in the next morning. Past the bacon, past the coffee, and apparently past Brandy slipping out of my room, because when I finally woke up, the other side of the bed was empty—except for a folded piece of paper sitting on the pillowcase. I fumbled for my glasses so I could read it:

> *A—Took car to get Theo. Lake probably,*
> *so we can talk about Stuff, just the 2 of us. Meet*
> *us later tho? Diner, like usual, 6ish?—B*
> *P.S. Last night was funnnnn. Encore soon?*
> *xo*

Hell yeah. She wanted an encore, *and* I was off the hook for going to the lake today. Thank god, because I was really kind of sick of hanging out there.

I checked my phone just in case she'd texted, too, but nope. Maybe she hadn't wanted the noise to wake me up. Maybe that was why she'd actually written a note by hand. The maybe-thoughtfulness of it made me smile.

It was almost noon by the time I made it downstairs and got the coffeemaker brewing. As I waited for the pot to fill, Grandma came in to meet me. "Ah. I was wondering when I'd see you."

"What's up?" I asked. "Is the Cliff broken yet? Because I'm ready to fix it whenever you are."

"Someone's awfully chipper this morning." Grandma threw me a smile that was almost . . . knowing.

Except she couldn't know, could she? Brandy and I had been so quiet. Painfully quiet, at times. Also, if she did know, I didn't want to know that she knew. Because *ew*.

"I'm not chipper," I said. "Anyway. Cliff?"

"Not until after dark," she replied. "The fault won't appear until then."

"Oh, okay," I said. "Wait, though. How do you know when it'll appear?"

"Past precedent," she replied. "Every Independence Day, hundreds of people gather atop the Cliff. All those bodies, all that weight? Of course there'll be a fault by the next day. Not right away, though," she added, her eyes going vague. "The Cliff holds itself together as best it can. It doesn't ask me for help until there's no other option left."

"Uh-huh." I was still a little unclear on how the whole communicating-with-the-Cliff thing was supposed to work. I didn't ask, though. Not now, when my caffeine-deficient brain probably wouldn't be able to retain the answer.

Speaking of which . . .

The first sip of coffee was, as always, like stepping into

a cold shower after a long day in the August sun.

"Are you going to meet your friends at the lake?" asked Grandma. "Your young lady left quite early this morning."

My young lady. Yeah, she totally knew. I tried my best not to let the thought of her knowing completely gross me out.

"Nah," I said, after another quick sip. "I think I'm just gonna stick around here today."

"Well, at least go outside and get some sun," she said, nodding toward the window. "It's a lovely day."

I knew she was talking about the weather, but I couldn't help thinking that it was a lovely day in every other sense, too. I mean, last night I'd hooked up with Brandy, who was basically the love of my goddamn life. I'd hooked up with Brandy, and I'd slept like a rock, and now I had a really good cup of black coffee in my hands. Everything was perfect. Everything.

Except . . .

No, not everything. Because hooking up with Brandy wasn't the only thing that had happened last night. Last night was also the third time I'd tried to steal something from that girl Leah—and the third time it had gone wrong.

"Yeah," I said. "Outside sounds like a good idea. Call my cell when it's ritual time, okay?"

Leah wasn't at Waterlemon Books when I got there. It was just the old guy—the one I'd seen shelving books the last time I'd been here.

"Can I help you?" he asked as I approached the register. Then he squinted, pushing wire-rimmed glasses up the bridge of his nose. "Ah. The phone thief. I think you'd better leave, son."

"I'm not a—" But I didn't finish. I was already sick of defending myself over that stupid phone thing. "Look, I just need to see Leah. Is she around?"

The old guy let out a sigh. "No, it's just me today. Even Mrs. Llewellyn isn't in town to cover shifts this weekend. Got family up in Toronto or . . . well, somewhere Canadian, at any rate. Keeps making noises about moving up there. Between her and Leah and Jesse, my entire staff will have left me high and dry by the end of the summer, just you watch." He paused, eyeing me. "No chance you're looking for a job, is there?"

"Even though I'm a phone thief?"

The guy let out a dusty laugh. "I don't care what kind of thief you are, so long as it's not books or cash."

That made me smile. This guy was weirdly cool. "Sorry, but no. I'm really just looking for Leah. You said she quit? Is she working somewhere else now?"

"No, no, she didn't quit! Just called in sick." Another sigh. "Jesse's the one who quit—or at least, that's what I choose to assume, given he's missed four shifts without calling in. But our Leah intends to find him and bring him back and then, presumably, talk me into not firing him. She's always had a soft spot for that boy, hasn't she."

My mind flashed back to the picture that Drunk Sadie

had shown me at the party last night. Leah, looking oddly shy as she cozied up to Jesse on that bench. "Suppose so," I said.

He blinked fast, eyes suddenly alert, like he'd just woken up from a daze. He peered at me. "I'm sorry. You're new here, aren't you. And here I am, rattling on about my employees as though you have the first idea who I'm talking about. Anyway. I'm Harry, and it's a pleasure to meet you, alleged phone thief or no."

He held out his hand, and I shook it.

"Leah," I reminded him. "Any idea where I can find her? Or maybe you could give me her number?"

Giving me a grandfatherly kind of smile, Harry shook his head. "I don't give out my employees' numbers. And I haven't the first clue where she's gone. Wherever Jesse went, I suppose, though she didn't seem too sure where that might be. One of his impromptu camping trips, likely enough. Weather's been good for it."

The rest of Sadie's pictures flashed through my memory. Jesse, crossing his eyes for the camera. Jesse, who would have been on the roof, literally, had he not been mysteriously missing from the party. Jesse, whose competitive streak I'd stolen away during the last triad ritual. . . .

". . . your name, son?" Harry was saying. It took me a second to process the question.

"Oh," I said, feeling suddenly flustered. "Aspen Quick."

"Quick, is it?" said Harry, his eyebrows shooting up. "I've known a few Quicks, and no mistake."

111

"Like my grandmother, probably, right?" I asked, and then immediately regretted it. Were you supposed to acknowledge that old people were older than you, or were you supposed to pretend that they looked younger than they did? I'd never been a good judge of that kind of thing.

Harry, though, just laughed. "I'd imagine so," he said. "Which one's your grandmother? Ivy or Lily? I went to school with both of them. Lovely girls. And those pretty names."

I frowned. "Neither, actually," I said. "My grandmother's name is Willow."

He peered at me, pushing his glasses up again. "Willow," he repeated, the name sounding full and fat as it rolled off his tongue. "Never met a Willow. But perhaps she was older, or younger. I swore there were only two of them, though. Ivy was sweet on me for a while, did you know that? All through our last year of school. She went to college down in the city, though. Big fuss about it. She never came back, and we lost touch. But that's the way of things, isn't it."

Actually, no. The way of things was that Grandma made a habit of not letting anyone remember her. Apparently that applied to this guy, too? Someone she'd maybe grown up with?

Damn.

But I just said, "I guess it is," and made a mental note to ask Grandma later if she had any sisters she'd never bothered telling me about. "Well, if you see Leah, tell her I was looking for her, okay?"

"Will do," said Harry, as I headed for the door. "And I'm serious about that job, you hear? You let me know."

When I got to the diner that night, Theo and Brandy were already there, sitting across from each other in our usual booth. As I approached, Brandy called out, "Hey there, cuuuutie!"

She was using that voice of hers, the one where I couldn't tell whether or not she was being ironic—but either way, Theo's only response was to roll his eyes, so I guess that meant they'd talked, and Theo knew, and he was okay with it.

"Hey, you," I replied, sliding into the booth beside her and giving her a peck on the lips. Just a peck. I mean, Theo was watching, and there's a huge difference between dating your friend's ex and rubbing it in his face. I didn't want to be *that* much of a dick.

"We ordered already," said Brandy. "You just wanted your usual, right? Burger with everything, medium rare, side of fries?"

"You got it," I said, pleased that she'd noticed. "How was the lake?"

"Good," said Theo. "Windy, but good."

"And entirely beside the point," said Brandy, a sly grin creeping over her face. "Theo has *news*."

"News?" I asked.

"Oh god," said Theo, shutting his eyes. "Not now."

"Why not now? Now's as good a time as any." Brandy

turned to me, blue eyes sparkling. "Apparently I wasn't the only one who got lucky last night."

Theo groaned, putting his hands over his face as he slumped down in his seat.

"Reeeeeally!" I said. "Way to go, man—but, wait, who was it? Not Natty . . . or, wait, *was* it Natty?" Because sure, last time I'd seen her, she'd been making out with that brunette girl, but that didn't necessarily mean anything. Maybe she swung both ways. Maybe she was just the kind of person who had a few drinks and started making out with everyone ever. Or maybe there'd been a threesome—

"No, dude, Natty's gay," said Theo.

Oh well.

"Then who?" I asked.

"Corey," said Theo, more to the table than to me.

"The girl whose house we were at," Brandy clarified, practically vibrating with excitement. "See, when Theo told me he had crash space, he neglected to mention said crash space was *in the hostess's pants.*"

I snickered, and Theo rubbed at his face again, so embarrassed that I almost felt bad for him. Almost. Mostly what I felt was happy, because Brandy looked so damn relieved. All that doubt from last night, when she'd thought that hooking up with me might hurt Theo? Gone. Theo was so far from hurt that he was hooking up with some girl named Corey, which meant Brandy and I were good to go.

"Sweet deal," I said. "So, was it a one-time thing, or you seeing her again?"

Theo parted his hands, just wide enough for a hint of a smile to peer through. "Called her a while ago. Taking her out tomorrow. Dinner. Hanging out under the stars. Maybe spot some constellations. Bet you can see 'em way better up here."

"Nice," I said. "Romantic. She'll dig that."

"Wait," said Brandy. "Dinner and stargazing? Seriously?"

Theo looked at her blankly. So did I. Apparently we were both missing something.

After a few seconds of thick silence, Brandy sighed. "That was what you did for *our* first date. What is that, like, just your standard thing?"

Theo hunched his shoulders a little. "Well. It *works*. So."

She sighed again, all pained and world-weary. "Boys. I swear."

"Hey," I said, nudging her arm with my elbow. "I don't do that."

"Uh-huh," she said, but gave me a smile.

"Hey, food's here," said Theo, looking intensely relieved.

But as we ate, that smile of Brandy's slowly gave way to something that looked . . . well, a little bit like worry. Or like wistfulness. A little bit sad.

That wasn't good.

So I reached over and brushed my fingertips against the sleeve of her hoodie. I touched it, and I reached, and I poked around for the thing that was making her look sad and wistful and worried.

There it was, just as I'd feared it would be: a tiny sliver

of jealousy, right on the surface of her thoughts. This wasn't leftover jealousy. It couldn't be, since I'd stolen away all her old feelings for Theo. No, this was totally new. So new that it hadn't even had the chance to grow big enough for her to notice.

Well, now it would never have that chance. I plucked it out, easy as anything, and let it drift away into nothingness. I gave Brandy's arm a little squeeze, closed my eyes for a moment as I waited for the reaching hangover to subside, and then went back to my burger—and she went back to asking Theo about Corey.

But I didn't pay much attention to her questions, or to Theo's curt, embarrassed answers. I was too busy thinking about that tiny piece of jealousy I'd just stolen from Brandy.

I should have known that was a possibility. I really should have. Sure, all Brandy's old love for Theo was gone. But he was still Theo, and she was still Brandy, which meant all the reasons they'd first been attracted to each other were still there. It made perfect sense that all the feelings I'd stolen might, if left to their own devices, grow right back.

Brandy had chosen me of her own free will—but if I wanted to keep it that way, I had to start being way more careful.

△ BEFORE △

I was eight years old and surrounded by roller coasters. I mean *surrounded*. They towered over me on every side, full of people who were screaming with joy and fear, and I remember thinking that I'd never wanted anything as much as I wanted to be one of those screaming people.

Because it was a weekday, the ticket lines were short, which meant my mom was back with our ride tickets before I could vibrate out of my skin with anticipation.

"Here are our passes for the rest of the day," she said, handing a couple cards over to my dad. "And . . . ta-da! Three tickets for the Cyclone."

The Cyclone was basically the Holy Grail of roller coasters. Theo had told me so, and Theo was basically a Coney Island expert. He'd been going there with his family since he was a baby. Me, though? This was my first time.

"Can we do the Cyclone first?" I asked.

Mom and Dad grinned at each other over my head, and we were off.

But when we got to the front of the line, this pimply, stupid-looking teenaged guy held out a hand. "Where d'you think you're going?" he asked me.

"Uh, on the Cyclone?" I said, pointing at the coaster looming behind him. "Duh?"

"Stand over there," said the pimply guy. I was totally confused until I saw what he was pointing at.

The sign said *You Must Be 54" to Ride the Cyclone*, with a mark to show exactly what fifty-four inches looked like. Heart sinking down into my shoes, I went over and stood next to the sign. I wasn't tall enough.

"I'm sorry, we didn't realize," Mom began—but Dad cut her off:

"Oh, come on, can't you make an exception?"

Pimples waved another adult couple through, then turned back to Dad. "No can do, buckaroo," he said. "It's a safety thing."

"He'll be perfectly safe," said Dad. "He's four foot five. Fifty-three inches. One inch doesn't make a difference."

"No difference at all," I added helpfully.

"It could make the difference between getting fired and keeping my job," said Pimples.

"Let's go talk about this somewhere else," said Mom, but nobody listened to her.

"Come on," said Dad, leaning closer to Pimples like they were best buds. "If we get caught, I'll tell your boss we snuck him in. Come on. . . ."

Pimples's face began to change. He'd been all smug just a second ago, like he was super proud of himself for catching us—but the expression was turning into something secretive. Something conspiratorial.

Then I noticed that Dad's hand was on Pimples's arm. He was reaching, changing the guy's mind, right before my eyes, and how cool was that?

"Just this once," said Pimples. "And you gotta cover for me if anything happens, like you said. Deal?"

"Deal," said Dad . . . and we were in.

As we waited to get loaded into our car, Mom said, "Andy." Her voice was equal parts weariness and warning—the kind of tone that, more often than not, led to a fight.

"I know, I know," said Dad. "But he's been wanting to ride this thing forever! And it's only an inch."

"That poor kid could lose his job because of you," said Mom.

I glanced back at Pimples, who didn't look like he was getting in any trouble. Why did Mom care about that guy? He was annoying and had a stupid face.

"He won't lose his job," said Dad.

"But he *could,*" Mom insisted.

"But he *won't,*" said Dad. "Let's just have a nice day out, okay? We'll talk about this later, just the two of us."

Mom glanced at me, and then back at Dad. I was sure she was going to insist on having a fight right then—but our car arrived before she could say anything. I sat next to Dad. Mom sat behind us, next to a stranger. We fastened our belts, and I was so happy that Pimples hadn't made me leave the line.

Or rather, I was so happy that my dad had made Pimples change his mind.

Just as the coaster started moving, I leaned over to Dad and said, "Hey. Thanks."

"Anytime, kiddo," he said, and we went up and up and up, the sky opening bright blue above us.

CHAPTER SEVEN

Grandma wasn't kidding about the Fourth of July messing with the Cliff. There was a small fault the next day, just like she'd said there would be, and that was just the beginning. Grandma, Aunt Holly, and I spent each of the following seven nights performing the triad ritual, centered around a series of tiny things that I stole from strangers.

I took away some woman's extreme dislike for pop music, and a third grader's shyness about answering questions in class. I took away a twenty-something guy's crush on a movie actress he'd probably never meet, and an old man's anger about having his driver's license revoked.

And then, every time the ritual was done and I could emerge from behind the locked doors of the den, I reached into Brandy and checked to see if any new feelings about Theo, feelings aside from plain old friendship, had emerged.

There'd been a few things. A tendril of admiration for Theo's arms. A wisp of nostalgia for the full-body hugs he used to give her. Things like that. I stole them away before they could grow into bigger feelings. That way, I was sure that when Brandy was with me, she wasn't . . . well, wishing I was someone else.

And she was with me a lot lately. More so, now that Theo was regularly ditching us to hang out with that girl Corey. We borrowed Aunt Holly's car and went to see *Blood of Jupiter* again. We wandered around Main Street, eating ice cream and seriously horrible pizza. We even had a picnic in the May Day field, where I tried my best to explain, without giving my family's secrets away, the presence of all the toys and papers and books and stuff piled under the tree.

"Oh, so it's like a good luck thing?" she said, after several minutes of mostly incoherent rambling on my part. "You leave a token there once a year for luck?"

Which, of course, was way simpler than anything I'd just said.

"Yeah. Something like that."

"That's really sweet," said Brandy. "I'm gonna leave something."

"No!" I said, as she got up and made for the tree.

She paused, clearly confused. "Why not?"

"Um." Obviously I couldn't tell her the truth. "Um. Because it's not May Day. You're only supposed to do it on May Day."

She rolled her eyes. "That's dumb." And she continued toward the tree.

"Brandy, come on, don't," I said, staying right where I

was, willing her back to me. But she kept going. She bent down and placed something on the pile, then she came back to me with a faraway look in her eyes.

"There. For luck."

"What'd you put?" I asked.

Brandy smiled. "It's a secret."

When I came back to the field with Grandma and Aunt Holly later that night, I kept a sharp eye out for anything that looked like Brandy's. I even reached into a few things, just to see if they felt like her. But whatever she'd left, I couldn't find it.

Finally, at the end of the seventh triad ritual in a row, Grandma sighed deeply and said, "There. That ought to hold it for a while."

"You're sure?" asked Aunt Holly.

"Of course I'm not sure," said Grandma placidly. "I'm never sure until the moment arrives, or until it doesn't. You know that."

But she sounded sure enough that I felt relief spread through my chest. Tonight had not been pleasant, thanks to the torrential downpour that had turned the entire May Day field into a flood zone. And the rain was supposed to keep going all night, if not longer.

I hoped it wasn't longer. My neck always got extra cranky when it rained.

But I also hoped it *would* last, because I liked the sound of rain, especially at night. I also liked the coziness of being inside with Brandy while, just beyond the walls that protected us, chaos reigned.

That night, like every night, Brandy eventually went back to her own room to go to sleep. She claimed it was because I snored, but I was pretty sure it was just because Heather's bed was so small. Totally fine for hooking up, but not great for actually sleeping.

Only when she was gone and the door was closed behind her did I realize something very important: I'd forgotten to close Heather's window before the storm had started— which meant that by now, the rug on the far side of the room was kind of soaked. That was easily fixed, since I could just roll it up and toss it in the dryer tomorrow. But I really wanted to keep the window open.

A bit of rummaging around in the basement yielded the perfect solution: a blue tarp that could catch the water. I spread it under the window before I took my contacts out, and I rolled my pillow under my head and fell asleep to the oddly soothing sound of raindrops on plastic.

And then I woke up again.

Someone was whispering.

I felt for my glasses on the bedside table, willing my thoughts to arrange themselves into the right order, to separate into sleep-thoughts and awake-thoughts. There'd been a voice, saying what sounded like a name, but that wasn't what had woken me up. There'd also been a dull thud, like a collision.

My fumbling fingers finally found my glasses, and I

pushed them onto my face. The room came into focus. Empty.

Almost empty.

There, in the space below the window, someone was crumpled on the tarp, like they'd fallen there and hadn't yet mustered the strength to get up.

Intruder. I needed to yell for someone. I needed to touch them just long enough that I could steal their desire to rob me or kill me. I needed—

But as soon as I turned on Heather's bedside lamp, the crumpled figure lifted its head, its long hair dripping water onto the tarp, and all those needs gave way to plain and simple confusion.

"The hell?" I muttered, sitting up and reaching under my glasses to wipe the sleep from my eyes. "Leah?"

"Aspen?" I saw Leah pressing her hand against her shoulder, and everything came together. She'd climbed in through the window somehow. She'd slipped on the tarp. Probably hit her shoulder on the wall, making the sound that had woken me up. "You're not," she said. "I mean . . . you were supposed to be Heather."

"And you were supposed to be . . . uh, not in my room," I finished stupidly. "How'd you get up here?"

"The tree outside," she said. "I climbed it."

She'd climbed it. Right. Swinging my bare feet onto the floor, I made my way cautiously over to the tarp and extended a hand to help her up. Ignoring it, she braced herself against the wall beside the window and stood up on her own.

"Why's that there?" she asked, glancing at the tarp as she stepped off it and onto the carpet. Her feet were as bare as mine, and speckled with wet dirt.

"To catch the rain," I said.

She leveled a look at me. "You could try closing the window instead."

"In a storm like this?" Between the sound of rain and the still-frantic pace of my heart, my voice came out almost giddy. "No way."

"Weirdo," she muttered, and wrapped her arms around herself. Her sky-blue pajamas were sopping wet. Wet enough that I could see, very plainly, that she wasn't wearing a bra. I would have averted my eyes, if I hadn't noticed something else at the same time.

"Hey, you're shivering," I said. "Here, come in."

Which was a stupid thing to say since, technically speaking, she was already in. But she took a few more steps away from the window, rubbing her hands vigorously up and down her arms, like a Boy Scout trying to start a fire.

I grabbed the first warm-looking thing I could find: a fluffy purple blanket from Heather's closet.

"Here." I held it out to Leah, but she didn't take it. She didn't even seem to see it. Whatever. It was probably too small to keep warm with, anyway.

"I should go," she said, looking uncertainly back at the window. "This was a bad idea."

"Wait," I said. "What did you mean, I was supposed to be Heather?"

Leah glanced back at me. "Um, hello. This is her room?"

"Um, *hello*," I said. "She's been dead since February?"

"Very funny," said Leah. "Hilarious, even. Just tell me where she is, and I'll get out of your hair."

"Where she *is*?" I repeated, feeling totally off balance.

"Or, wait, don't tell me. She's off on another crazy European vacation, right? Figures. People with money. Honestly."

"Leah—"

"When's she back, so I can—"

"*Leah.*"

Her mouth snapped shut, even as I cringed at the sound of my own voice. I don't think either of us expected that to come out so loud. I took a few seconds to listen for movement outside the bedroom door, just in case.

Only when I was satisfied that the house was just as still as before did I register the look on Leah's face. Total confusion. She really thought I'd been kidding.

"You didn't know?" I asked.

She stared at me. "Know what?"

"Heather died," I said again. "First week of February. Some kind of lung disease."

Leah stared some more. After a few seconds, she began shaking her head slowly, back and forth, almost like she didn't even know she was doing it.

"February," she said.

"Yeah," I said, studying Leah. Something was missing here. For someone who felt comfortable climbing through Heather's bedroom window at—I glanced at the clock on

127

the dresser—almost two in the morning, she'd missed an awfully huge piece of news.

"Right before Valentine's Day. Yeah, that's when . . ."

I stayed quiet this time, watching her brow furrow, waiting for her sentence to end.

"That's when she stopped coming to school."

"Well, yes," I said. "Because she was dead."

"But I asked," continued Leah, like she hadn't heard me. "They said she'd transferred to another school. I figured it was one of those fancy art schools down in the city. She used to talk about applying for scholarships, and I thought she finally . . ." But then her eyes went sharp again, focusing intently on me. "Why'd they lie? Who lies about something like that?"

I put my hands up, palms out, like I could keep her at bay. "Dude, you're asking the wrong guy."

I remembered, then, how few people had been at Heather's funeral. I remembered noting that none of her friends had shown up. Only family. But why?

"And she . . ." But Leah trailed off again, her hand creeping upward and pressing flat against her chest, just below her collarbone. She looked like she was about to have a panic attack. I closed the window, then went over to Heather's closet and rummaged inside until I found a bathrobe. It was very pink.

"Not quite your style, probably," I said, holding it out to Leah, "but it looks warm."

She hesitated a moment, saying, "That's Heather's." But

then she took it and wrapped it around herself. "Thanks," she muttered, more to the floor than to me. Now, instead of shivering, she'd gone entirely still. "I just can't believe . . ."

"Yeah," I said. "Um, listen. Not to be rude, but, uh, if you and Heather were climbing-through-each-other's-windows-type friends, how did you not figure out . . . I mean . . . didn't you notice she wasn't, like, calling you anymore? Or whatever?"

Leah's mouth fell open, and for a second she looked ready to murder me. Or to cry. But all she said was a curt, "I should go."

"Like hell you should," I said, pointing at the window behind her. "It's insane out there."

She turned to look. On the other side of the glass, the storm was getting worse. The rain was practically horizontal. There was no way I was letting her go back outside. "Leah," I said. She didn't answer. Brow furrowed, she stared almost blankly at the sheets of rain whipping past. "Leah. Hey. Sorry for being insensitive or whatever."

Still nothing.

"Leah!"

She started violently, brushed her hair almost angrily away from her face, and squinted at me. "What?"

"Why'd you come over here, anyway?" I asked.

Leah opened her mouth, just a little bit. Then closed it again. Her eyes looked sort of past me, and sort of through me, and suddenly I couldn't tell if she was about to keel over or start crying or just pull out a gun and splatter my brains across Heather's wall. Anything could happen tonight, with Heather's death so fresh in Leah's mind, and with the wind howling like it was. Anything at all.

If it'd been anyone else, I'd just reach into her and take away her sadness, or her shock, or whatever. But last time I'd stolen something from Leah, I'd ended up passed out in a stranger's backyard. So instead I just said, softly as I could, "Leah? Come on, what is it?"

"It's Jesse," she said, voice choked with some emotion I couldn't quite make out. "He's . . . god, no, it seems so stupid now. I didn't know about Heather. I didn't know."

"Jesse," I said loudly, trying to focus her. "Glow-stick hula hoop Jesse?"

"My *friend* Jesse." Her expression shifted from defensive to angry to devastated, all in less than a second. "Something happened to him, and I thought . . . well, I thought Heather could help. Or maybe Heather did it in the first place. Or maybe both, I don't know. But neither now, I guess. God. Sorry. I sound like a crazy person."

"No, you don't," I lied, trying to sound as gentle as I could. "What happened to Jesse?"

Leah sniffled. "It'll sound stupid. To you, I mean."

"I bet I've heard stupider."

"Like *seriously* stupid."

"It's after midnight," I said. "Nothing sounds seriously stupid after midnight."

She looked at me for a long moment. Then:

"Jesse went blind."

"Like . . . recently?" I said carefully, trying to remember the pictures that Sadie had shown me. Jesse, on the roof, colored lights all around him. It was a ballsy stunt to pull even if you *did* have sight. And if you didn't? *Eesh.*

"Yes!" Leah said, throwing her hands up. "See, that's it. You don't get it."

"Get what? Leah. Tell me."

She began to back away, slowly, toward the window. "Never mind. I should . . . Hold on. Wait a sec." She stopped. Narrowed her eyes at me. "February. She's been gone since February. How long have *you* been here?"

"Me?" I said. "Just a few weeks. End of June. Why?"

Leah drew in a soft breath, and I could see something clicking into place behind her eyes. "Ohhh," she said. "It wasn't Heather. It was *you.*"

"Whoa, hold up," I said, taking a small step back. "What was me? What'd I do?"

"What'd I do?" she mimicked, her voice snotty and high. "Oh, come on."

"Okay, seriously, though. What did I do?"

She tilted her head a little, looking at me like she couldn't decide if I was messing with her. Which I wasn't. I totally wasn't.

"My cup at the party," she said. "And my phone, when you came into the bookstore."

"I told you, I was putting my number in—"

"Your number isn't in my phone," she interrupted smoothly. "I checked."

"Well, you have a different phone than me," I said. "You caught me before I could figure out how it worked."

"So you're saying you *can't* do what Heather could do."

I blinked, dumbfounded. She knew. Grandma had insisted that nobody in this entire town knew what the Quick family was capable of, but she was wrong.

Leah totally knew.

"Um." I tried willing my voice back toward normalcy. "What, ah . . . what is it that Heather could do?"

Leah raised an eyebrow. "Are you asking because you want me to tell you her secret? Or are you asking because you already know, and you want me to say it first?"

A chill swept over me. She knew, she knew, she knew.

Before I could think of a suitable answer, she went on: "Heather can take things away from people. She reaches— *reached*—into their possessions, or things they've touched, and she took pieces of them away, and she fed them to the Cliff for that weird ritual thing."

"I . . ."

"And you can do it, too," she added. It wasn't a question anymore. "Can't you."

An eternity passed between us. Leah, looking all goddess-of-truth-and-justice despite her drowned-rat hair and the stupid pink bathrobe. Me, in my glasses and pajamas and bare feet.

I'd never told a single person my secret. Not Theo. Not Brandy. Not anyone.

I tried to smile, but all it did was make my face feel

stretched out. So I took a deep breath and said, plainly, "Yeah, I can."

And then, before I could even process what was happening, Leah was running at me, shoving me with both hands, sending me stumbling back far enough that my legs banged into the wooden framework of Heather's bed.

"Why did you do it?" she demanded, dark brown eyes alight with fury. "Why his sight, of all the—"

"I didn't do anything!" I said, my hands flying up instinctively to protect my chest, in case she decided to hit me again. "Well, I mean, that's maybe not *exactly* true, but I didn't take his sight. I swear I didn't."

"Then tell me who did!"

"Shh!" I hissed, glancing toward the door. "Keep it down, okay? I don't want them hearing this."

"Them? Heather's mom?"

"And my friends, *and* my grandmother. Everyone's sleeping."

She blinked. "Since when does Heather's grandmother live here?"

"Since..." Oh. Right. Leah had probably been one of the legions of people who'd had her memories of Grandma stolen away. Oops. "Eh, I don't know. But okay. Listen. Why'd you think it was Heather who made him blind? Couldn't it have just... you know... happened? Somehow?"

"Happened somehow," Leah repeated flatly, like she was willing me to hear exactly how dumb the words sounded. It worked. I winced. "So what *did* you do?"

"Um . . . ?"

"You just said you didn't do anything." She crossed her arms impatiently, glaring. "Then you said that wasn't *exactly* true. So? What did you do?"

"He had a competitive streak," I said. "That's what I took. That's *all* I took."

"Then why . . . ?" Leah began, but this time the unfinished question seemed directed more at herself than at me.

"I have no idea why. It was the same ritual as always."

"His competitive streak," said Leah, with a weird look that was almost a smile. "Man. His coaches'll love that. Just in time for senior year. He's captain of the basketball team, you know." She swallowed hard, dropping her gaze to the floor. "Although, now that he can't see . . ."

"Yeah." And that was when I remembered the hunch I'd had. The reason I'd gone back to the bookstore to look for Leah. "Wait, can you do it, too?" I asked her. "I mean, taking stuff from people. Are you—"

"No." Her shoulders sagged. "I mean, I wish . . . but no."

"Then how'd you know?" I asked. "My grandmother said nobody in town knew about . . . about . . . you know. Us. What we do."

"Heather told me. Back when we were best friends. She wasn't *allowed* to tell me, technically," she added—then winced. "Sorry."

"Sorry?"

She hunched her shoulders. "Speaking ill of the . . . you know. You're not supposed to."

"Oh," I said, even though I was pretty sure that stating facts didn't count as speaking ill.

"But yeah, nobody else knows," said Leah. "Just me. Even Jesse only knows that he can't see anymore. He doesn't know why."

Jesse. Right. As I heard his name again, my thoughts began to put themselves in order. I narrowed my eyes. "Yeah. About that. What exactly happened tonight? Since it was apparently enough to send you racing over here in the middle of . . ." I gestured toward the window, toward the storm.

Leah sighed and sat on the floor, leaning her back against the dresser. I sat down on the bed opposite her. She drew her knees up toward her chin, like a shield.

"He'd been missing for almost two weeks," she said. "Not answering my calls. Not even answering Sadie's calls, or Harry's. That's our boss at the bookstore. And nobody could find his parents, either."

I nodded.

"And then tonight, just when I'm getting ready for bed, my phone rings. It's him. He says he just got back, and he's sorry he didn't call, but . . ." She trailed off, then shook her head sharply, like she was trying to focus. "So apparently, this one morning, he just woke up and couldn't see. Simple as that. His dad took him to the eye doctor, but the guy had no idea what to make of it. Took him to a different eye doctor—still no dice.

"So they made an appointment with a specialist down

in the city. Still nothing. They stayed there for more than a week, seeing doctor after doctor after doctor, and nobody could find anything wrong. No detached retinas, no diseases where sudden blindness is a side effect, no nothing. In the end, it was a choice between staying and being a lab rat for some university scientist, and coming home."

"Yeeeah, I wouldn't have picked the lab rat thing, either," I said.

"Right?" said Leah. "He said he didn't call because he didn't know what to say. Like, he didn't want to tell everyone he was fine, and then find out two days later that he had some weird rare disease, you know?"

"That makes sense, I guess."

"No, it doesn't!" said Leah. "I gave him hell for it, too, the bastard. But I also tried to be reassuring . . . and then, when he hung up to call Sadie, I hauled ass out the door and came over here and climbed in through the window, and here we are."

And she hadn't even stopped long enough to put on a pair of shoes.

"Why here?" I asked.

"Because," she replied immediately, "Heather's family is the source of everything weird and supernatural that's ever happened in this town."

I frowned. "Is there a *lot* of weird supernatural stuff that happens here? I mean, obviously there is, but like . . . noticeable stuff?"

"Well, maybe not noticeable to anyone but me," she

said. "You know. Someone'll stop being into something they used to love, or vice versa. Little stuff. I dunno. Some of it's probably not because of the ritual at all. But I guarantee some of it totally is. Especially when it's big stuff."

"Huh," I said. "What kind of big stuff?"

"Well, Jesse's eyesight, obviously," she said, anger creeping back into her tone. "And other things, too, like there was this one time our algebra teacher suddenly forgot how long division worked. Heather hated that guy, so I know it was her. Or when that girl—god, what was her name?— anyway, this girl who used to star in all the school musicals. One day, the most annoyingly gorgeous singing voice ever. The next day? Tone-deaf."

"Whoa," I said.

"Like I said, it's not very often." She paused. "Or, I dunno, could be all the time. But half the stuff under the May Day tree gets left by tourists, so there's really no way to be sure."

"Tourists? Seriously?"

"Uh, yeah?" said Leah. "May Day's kind of a big deal . . . ?"

"Oh, I didn't know—"

But just then, a loud *crack* boomed through the house. I swore I could feel the floor shaking under me—and if the way her body tensed up was any indication, Leah could feel it, too.

"What the hell was that?" My voice came out about seven octaves higher than usual. The wind was whistling so loudly that it sounded like a chorus of people shrieking.

"A tree," whispered Leah. "Big one, from the sound of it."

My first thought was the May Day tree, but that was much too far away for us to have heard it here. Besides, I had no doubt that some kind of magical something-or-other protected it from mundane things like storms. My second thought was of the tree right outside my window—the one that Leah had climbed to get up here. But I could see its branches whipping madly in the storm. It was still intact.

"Shit," said Leah, standing up abruptly. "My bike." Her face suddenly looked a whole lot whiter than before.

"You *biked* here?" I said. "Are you crazy?"

"I left it under the eaves. I have to go check—"

"No way," I said. "You are so not going out there."

She narrowed her eyes. "And you so don't get to tell me what to do."

Rising from the bed, I moved to stand between Leah and the window. "Look, if your bike's already survived this much, it'll still be fine when the storm's over. But if it's already gone . . . well, not much you can do about it now, right?"

She frowned, first at me, then at the window. "I guess not. . . ."

"Really, though. You shouldn't have biked here."

"You're right, Aspen. I should have taken my nonexistent car instead."

The narrowed eyes. The sarcastic tone. The wry smile pulling at the corners of her mouth. She suddenly reminded me a whole lot of Brandy—except annoying instead of hot.

Which made it that much harder to say what I had to say next:

"You think maybe you should spend the night?"

The air between us seemed to go taut. "Don't tell me you're trying to flirt again," she said, except this time it came out uncertain instead of sarcastic.

"No. And I wasn't flirting before, either," I said. "Anyway, I've got a girlfriend now."

After a few moments of staring at me, Leah said, "If you're telling the truth, and you didn't steal his sight, then what is it? Just a coincidence?"

"It has to be, right? I did the ritual the same as always." I held my hand up like I was in court. "I swear, if anything happened differently, it wasn't me who did it."

She bit her lip. Glanced over at the window again—just in time for what looked like an entire tree branch to ricochet off the window with a *clunk*. "Yeah, I probably should stay over. Thanks for offering."

"I'd say stay in one of the guest rooms, but my friends are in them right now." I smiled and corrected myself: "My friend and my girlfriend. But here, you take the bed and I'll—"

"No way," she said abruptly, eyes widening. "Sorry, I know it's dumb, but . . . that's Heather's bed."

"So?"

"So you don't think it's weird? Sleeping in Heather's bed when she's . . . and with all her sheets and stuff still on it?"

Ah.

"I'm sure they washed the sheets. Plus it's been five months."

"Yeah," said Leah slowly. "It's only been *five months.*"

Right. She'd just found out like two seconds ago, where I'd had five months to process it. Not that much processing had to be done, since I'd barely known Heather. Usually, when I'd come up here for the summer before this year, it was to complete the triad for a little bit while Heather took a vacation. We'd intersect for a few hours here and there, but never long enough to actually spend time together.

But it was past two in the morning, and the adrenaline rush I'd gotten from Leah waking me up had long since faded. I was very, very tired.

"Well, hey," I said, "if you want the floor, I'm not gonna argue."

△ BEFORE △

I remember thinking it was weird that Dad came to meet me at the door when I got home from Theo's place. He never did that. But that one random evening, more than a month after Mom had left, he did. He watched as I took off my shoes and put my umbrella on the drying mat, and he said, "Your mom emailed."

My insides did a weird flippy thing. "Oh yeah? What'd she want?"

"To know if you're okay," said Dad. "Apparently she's been trying to get in touch with you? And you've been ignoring her?"

This was very true. It was the end of spring break, right in the middle of March, and aside from the one time I'd picked up the phone and she'd said that weird thing about Heather's funeral, I'd been ignoring all her calls, all her emails, all her texts.

"I guess," I said.

Dad nodded. "Well. That's understandable, I suppose. And it's your decision, obviously. But your mother does have a right to know that you're still alive."

"Obviously I'm alive," I said, heading into the kitchen for some water. "Doesn't she think you'd tell her if I died?"

Dad sighed. "That's not the point, son."

"Then what is?"

"If you're not going to talk to her, at least—I don't know—update your profile once in a while? So she can see it?"

I thought about that. It was true that I hadn't posted anything online in a while. But who could blame me? Everything in my life basically sucked right now, and I didn't want to be one of those douche bags who always posted shit like *People are the worst* or *Hate everything right now, don't even ask* or whatever, in hopes of getting some internet sympathy. Brandy's friend Lauren did that all the time, and it drove me nuts.

Still, Dad had a point. I didn't want to talk to Mom, but I also didn't want her worrying about me.

So I pulled out my phone, snapped a picture of the glass I'd just filled from the tap, and posted it with the caption, *Dinner = one pint of pure vodka.*

"There, happy now?" I asked, showing Dad my phone.

He peered closer to read the caption, then laughed softly. "I just hope Child Services knows you're joking."

I shrugged. "If they don't, I'll steal their memories. Whatever."

"There you go," said Dad, shaking his head. "Anyway, speaking of dinner, did the Valdezes feed you?"

"Yup," I said. It had been spaghetti night at Theo's place, and Mr. Valdez made the best garlic bread in history. So obviously I'd said yes when they'd invited me to stay.

"In that case, in honor of your pint glass, how about joining your old man for a nightcap?" I gave him a blank look, and he clarified: "A drink. I just picked up a new Scotch that I've been wanting to try."

Scotch? I'd never had Scotch. Beer, sure. Fruity mixed drinks, sure. The cheapest liquor my fake ID could get me, sure. But never anything as classy as Scotch.

(Also, I was kind of unsure what to make of the question. Was this a peace offering after the other night, when I'd stayed out too late without calling? Had my dad forgotten that I wasn't legal? Did he just miss having another adult in the house?)

"Um," I said.

"Come on, try it," he said. "If you hate it, you can have something else."

As it turned out, I actually kind of liked Scotch. It tasted like fireplaces smelled—in a good way. After I told my dad as much, he clapped me on the shoulder, steered us into the living room, and turned on the TV. He flipped through the channels until he found some old show about mobsters, and we watched an entire episode, sipping our drinks the whole way through.

"You see?" Dad muted the TV. His voice had gone a little blurry. That was fine. I felt blurry, too.

"See what?" I said.

"Father-son time," said Dad, gesturing to me, then to himself. "It's *important*. And you'd've missed out on it, if you'd picked your mom."

"Picked?" I frowned. "There was nothing to pick. She left."

"Ehhh!" He gave an expansively dismissive wave of his hand. "Here, let me get the bottle. I'll top us off."

As he went into the kitchen, I thought about what my mom had said before she'd left.

If you ever want to leave, too . . .

If you want to get out of all this . . .

I can help you . . .

Dad came back with the Scotch bottle. He tipped more fireplace-smelling liquid into my glass, then into his, and then he clinked his glass against mine. "To father-son time," he said.

"Cheers," I said, because that's what you were supposed to say. And, yeah, because I was pretty sure Mom was out of her mind. I didn't want to leave, and I didn't need her help. I had everything I needed, right here.

CHAPTER EIGHT

I got Leah a giant pile of spare blankets from the linen closet, plus a pillow. Then she made me swear that I wouldn't steal anything from her while she slept. I swore. And I meant it, too.

When I woke to the warm smell of bacon cooking downstairs, and the sounds of rain on the roof and Leah snoring softly on the floor, it took me longer than it should have to remember what'd happened the night before. Probably because I hadn't gotten much sleep, thanks to Leah's break-in.

And when the pieces clicked together, two facts came into very sharp focus in my sleep-deprived brain:

First: Nobody was allowed to find out about Leah being here. Definitely not Aunt Holly or Grandma, since they hated her, but preferably not Theo or Brandy, either. Trying to explain her presence to them would just be awkward.

Second: I needed to shower. Immediately. And probably shave, too. I hadn't done that in a while, and somehow the presence of an almost-stranger in my room turned that simple fact into a problem that required immediate solving.

Right.

Taking care not to wake Leah as I crawled out of bed, I dug out some fresh clothes, then closed the door behind me as I left. I could hear the faint sounds of Aunt Holly and Grandma talking downstairs. Over in the east wing, though, it was still quiet. Both guest room doors were closed. Brandy and Theo were still sleeping.

Once I was safe in the bathroom, I ran a quick finger over the stubble that had accumulated on my chin over the past few days. More than a few, actually. It had been at least a week since I'd last shaved, and the result didn't add up to much more than a normal guy's five o'clock shadow. My dad, who could grow a full beard in about ten seconds, enjoyed telling me that I should stick to warmer climates. And never become a lumberjack.

Maybe it was because I didn't do it very often, but shaving always put me in this zen sort of mindset. Something about the buzz of the razor combined with the level of concentration. Tilt jaw just so. Lift chin. Make sure hair doesn't get in the way. Make mental note to get a haircut. Be extra careful around the mole tucked way under the left side of my jaw—

Except—

I leaned closer to the mirror for a better look. There was no mole there. I'd had a mole just under my jaw for my entire life, and now it just

Wasn't

There.

I'd tried to steal Leah Ramsey-Wolfe's mole just the other day, and it hadn't worked. Now mine was gone.

It wasn't until after I'd turned the shower off and grabbed a towel that everything clicked into place.

At the bookstore, I'd tried to take Leah's mole away, and mine had disappeared instead.

At the party, I'd tried to take some of Leah's sobriety away, and what little remained of my own sobriety had disappeared instead, leaving me so drunk that I'd actually, for the first time in my life, blacked out.

And in the course of my first triad ritual of the summer, I'd tried to take away Leah's love of being out on the water—but it wasn't Leah who'd suddenly lost her desire to keep going up to the Elmview lake.

It was me.

I toweled off as fast as I could, got dressed, and dashed back into the bedroom.

"Leah," I said, not even caring who heard me. "Leah!"

Her tangled hair stirred in the little blanket-nest she'd made on the floor, and she looked up at me with one bleary eye.

"Mmmmsleep," she said, and the eye closed.

"Leah," I said again . . . and then stopped. Because while I really, really wanted to know how she was deflecting my magic, pushing it all back on me, I was suddenly sure that she wasn't the one who could give me that answer. She'd looked awfully surprised last night, when she'd realized I had the same abilities as Heather—which meant that if she was doing something to make my magic bounce back on me, it probably wasn't on purpose.

Of course, as soon as I'd decided not to say anything, Leah was sitting up, rubbing sleep out of her eyes. "Fine, fine, I'm awake. What's up?"

"Um. It's morning." I pointed toward the window, where faint light was sneaking in around the edges of the curtain. "Think maybe you should go before someone finds you here?"

Leah groaned. Rubbed her eyes again. Then sighed and said, "Yeah, guess so."

"Good. Aunt Holly and my grandma are downstairs. I'll go down and keep them distracted so you can get out."

"My hero," muttered Leah, and heaved herself to her feet as I left the room, shutting the door behind me.

Coffee. I needed coffee. Then I could actually think, with my actual awake brain, about what to do with all this . . . whatever it was that Leah was doing to my magic.

Luckily, coffee was being made right now. I could smell it. So I closed the door quietly behind me, and headed downstairs. Maybe, since Grandma was already up, I could ask her about the Leah situation—without naming names, of course. Maybe she was a distant relative or something. Maybe she had just enough Quick blood that she had magic of her own, but not enough that she could use it consciously.

But when I reached the kitchen, four heads turned to look at me.

"Oh," I said, looking at Brandy, then Theo. "I didn't know you guys were up."

"Bacon," said Theo simply, shoving a piece into his mouth.

Brandy, though, didn't say anything. She just looked at me, head to toe and back again, like she couldn't decide whether to laugh at me or not.

"What?" I said.

"You're all . . . neat and tidy," said Brandy, who was still in her rumpled polka-dot pajamas. "Spick-and-span."

"So?" Sure, I'd showered before breakfast, and sure, I didn't usually do that, but she was giving me this weird smile, like I was an adorable puppy who'd finally figured out what the newspaper was for.

"So it's different. In a good way. Come on, sit down."

I poured some coffee into a mug, and sat next to Brandy, who leaned over and gave me a peck on the lips. Which made me feel slightly less like a puppy, slightly more like a guy with a hot girlfriend. So that was something.

There were eggs cooling on the stove, and bread on the counter for toast, but those things were for days when my stomach was less jumpy. When I hadn't just learned, half-way through shaving, that my own magic could be turned back on me.

Today, all I wanted was the big plate of bacon in the middle of the table.

Aunt Holly grunted as I crammed a few long, crunchy strips into my face.

"Boys," said Brandy, offering her a sympathetic look.

But Aunt Holly ignored her. She just took a delicate sip of her tea—Aunt Holly wasn't a coffee drinker—and regarded Grandma coolly. "Well?" she said. "The bridge?"

"I haven't finished my eggs," said Grandma. "Simmer down. A few more minutes of human interaction won't kill you."

Aunt Holly looked at me, drinking my coffee. At Theo, still stuffing bacon into his mouth. At Brandy, who smiled at her. Aunt Holly didn't smile back. She just stirred her tea with her spoon.

"What bridge?" I asked, more to cover up the awkwardness than because I actually wanted to know.

"The one that crosses the creek going into town," said Grandma, as Aunt Holly rolled her eyes at me. "One of the supports was damaged in the storm last night. Old wooden structure like that, it won't be able to hold any weight until it's fixed. Not safely, at least. Holly and I have to mend it before it breaks completely."

I blinked at them. "*You're* going to fix it? I thought that was the town's job. Or the . . . the county, or something."

"It is," said Grandma. "And I'm sure they'd do a perfectly fine job, if we don't mind waiting the rest of the summer for them to get around to it. Your aunt will have it done in minutes."

"You do carpentry?" said Brandy, her face brightening

a little as she peered at Aunt Holly. "That's so cool. I've always wanted to learn that kind of stuff."

She had? Yeah, right.

"No, I—" But Aunt Holly cut herself off at an *ahem* from Grandma. She sighed. "Only as a hobby."

Ahh, okay. Probably there was just some hairline crack in the bridge's support, and Aunt Holly was going to reach in and steal it away. More power to her, I guess. Reaching into sentient beings was so much easier, and the reaching hangover wasn't nearly as bad. The few times I'd reached into inanimate things—opening locked doors, mostly—the process had left me practically catatonic for a solid five minutes. I didn't do it anymore, as a rule.

"That's so cool," said Brandy again. "Can I come watch?"

"No," said Aunt Holly, standing abruptly. "Ma, are you ready yet? I'd really rather get this over with."

"Such a rush," murmured Grandma. She forked another bite of eggs into her mouth, but then stood up, too, leaving the rest unfinished. "Fine. Go on. I'll meet you outside."

That was all Aunt Holly needed. Without another word, she turned and tromped out of the kitchen. I heard the screen door slam on her way out.

"You'll pardon my Holly's rudeness," said Grandma, mostly to Brandy. "She still hasn't quite recovered from . . . events."

Brandy's face softened. "Well, of course she hasn't. She lost her only daughter."

Grandma squeezed Brandy's shoulder. "Sweet girl," she

said. "Aspen, keep an eye on the house. We won't be gone long."

Only once we'd heard the screen door slam a second time did Brandy ask, "Keep an eye on the house? Does she think we're gonna set it on fire?"

More like she thought Brandy might try to sneak out and see Aunt Holly's carpentry skills in action, and I was in charge of preventing that. But the difference between me and Grandma, in this case, was that I could tell Brandy had just been faking interest to be polite. So I just shrugged and kept chugging my coffee.

Once we'd all finished, and Theo called first dibs on the shower, I said, "Hey, I have to make a phone call upstairs. Brandy, you good on your own for a while?"

Theo snorted as he disappeared upstairs. Brandy just tilted her head a little. "Who are you calling at nine in the morning?"

Nine in the morning. God. No wonder I was still so tired. Usually that bacon-and-coffee smell didn't wake me up before ten thirty.

"My dad. He called last night and I didn't get it. So I'm calling back."

It was partly true. My dad *had* called last night, just like he did every few days or so, just to check in. I'd picked it up halfway down to the May Day tree, and we'd had our usual boring yeah-everything's-fine conversation as Grandma listened in and Aunt Holly glared at me.

Right now, though, my priority was putting Leah's

blankets away before anyone saw them and started asking questions.

"Ah," said Brandy. "Tell him hello for me. I'll get started on the dishes."

"Eh, leave them for Theo," I said. "He never takes a turn."

"Touché," said Brandy. "In that case, I'll just be reading."

As soon as she was gone, I poured myself another cup of coffee and headed upstairs.

But when I pushed the door open, the room wasn't empty. Leah was still there, sitting on the floor with the comforter pooled around her like a half-melted cocoon. There was a notebook open on her lap, and as I watched, she flipped a page, reading its contents with the kind of concentration usually reserved for standardized tests.

I shut the door behind me, fast as I could. "What are you still doing here?"

She looked up with a start, snapping the notebook closed like it was a porn site and I was her mom. I glanced at it, suddenly curious; it was one of those marble composition books, and someone had written the words *CASE FILE 6* on it, all in capital letters.

"Sorry," she said. "I . . . got distracted."

"What's that?" I asked.

"Nothing," she mumbled, and shoved the notebook under Heather's dresser. There were about eight inches of space between the dresser and the carpet—and nearly all of it was taken up by papers. Notebooks, folders, loose leaf. "I heard the door. Did they leave?"

"Aunt Holly and Grandma did. My friends are still around. So keep it quiet." As she got up and moved toward the window, my eyes wandered back to the papers under the dresser. I set my coffee down on the nightstand. "Are those Heather's?"

"And mine," she said, following my gaze. "We used to . . ."

But her mouth contorted, and she stopped speaking, and suddenly I just knew that she was right on the verge of crying.

"Hey, do you think we're related?" The question tumbled out of my mouth before I'd even decided to ask it. Anything to stop her from crying, I guess.

Leah blinked, startled. "Huh?" she said.

I shrugged, like it'd been a perfectly normal question. "I just meant, you know, my family's from here. And I was wondering if this is the kind of town where everyone's related to each other."

Leah laughed—not entirely kindly. "Are you saying we all look the same to you?"

"I'm just asking a question. It's a small town, you know? You hear things about small towns."

"Sure thing, newbie," she said, putting one hand on her hip, posing a little. "Come to think of it, I do have this brother who's also my uncle, and two of my thirteen sisters are engaged to the same guy because there aren't enough men to go around, and—"

"Oh, shut up," I said with a laugh.

"And I also cook meth in my secret cabin in the woods," she continued, "because a girl's gotta make money somehow, right, and they won't let me work down in the coal mines with the menfolk because it's so terribly horribly unladylike."

"Okay, okay, I get it," I said, laughing as I held my hands up in surrender. "Not all small towns are inbred cesspools."

She grinned. "Nope."

I shook my head and finished off my coffee.

"But to answer your question," she went on, her face settling into a more serious expression, "your family's been here since basically the dawn of time, right? So for you, probably, yeah, lots of relatives. You should ask your aunt. But my family moved here from Pennsylvania when I was five. Both my parents grew up in Europe."

"Hmm." So much for that theory.

"Why?"

"No reason. Just wondering."

"Weird thing to wonder." She cast a glance over at the window. "I guess I should probably see if my poor bike survived the night."

Without waiting for a reply, she heaved herself to her feet, opened the window, and crawled out onto the roof, leaning over far enough that I felt the urge to reach out and pull her back in. But she knew what she was doing, so I stopped myself.

After a moment, she crawled back inside, looking distinctly relieved. "Looks like it's fine! Thank the Great

Muppet God. I should go. Maybe visit Jesse, make sure he's as okay as he says. . . ."

"Ah yeah, Jesse," I said. "How long have you two been together, anyway?"

"Together?" she echoed blankly. "Wait, me and Jesse?"

"Well, yeah," I said. "I mean, a single phone call from the guy sent you biking over here without even bothering to put shoes on. I just figured . . ."

"We're not—ha—no, he and Sadie have been together since ninth grade. He's my best friend. That's all. They're *both* my best friends."

But she'd suddenly lost the ability to look me in the eye. And when she said, "Hey, you want to make sure the coast is clear?" it was in this cagey way that reminded me of . . .

Well, actually, it reminded me of *me*. Of how I used to change the subject as fast as I could, whenever Brandy-and-Theo-as-a-couple came up in conversation with basically anyone ever. And why had I always wanted to change the subject?

Because I hadn't wanted to let on that I was madly, crazy, head-over-heels in love with Brandy, that's why.

A secret crush. Interesting.

All I said, though, was, "Sure."

That was when the bedroom door opened. On the other side of it was Brandy.

△ BEFORE △

I remember the first time my mother tried to talk to me about girls. My dad had taken the reins for most of my life, telling me where babies came from when I was little, giving me the Real Men Respect Women speech when I was in junior high, all that stuff. But it was Mom who came to my room one day last fall, stood in my doorway, and said, "When are you going to start dating?"

No intro. No segue. Just that.

The answer, of course, was, *As soon as I work up the nerve to ask Brandy McAllister out*—but obviously I couldn't say that. Not to my mom. Not to anyone, really, but especially not to my mom.

So I paused my computer game and said, "I dunno. Why?"

"I'm just curious. Can't a mom just be curious?" She sidled into my room, parking herself on the edge of my bed.

"In theory, sure," I said. "But in practice? Like from experience? No."

She gave me a small smile, taking a moment to tuck her jet-black hair behind her ears. "I was just talking with your aunt Mona about when your father and I first started dating. It got me thinking."

My neck tensed up. The rest of my body followed. This was going to be a sex talk, wasn't it. I wondered if I could make it to the fire escape in time.

"Thinking about what?" I said, my voice coming out a little higher than usual.

"Your father didn't tell me right away," Mom said slowly, her eyes going distant, her voice growing delicate. "About his . . . *abilities*."

"Oh, the reaching thing," I said, relieved beyond belief.

"Yes. That. He didn't tell me until after we were engaged. We worked it out in the end, of course, but for a little while there . . . well, let's just say I wouldn't wish that feeling on anyone else. So I was wondering how you were planning to approach the situation, when it arises."

"Mom. I'm not even dating anyone. The situation couldn't be any further from arising."

"And the longer it stays that way, the happier I'll be," she said. "But the question still stands."

"I dunno!" I said. "I guess I'll . . . figure it out when I get there."

Disappointment flickered behind her eyes, just for a second. She sighed and stood up. "Well. As long as you keep in mind what I just told you. Will you?"

"Um, sure." When she raised an eyebrow at me, I added, "Definitely."

"Good," she said, and finally left me alone.

CHAPTER NINE

Confusion crinkled Brandy's forehead as she registered Leah, with her rumpled pajamas and sleep-wild hair. "So, um . . . this is when you tell me it isn't what it looks like, right?"

"Does it look like I should have left by now except I didn't?" asked Leah, without missing a beat. "Because that's exactly what this is."

Oh, for the love . . .

"Leah, come on, be nice," I said. "Brandy's cool. Plus she's my girlfriend."

Leah rolled her eyes at me, but her voice was significantly less sarcastic when she spoke again. "Okay. Fine. No, this is definitely not what it looks like."

Brandy stuck a hand on her hip. "You sure? Because it looks kind of like Aspen's got a girl in his room, and he lied about it by saying he was gonna come up here and call his dad."

I winced. When she put it like that, it did sound pretty bad.

Leah turned to me, shaking her head. "You lied to your girl about me? Dude. Come on."

"Well, you were supposed to be gone by now!" I shot back.

"I told you, I got distracted!" she said. Then, to Brandy, "I'm sorry. This is so awkward. But I'm not screwing your boy toy, I promise."

"She just slept over," I cut in, before Leah could make this any worse. "On the *floor*. That's all. Storm was really bad last night, and I wasn't about to let her back out there on her own."

"Um." Brandy looked back and forth between us, uncertainty slowing her speech. "Sorry. It's just. It's not the sleeping-over thing. Not *just* the sleeping-over thing. I mean, I didn't know she was coming over, is all. But why'd you lie just now?"

"He was covering for me," said Leah, before I could come up with anything good. "I'm not exactly welcome here, see. Heather's mom sort of—well, not sort of. She straight-up hates me. So your boy here was just being a good friend."

"Oh," said Brandy, trying for a smile. It looked kind of fake. "I, uh . . . guess I just didn't know you guys were friends now."

"Surprise," said Leah drily. "And to be fair, he didn't know I was coming over, either. Another friend of mine got hurt, and I only found out last night, and I came over because this family's the source of every—"

"She needed a shoulder to cry on," I said loudly. "And she knew I'd still be awake. And here we are."

Leah shot me a look. So did Brandy. Yeah, I hadn't exactly been subtle, interrupting her like that.

"Soooo anyway, I was just leaving," said Leah. "Must erase all traces of my presence before Heather's mom comes back and gets all vengeancey on me. Aspen, wanna walk me out?"

"Sure." I touched Brandy's shoulder as I passed her. The sleeve of her T-shirt was soft against my fingers. "I'll be right back, okay?"

I reached into her, just for a second. Just long enough to find Brandy's memory of what Leah had started to say, and her ensuing curiosity about what, exactly, my family was the source of.

"Mmhmm," she said—but averted her eyes. Despite what I'd just taken from her. Okay, this was going to require a little more digging on my part. But first, I had to get rid of Leah.

When we got downstairs, I went outside first and did a full scan of the property. Aunt Holly and Grandma were still nowhere in sight, so I gave Leah the all-clear. Together, we went around to the side of the house, where her bike was sheltered by both the eaves and the thick-trunked tree that she'd climbed to get up into my room last night. She checked the bike for damage, and then, when she was satisfied, lifted one leg over and settled herself on the seat.

"Get home safe," I said. "And see you around, I guess."

Leah peered at me. "So your girlfriend doesn't know."

"Huh?"

"Your magical stuff. Your family. The Cliff. Whatever. She doesn't know, right? That's why you cut me off before? And lied?"

"Ah," I said, rubbing at my neck. I really wished it would stop tensing up all the time. "Yeah, she doesn't know. And I'd really appreciate it if you didn't say anything, okay?"

Her eyebrows lifted a little, her head tilting to the side. "You don't plan on telling her?"

"Um, hell no," I replied.

"Ohhh, okay. Yeah. This'll end well."

"Hey, don't do that. You don't know her. You barely know *me*. So don't judge."

Leah shrugged. "I wasn't judging. Just predicting. Anyway, give me a call, okay? If you wanna talk about . . . anything. People we have in common. Whatever."

In other words: Heather. She wanted to talk about Heather. Maybe the shoulder-to-cry-on thing would turn out to be more truthful than I'd thought.

"Sure, if you want," I said. "What's your number?"

"You already have it."

"I do?"

"I programmed it into your phone this morning." She grinned. "You're not the only phone thief around here, dude."

Leah used her foot to flip up the kickstand, and I watched as she rode down the driveway, gravel flying in her wake.

Sure enough, when I checked the contacts in my phone, there was a new number. A new number from which I'd just gotten a text:

Aw thaaaaanks! You're not bad yourself!

Confused, I opened the message. And laughed. Leah's text was in response to a text from my number to hers:

Leah, this is Aspen. Don't tell my pretty blond girlfriend I
said so, but you are hawwwwt stuuuuuuff.

Shaking my head, I sent her a middle-finger emoji, followed by a smiley face. Yeah, my first impression, back in the bookstore, had been right. This girl was cool. Funny, too.

"Whatcha laughing about?" came Brandy's voice from my doorway. She was smiling softly, and it didn't look fake anymore. Not entirely, anyway.

"Stupid internet thing," I said, and beckoned her closer. She sat beside me on the bed, and as I set my phone aside, I thumbed the button that put it on silent, just in case Leah texted back. "Hey, listen. Sorry I lied about Leah being here. I really just didn't want the relatives knowing. That's all. I'm not, like, cheating on you or anything."

Brandy laughed. "Aspen. God. I didn't think you were cheating. I just thought it was weird that you lied. Come on, you can't tell me that isn't a weird thing to lie about."

"Yeah, fair enough," I agreed.

From down the hall, there came the sound of the shower turning off. Theo.

"So what's her deal?" asked Brandy. "You guys didn't

seem all that friendly last time you saw her. And didn't you call her a jerkwad?"

I shrugged. "Sometimes she's a jerkwad. Sometimes she's not."

"So she's your frenemesis," said Brandy, which made me laugh. "How long have you guys known each other?"

"Oh. Well, she used to be besties with Heather." Truth. "Then they had some sort of huge fight, and now Heather's mom hates her." Truth, as far as I knew, but details not yet confirmed. "I met her at Heather's funeral, and we've been keeping in touch." Lie. "We've been texting each other at all kinds of hours ever since then, so I guess I just didn't think it was that weird that she came over in the middle of the night." Complete, total, utter lie.

Brandy squinted at me. "In a storm like that?"

I shrugged. "Leah has a lot of feelings. Sometimes they can't wait for better weather, I guess."

"Sounds like it." She frowned again. The kind of frown where there was obviously something she wanted to say, but she wasn't sure how—or maybe she wasn't sure if she wanted to. That couldn't mean anything good.

I touched her shoulder, like I was trying to comfort her, and reached into her sleeve again. There, right on the surface: her vivid memory of Leah standing in my room, her memory of Leah being all awesome at the bookstore, her memory of Leah kicking us out of the bookstore, her suspicion that I wasn't telling her everything . . .

Well, that last one definitely had to go. I stripped the suspicion away, digging my will into its edges to make sure I got all of it. As soon as I let it go, she leaned into me, resting her head on my shoulder. A kind of sideways hug. I put my arm around her and held her tight, closing my eyes until the reaching hangover faded away.

"I think it's great that you're being such a good friend to her," said Brandy. "You're a sweet guy."

She sounded like she really meant it—which meant my work was done. I didn't have to take anything else away from her. Not today, at least.

"Well, you're a sweet girl," I said, and kissed her forehead. Which led to her straightening up again and giving me a real kiss. The kind with tongue. The kind that lasted.

At least, it lasted until Theo appeared in the doorway and went, "Ugh, get a room."

"We did," I said as Brandy broke the kiss with a laugh. "We're in it."

Theo rolled his eyes. He was already dressed in real clothes, and his hair was still slick from the shower. "Was gonna say let's go to the lake. But . . ."

"Yes yes yes, lake lake lake," said Brandy, getting to her feet. "Let me just shower first. Ten minutes, okay?"

As she darted into the hallway, Theo shook his head at me. "Ten minutes. That'll be the day."

"You should talk," I said. "You were in there for like half an hour. And go wash the dishes, okay? It's your turn."

"Mmkay," he said, and walked away, scrubbing his still-drying hair with a towel. Only when he was gone did

I check my phone again. There was a new text from Leah:

> OK, really, why did that counselor tell me Heather trans-
> ferred to another school? The more I think about that,
> the weirder it is. Who covered up her death? Her mom?
> And WHY?

Those were good questions. But I had another question to add to the pile. Was it just Leah who'd been prevented from knowing about Heather's death—or was it everyone in town? Now that I was thinking about it, hadn't that girl Natalie even said *I know Heather,* present tense? Maybe Leah was onto something. Maybe this actually was a cover-up.

But as for the why of it . . . I really had no idea.

I hadn't been up to the lake in almost two weeks. Not since before I'd started hooking up with Brandy. And I hadn't been in a boat since well before that. But now that I knew my aversion to boats was totally fake, just a product of that weird bounceback thing, I knew I had to fight it. So when Theo decided on a paddleboat, I didn't object, even though I desperately wanted to. I just went with it.

And it *sucked*.

Like, sucked to the point where Theo kept waxing poetic about the awesomeness of Corey, his summer girlfriend, and Brandy was basically the only one who said anything in return. I was too busy fixating on the rocking of the boat, imagining what would happen if—*when*—we tipped over and fell into the water, trying to convince myself that the lake was not, in fact, filled with eels or toxic chemicals or sewage or the remnants of other people's barf. All because of the stupid bounceback.

But I sucked it up, and I swore never to go up to the lake ever again *ever*, and soon we were all safely back in Theo's car, driving toward Three Peaks and the diner. The safe, dry diner.

By the time we put in our orders, I had two new texts from Leah.

> OK, long shot idea time. Can you check something for me?
> Back of Heather's closet door, there should be a manila envelope taped to the back of the mirror. See if it's still there? See if there's anything in it?

I frowned at my phone, confused, but replied—Sure—all the same. I had no idea what Leah was getting at, but it was no skin off my back, so whatever.

"Hey, no texting at the table, Rudey McRuderson," said Brandy. "We've got company."

Sure enough, when I looked up, there was a familiar-looking girl heading our way.

"I invited Corey," said Theo. "Hope you guys don't mind."

Actually, no, I didn't mind at all; Theo had just given me the perfect way to find out the answer to the how-many-people-know-about-Heather question. So after introductions were made, and after we'd placed our orders, and after Theo and Corey shared a long, sloppy kiss that seemed to happen for the sole purpose of showing off, I spoke up:

"So hey, Corey. Have you lived up here for long?"

"All my life," she said, dabbing at her lips with her napkin. "Why?"

"Oh!" I said, feigning surprise. "I mean, I was just curious. I've been coming up here for years—you know, to visit my family—and I've never met you before. So I thought you might be new."

"Ooh, who's your family? Anyone I know?"

"The Quicks. Actually, my cousin was our age. Heather?"

"Heather Quick," said Corey, her brow creasing as she thought about it. "Yeah, that's ringing a bell. I think she's a grade below me? Maybe? Or, wait, does she still even go to TPHS?"

And there it was. The answer I needed. If it had been public knowledge that Heather had died, in a tiny town like this, everyone would've known her name. So it wasn't only Leah who didn't know the truth.

Beside me, Brandy looked mildly horrified—and I immediately realized the flaw in my plan. Whatever weird cover-up shit my family had pulled, I didn't want my city friends knowing about it. Not until I knew what was going on, at least.

So I just averted my eyes, like I was super uncomfortable talking about this, and said, "No. She doesn't." Then I let the ensuing awkward silence go on for just a moment too long before clearing my throat, smiling, and changing the subject.

But for the entire length of dinner, I couldn't stop thinking about how bizarre it was. I mean, what reason could my family possibly have for covering up Heather's death? Unless . . .

Well, unless one of them had killed her. Something stupid like that. But that was out of the question, because, just, obviously. Still. Something was going on, and I wanted to know what it was.

As soon as I'd scarfed down my burger and fries, I pretended to hear my phone buzzing in my pocket. I picked it up and faked answering a phone call, then nodded and said I'd be there as soon as I could.

"Your aunt?" asked Brandy, when I faked hanging up.

"As always," I replied. "I gotta run. But I'll see you guys back at the house later, yeah? Good to meet you, Corey!"

"You too, Aspen. Oh! *Aspen*!" Her face brightened, a little laugh escaping her. "That's where I've heard that name before!"

"Wait, where?" My stomach twisted. Another piece of the puzzle was coming. Corey was about to say something about Heather. I could feel it.

But all she said was, "You're the one who passed out on my deck at the party!"

Brandy put her hand over her mouth and giggled into it. Theo didn't bother covering his snort-laugh. Half mortified and half relieved, I said, "Yeah, that was me."

"Man, I'm sorry I missed that," said Corey. "Anyway, see you around!"

"See you," I replied, and headed for the door.

I walked so fast that I made it back to the house in just over ten minutes, instead of my usual fifteen. But when I got there, I discovered . . . nothing. The lights were off, and nobody was home. I checked the whiteboard on the fridge, in case anyone had left a note, but nope. Then I checked the driveway—and, yeah, Aunt Holly's car was gone. Apparently I'd missed that on the way in. There was nobody I could ask about the Heather cover-up, which meant I'd ditched my friends early for nothing.

Well, at least that gave me time to do the favor that Leah had asked of me. Taking the stairs two at a time, I flipped the light on in Heather's room and made for the closet. I opened the door. The mirror, a thin little thing that only showed my reflection down to the knees, was suspended from the top of the door, not stuck onto the door itself, so it was easy to lift away. Taped onto the back, just as Leah had said, was a large, well-worn manila envelope.

Inside the large envelope was a smaller envelope, this one new-looking. On the front, it said:

For Sherlock's Eyes Only.

Sherlock. Yeah, because that made sense. But whatever. I sat down on the floor, my back against the door, and opened the envelope. There was a letter inside, written on lined paper that had been torn unevenly out of a notebook. I recognized the handwriting easily, from the datebook on the nightstand and the backs of the photos I'd found in the dresser drawer. It was Heather's.

February 3

Dear Sherlock,
*   I think I'm going to die soon.*
*   Super dramatic, right? Haha. But I'm*
actually serious. That's why I'm writing this
letter to you—because if I do die, I want
someone to know what happened to me. Even
my mom and Willow don't know all of it,
although I guess they suspect it's ritual-related
(which it is). But I want someone who isn't
family to know, and I want that someone to be
you.
*   If you're reading this, I imagine I'm dead.*
You went to my funeral, and you were sad.
(You should definitely be sad, but not for
too long, okay? You should totally move on
and be happy and stuff! Eventually!) And
when you asked my mom how I died, she got
all weird and wouldn't tell you . . . so you,
being the world's greatest detective, decided to
investigate for yourself. The first places you
checked were our three old hiding spots. There
wasn't anything in your air vent or in the tree
on the school playground (because I couldn't
stand up long enough to get there . . . sorry)

but there was something behind my mirror.
Congratulations, my dear detective! You did it!
(Am I right so far?)

I also imagine you think I'm dead because
of my family, and you want to blame them for
it. Please don't. It's a little bit Willow's fault,
because she picks the objects from under the
May Day tree, but she didn't know what I was
going to do, so don't be mad at her, okay?

A few days ago, there was a triad ritual. It
would've been the same deal as usual, except
this time Willow picked something of <u>yours</u>
from under the tree. It was this little wooden
doll thing. I didn't even know it was yours
until I reached inside. I said we should go
back and get something else, and that I didn't
want to steal something from you, but Willow
wouldn't listen. She said the Cliff wanted "this
energy in particular" and that we couldn't
switch it out for something different. She said
the Cliff would collapse if it didn't get what
it wanted. And trust me, the Cliff can NOT
be allowed to collapse. I didn't find out the
real reason why until after we stopped being
friends, but just . . . trust me.

So I reached into your wooden doll, like

Willow told me to, but instead of reaching into you, I made the path from the doll go back into me instead.

I explained that badly. But I'm not sure how I'm supposed to explain it, because I'm still not sure how it worked. Or why it worked. Or why my mom and Willow couldn't tell the difference. But the point is, I made it so that when I stole something through the doll, I'd be stealing from myself instead of you, and you would be safe. And if it works like I think it'll work, you'll be safe from us forever. Nobody will ever be able to steal from you again.

See? You were wrong about me. I'm not a parasite. Especially not to you, especially not after what happened with Rachel. I didn't want to do that to you again.

Anyway, I reached in and tried to pull out the color of my hair. (I thought maybe it would leave me with unpigmented hair. Is that even a word? Unpigmented! I thought it would look so cool, and I thought maybe you would think so, too. And maybe you'd start talking to me again. But anyway . . .)

Anyway anyway anyway. I reached in and I tried to feed the color of my hair to the Cliff.

But the Cliff wasn't interested. It left my hair alone and took something bigger instead. The kind of something where about an hour after the ritual was done, I stopped being able to breathe right. I don't know <u>why</u> exactly—and get this: I tried fixing myself, and it didn't work. Like I reached into some random stranger and tried stealing his healthy lungs for myself. My mom did the same thing. It just didn't work. And the reaching thing <u>always</u> works.

Maybe when <u>the Cliff</u> takes something, it can't be replaced. I can't think why that'd be true, but it's the only theory I've got. Either way, this is just . . . not good. Incredibly, stupidly, OMGWTF not good. The kind of not good where you should go back and read the super dramatic but 100% true sentence that began this letter.

But see? That's why I wanted you to know. Maybe it's selfish, because now I know you'll feel all guilty, but DO NOT WORRY YOU ARE NOT THE REASON I AM DEAD THIS IS WHAT I SAY THEREFORE IT IS TRUE. Plus I don't blame you, so you are not allowed to blame yourself. Okay? <u>OKAY</u>?

*If I'm right about my funeral being the
reason you found this letter, then I hope we got
to talk one more time before I passed into the
great beyond. No big deal if we didn't, I guess.
But I hope we did.*

*Anyway, I just wanted you to know the
truth: that I'm still so so so sorry about Rachel,
and that I wish we could've stayed friends,
and I'm even a little sorry about saying no to
the Jesse thing—but most of all, that I tried to
protect you from the Cliff.*

I hope it worked.

Love always,

Dr. W

*P.S. If it didn't work . . . good luck with
your brand-new white hair! Haha!*

△ BEFORE △

When Heather got back from her summer vacation last year, she dragged her suitcase up to her room without even stopping to say hello. I remember feeling kind of annoyed—I mean, I'd been covering her role in the triad ritual for three whole weeks, and she couldn't even say hi?—so obviously, I followed her upstairs. The door to her room was open, and she'd already started unpacking. Except the stuff she was unpacking definitely didn't look like regular vacation stuff.

"What's all that?" I asked, apparently suddenly enough to make Heather jump. I snickered as she pressed her palm to her chest, like an old lady clutching her pearls.

"Creeper," she said, lifting a hat out of her suitcase. It was a tricornered one. The kind favored by movie pirates. She inspected it quickly and, apparently satisfied, set it down on the floor beside a fancy cup thing. "What are you doing in my room?"

"I'm not in your room. I'm in the hallway. See?" I pointed to the floor, where the line between the bedroom carpet and the hallway carpet was very apparent.

Heather rolled her eyes and kept unpacking. A shiny flask. A whole bunch of jewelry. And . . . whoa . . .

"Is that a *sword*?" I said, crossing the carpet line and kneeling down to touch the hilt.

"It's a dagger. Swords are bigger, duh." She snatched it out of my reach. "And get out of my room."

Ignoring her order, I followed the dagger with my eyes. "It's so cool. Did you get that in Hawaii?"

She shrugged. "There was a guy making replicas there. This one's Frodo's dagger from *Lord of the Rings*. It's called Sting."

"Nerd."

"Moron."

"How'd you get that past security, anyway?"

Heather grinned. "Same way I got it out of the store. Well, not exactly the same. With the store, I took away the guy's memory of letting me hold it. At the airport, I took away the security guy's sight."

"You *what*?" I gaped at her. Dad would kill me if I ever did anything like that.

She laughed. "I'm kidding. Totally kidding. I just took away his knowledge that sharp objects weren't allowed past security."

"That's . . . kind of terrible," I said, impressed.

Heather just shrugged.

"Did you steal all the rest of that stuff, too?" I asked, pointing at the jewelry and the cup and the pirate hat.

"What are you gonna do?" she asked, raising an eyebrow. "Tell my mom? Because she already knows."

But before I could reply, Aunt Holly's voice rang out

from downstairs: "Heather, honey! There's a fault in the stone!"

Heather's whole body seemed to sag. "Mom, come on, I'm all jet-lagged! Make Aspen do it!"

I heard a chuckle from downstairs. My dad. He and I had been staying here for the past three weeks while Heather and Aunt Holly had been snorkeling with dolphins or sky-diving off volcanoes or whatever people do in Hawaii.

Then, Aunt Holly's voice again: "Aspen, honey? You up for one more triad before you leave?"

I checked my watch. My dad had said he wanted to be on the road by six. It was almost five already. I didn't re-ally feel like doing a ritual right now—it hadn't even been twenty-four hours since the last one—but I knew that when I was back home, stewing in Brooklyn's rancid August hu-midity, I'd miss this. I'd miss being up here, doing some-thing I was good at.

"Coming!" I shouted. "Guess I'll see you next year, Heather."

"At least hug me before you go," she said. "God, didn't your parents teach you any manners?"

"No, they didn't. I'm basically a caveman." But I leaned over and gave her a hug anyway.

"Go forth, caveman," she said. "Build mighty fire. Make rocks not fall down."

"Oh, shut up," I replied. Heather laughed as she went back to unpacking her stash.

That was the last time I ever saw her.

CHAPTER TEN

One floor below me, the front door opened, then shut again. Someone was home. God, I hoped it wasn't Brandy yet. I'd barely had any time to process Heather's letter.

"Hello?" I called, in the general direction of the stairwell.

"Hi, honey!" Grandma called back.

Letting out a breath of relief, I went downstairs to meet her—but not before tucking Heather's letter back into its hiding spot. She and Aunt Holly were in the kitchen, unloading groceries from plastic bags.

"I didn't see Theo's car." Grandma rubbed her hands together, like she was trying to warm them. "Are your friends still out?"

"Yeah, I just didn't feel like . . ." But I trailed off. This wasn't the time for made-up excuses. So I sat down at the kitchen table and asked the question I wanted to ask:

"How did Heather really die?"

Silence. The too-loud *thud* of something falling to the

floor. Aunt Holly, slack-jawed and wide-eyed, staring at me like I'd just killed Heather all over again. Staring, and staring, and then turning around and stomping out of the room. A few seconds later, her bedroom door slammed.

Grandma stooped and picked up what Aunt Holly had dropped. A tub of butter.

"Aspen," she said.

". . . Sorry?"

"She's still grieving."

"No kidding, Captain Obvious."

"*Aspen.*"

I sighed. "Sorry," I said again, and meant it this time. "But I still want to know."

"We all do," said Grandma, resting her hands on the countertop. "But nothing has changed since the last time you asked. I told you I would let you know if we found out anything more, and I meant it. There's been no more progress." She smiled sadly. "And given what we had to do to her doctors' memories, it seems unlikely there'll ever be."

"Her doctors?" But no, that wasn't even the most confusing thing Grandma had just said. "Wait . . . what do you mean, the last time I asked?"

Her eyebrows shot up. With a dry huff of laughter, she started piling things into the fridge. "After the funeral, Aspen dear. Don't you remember?"

I stayed quiet, because no. I didn't remember. Rubbing at my increasingly tense neck, I waited for Grandma to keep talking.

"You said her cause of death was too 'vague'"—she used finger-quotes to emphasize the word—"to sound real. You wanted to know if there was a supernatural origin instead of a medical one. I told you what I knew, of course: that Heather's doctors had been just as perplexed as you were, and they'd been unable to diagnose her with any certainty before she passed."

I remembered nothing of this conversation. Nothing at all.

"The doctors' memories?" I asked. "What'd you mean by that?"

"We had to wipe them," said Grandma, giving me a hard look. "You know that."

"I do?" I said.

"Aspen, sweetheart, are you all right? You look . . . unwell."

I felt pretty unwell, too. I slumped a little in my chair, which only deepened her frown.

Abandoning the groceries, Grandma came over and put her hand on my cheek. Her fingers vibrated against my skin. I jerked away.

"What is it?" she asked, alarmed. But then she saw me eyeing her hand, and she shook her head. "Ah. A small tremor of the hands. Old age. You understand."

Sure, whatever.

"Why'd you wipe their memories?" I asked.

Grandma sat down in the chair opposite mine. "Aspen," she said delicately. "Is something wrong?"

Oh, so many things were wrong.

"You said we talked about this stuff at the funeral. I don't remember that."

"How can you not?" she asked. "You called me every day for weeks, trying to piece together an unsolvable puzzle. You were determined to believe that Heather's death was a mystery, and you were determined to solve it."

It wasn't a mystery. Not anymore. Now that I knew it was a triad ritual gone wrong, the real mystery was why nobody knew that except for me—and why Leah and Corey hadn't even known that she'd died.

And the real *real* mystery:

"I don't remember that," I said. "Why don't I remember?"

Silence again. Then, slowly, Grandma's eyes fluttered closed. Her shoulders sagged, and she rubbed at her temples with her hands. "Your father," was all she said.

"What about him?"

"This is only speculation," she said. "But your father has never been entirely comfortable with our family rule."

"What are you talking about?"

She lifted an eyebrow. A second passed.

Then, all at once, I understood what she was getting at. "You mean he stole my memory of the funeral?"

"I'm only speculating," she said again. "But it certainly would explain a lot, don't you think? I'll call him tonight. I've been meaning to have a word with him anyway."

"No, I'll call," I said. "He makes *me* follow that rule.

Hell, he *taught* me that rule. Why would he do that?"

Grandma shook her head and murmured, "Do as I say, not as I do."

God, I hoped she was wrong. But the more I thought about it, the more right it seemed. I wasn't the kind of person who went around forgetting stuff. Especially important stuff.

"Why'd you have to wipe the doctors' memories?" I asked.

The look on her face was confusion-pity-anger, all in a row, rapid-fire. "The same reason we clear our names from government records, Aspen. You know that." When I gave her nothing but another blank look, she sighed. "We have to strike a balance. We always have. A balance between being a present and active part of the community, and living off the grid."

"Does my dad do that, too?" I asked. "Do I just not know about it?"

"No, goodness, no," said Grandma. "Your father lives exactly as your government wants him to. Everything documented, everything out in the open. He even pays *taxes*." This last with a wrinkle of her nose, like she'd just caught a whiff of ripe garbage. "No, it's only us. The Quicks of Three Peaks have always had another layer of protection in place—a degree of anonymity, if you will—because of the work that we do."

"The triad ritual?"

"The very same. It's secret work, and it's dangerous. If

anyone ever figured out what we do, or what we *are* . . .
Well. It would end badly for us, I can assure you of that
much."

That wasn't the only reason it was dangerous. Heather's
letter was proof of that. But unless Grandma was a better
liar than I'd ever given her credit for, she didn't know anything about it.

"Aspen, sweetheart," said Grandma, reaching over to
take my hand. The trembling was less of a shock, now that
I knew to expect it. "I'm so sorry for what happened to you.
Your father, if I'm correct about what he did, had no right
to dig into your mind like that."

Damn straight. Stealing memories was a thing we did to
other people, not to each other. That was the opposite of
how things were supposed to be. It was just *wrong*.

"And for whatever it's worth, I want you to know that
you can trust my Holly to follow the rule. Me too, obviously, since I can't reach at all," she added with a smile.
"Just don't let one incident mar your trust of our family, all
right? You're safe while you're up here."

I hadn't even thought of that—that Dad might not be the
only Quick who broke our family's cardinal rule.

"Thanks," I said, letting her squeeze my hand. Despite
the weird tremor thing, despite how old she was, I was
struck with the sudden sense of being absolutely understood, maybe for the first time ever. My grandmother, of
all people, totally got how I felt about all this. And I hadn't
even had to tell her.

I went upstairs, ready to fling accusations at my dad—but when I got there, I found a missed call on my phone. Not from Dad.

From Mom.

She hadn't called in a couple of days.

All at once, the rage leaked out of me, leaving my legs so weak that I sank down onto the bed. She'd called, and she'd left a voicemail, which I'd obviously delete, like usual, because it would just be the same shit as always: She loved me, she missed me, she wanted me to visit, blah blah.

But this time, for whatever reason, I pressed PLAY.

"*Aspen, it's Mom. I'm just calling to say I love you. You know everything else I want to say, so I won't say it all again. But that's the one thing that's always worth saying, isn't it? Even though you're mad at me. I love you. Call me back. Please call me back.*"

Yup, same old same old. Except, just, I hadn't heard her voice in *so long*. I'd been deleting her voicemails since before spring break.

Suddenly I didn't have the energy to call Dad anymore. Maybe I could just stay in Three Peaks, live in my dead cousin's room, and forget I ever had parents. Or maybe I could steal Dad's memory of me, so he'd forget he ever had a kid. It would serve him right.

I lay back, staring at the ceiling, trying to convince myself to suck it up and call my father and ask what I wanted to ask. Or, barring that, to call Leah and tell her I'd found Heather's letter.

But before my mind could triumph over the lazy matter that was my body, Brandy appeared in my doorway.

"Hey," she said.

"Hey," I replied, waving feebly. "Sorry I had to ditch you guys before."

"No biggie." She came over to sit beside me—after shutting the door behind her, which usually meant good things were about to happen. "You feeling okay?"

"I am now," I replied truthfully.

She leaned over, kissing me long and deep. "Glad to hear it," she said. "Because that was a long time that I had to sit there just now, watching Theo and Corey flirt. You have *no idea* how much it sucks being a third wheel during someone else's honeymoon phase."

"Um," I said.

She looked at me blankly for a second, before her expression turned sheepish. "Oh yeah. I guess you do have a pretty good idea. . . ."

"Maybe a little," I said. "But did it work? Did my absence make your heart grow fonder?"

"Oh my god. So fond. I have the fondest heart *ever*. You don't even know."

Her hand moved higher up my leg, inch by inch. Her pretty hand, with its soft, warm skin and nimble, talented fingers. Yeah, this was exactly what I needed right now. I could deal with Leah and the letter tomorrow. Maybe I'd even deal with my dad tomorrow.

Tonight, though? Tonight was all about Brandy and me.

⚠

I left early the next day, excusing myself from the break-fast table with Heather's note folded up in my back pocket. Brandy asked where I was going, but I just told her I'd be back soon.

Leah was counting bills behind the register when I walked in, and she looked up at the sound of the little bell above the door. "Aspen," she said, lowering a small stack of fives into the till. "Hey."

Instead of answering, I just held up the envelope. For a few seconds she looked confused—and then she got it. Bumping the register closed with her hip, she darted out from behind the counter and snatched the envelope from my hands.

"You read it already," she said, frowning as she ran her fingers along the torn edges of the envelope. "Didn't you."

"Good morning to you, too," I said, a little annoyed at her tone. I mean, I'd done her a favor by finding that thing, hadn't I?

"She wrote it to me, not you," said Leah. "You shouldn't've read it."

"Look, I had to know what was going on—"

"It's my letter," she said. "You had no right to read it first."

"Is this young man bothering you?" came a familiar voice from behind me. Harry, the owner of the store, wearing an expression that was half joking, but also half not.

"No," said Leah, rubbing a hand over her forehead.

187

"Sorry. Didn't sleep well last night. D'you mind if we use the back room for a bit?"

Harry gestured at the empty store around us. "I'll yell if there's a stampede."

Leah didn't reply, just nodded and marched toward the back of the store. Then I realized that she'd just said *we*, so I followed.

She led me through a seventies-style beaded curtain, into a dusty hallway full of tall metal shelves crammed with more books than I would've thought possible. We ended up in a tiny office, just big enough for one wheely chair, a desk, and another narrow bookshelf. An orange cat was curled up on the desk, its head pillowed on a crusty-looking computer keyboard; it blinked at me a few times, but then went right back to sleep.

"This is Chekhov," said Leah, running a hand fondly down its spine. "He's the laziest animal in the known universe."

"Hi, Chekhov," I said, and gave his head a quick scratch. He didn't seem to notice.

Leah sat down in the only chair, pressed her lips together, and began to read. The clock on the wall ticked. The cat purred softly as he slept. I leaned on the doorframe, watching Leah.

"A parasite," she murmured after a moment, then fell silent again. I couldn't tell if she'd meant to read the word out loud.

She flipped the paper over to the other side.

After another moment, she muttered, "Super dramatic, a hundred percent true." She was blinking faster now. I wondered if I should leave.

Finally she laughed, sort of wetly, then touched her hair and looked up at me. She looked like she wanted something. Tissues? A profound statement that would magically make her feel better about the whole thing? A hug?

I made myself speak. What came out was: "So . . . yeah. That's the letter."

She put it carefully, first page up, on the desk. Smoothed it out with her hand and said, slowly, "So it's really true. She's really dead. And it's because of me."

"No, see, that's exactly what she wrote," I said, pointing to the paper under her hand. "She said not to feel guilty."

"Oh, good," said Leah flatly. "Poof. I don't feel guilty anymore. Magic."

"I'm just saying, it wasn't because of you. It was because of something *she* did *for* you."

"Yeah. This is totally working. You should be a professional therapist."

I threw my hands up. "God. Fine. Never mind."

Leah shook her head. "Sorry. Sorry. Just . . . cut me a little slack, okay? This is a lot to take in all at once."

"I know the feeling," I mumbled, thinking of my conversation with Grandma yesterday evening. The one about my dad.

"Hm?"

"Nothing." I straightened up, watching as she ran her

index finger over the first line of the letter. "Hey, I wanted to ask you . . ."

She swallowed. "Ask me what?"

"That stuff she said she was sorry about. A 'Jesse thing.' And also someone named Rachel. Who's Rachel?"

"My sister."

"Oh. What happened to her?"

She splayed her hand over the letter. Hesitated a moment. "I'm . . . I'm not sure anymore. I thought she was lying. Heather. I really did. But she talks about the Cliff like . . . oh god . . . and I didn't believe her. . . ."

Pushing myself off from the doorframe, I braced my hands on the desk and leaned over, trying to catch her eye again. "What happened to Rachel?" I asked again, soft but firm.

"Rachel's mute," she said. "For five years now."

"She lost her voice?"

"She didn't *lose* it, you moron," Leah snapped. "You people stole it from her."

Oh.

I straightened up slowly, a zillion things sliding into place in my head, all of which added up to:

"That's why you and Heather stopped being friends."

Leah nodded. "Well, that was the beginning of it, anyway. This one day, about five years ago, Rachel woke up without a voice. I asked Heather if she knew why. Heather said she hadn't meant to take away her voice—she'd meant to take away Rachel's preppy fashion sense, because she knew that would make me happy. It *would* have made me happy, is the thing, because Rachel always dressed like a freaking senator or something. Still does. But . . . but that's not the point. The point is, Heather said she didn't mean for Rachel's voice to get stolen. She told me so, right after it happened, and I didn't believe her." She paused. "I should have, but I didn't."

Rachel's voice. The result of the Cliff taking something bigger than what my family had offered it. Heather hadn't been the first victim of that kind of situation. It had happened before.

"And she kept bugging me to be friends again. For *years* she bugged me, and I just kept blowing her off, until . . ."

"Until?"

Leah swallowed hard. "Until I changed my mind. I tried to make a deal. At first, it was just, you know, if Heather could steal someone else's voice and give it to Rachel, we could be friends again. She said no. Then I said if she made Jesse fall in—" She cut herself off, eyes wide.

But she'd already said more than enough. "Fall in love with you?" I finished for her.

She nodded, cheeks going pink as her eyes fixed firmly on the unmoving Chekhov. "She said no to that, too."

"Well, we can't exactly do that stuff. I mean, the voice thing, maybe. But then Rachel would sound like someone else. And the falling-in-love thing?"

"She could've found a way," said Leah, in a tone that allowed for no argument. "But she didn't want to. She didn't even want to try—and trying would've been enough, you know? So I just kept ignoring her. For five years, I ignored her."

"Well, that's—"

"Sorry, wait, did I say *ignored*?" Her eyes were narrowed as she got to her feet, her voice sharp, her hands clenched. "I didn't ignore her. Who am I kidding. I was so . . . so *mean,* and . . . and what the *hell* kind of stupid *asshole* of a person *dies* for someone who's been *mean* to them for five whole *years*?"

"That's not what she meant to do, though," I said, holding my hands up like that might somehow stop her from yelling. "She meant to—"

"*I know what she meant to do, Aspen! I can read!*"

And then, with no warning, Leah was crying. Sobbing. Hiding her face in her hands as her shoulders shook.

Run away run away run away, said a little voice in the back of my head. *Run while you still can.* Crying people scared the shit out of me.

Quietly, ignoring the voice, not to mention the death glare that the orange cat was now giving us, I moved around the desk and reached for Leah. She flinched when I touched her shoulders. But I didn't move away. Just gave her a small smile and left the next move up to her.

One heartbeat passed. Then two. Then Leah melted into me, cheek on my shoulder, tears soaking through the thin fabric of my shirt. "I didn't even get to say I was sorry," she murmured, her voice thick as I held her tight. "So many times . . . in school, around town . . . I'd see her and . . . she looked so lonely and . . . but . . . but I just couldn't do it . . ."

"It's okay," I said, because that was what you were supposed to say in situations like these. Wasn't it? "It's okay, it's okay."

"No, it's not," she said, pulling away and looking at me with dark, watery eyes.

And before I could figure out how to reply, Leah was kissing me.

Leah

Was

Kissing me.

And then I was kissing her back. My lips against hers, her chest against mine, her hand in my hair, my hand on her back, my fingers digging into the muscles of her shoulders as sparks flew through my brain, growing brighter every second.

Kissing Leah hadn't been an option. That was what I'd thought, because she wasn't my type, and she was kind of abrasive, and she didn't even seem to like me all that much anyway. It hadn't been an option at all, despite how weirdly magnetic she was, because I had too much other stuff going on. I had a *girlfriend,* for god's sake. I was dating the girl of my dreams. So of course it hadn't been an option.

Until, suddenly, it was.

She pulled away first, leaving me with a racing heart and a mouth that had forgotten how to say words and a pair of hands that didn't have anything to hold on to. She looked calm. Vaguely perturbed, in a thoughtful kind of way, but calm.

I had to be calm, too. Calm enough for my brain to remind my body that this was a completely horrible idea. That kissing other girls was not allowed. That I loved Brandy, and always had, and always would.

Chekhov was calm. I rested my hand on his fur, letting my ring finger land on his collar like it was no big deal, and I reached into him and found his calm laziness resting right on top.

I skimmed a little bit off, absorbed it into myself, and let my hand fall to my side again.

"So," said Leah, looking at me thoughtfully. "Yeah."

I resisted the incredibly strong urge to rub my whiskers with my hand. This was why I didn't reach into animals very often. Thanks to the reaching-hangover thing, there were always a few seconds afterward when I had the disorienting sensation of being covered in fur.

"Yeah," I made myself say. "Uh." I looked down at Chekhov again. Then back up at Leah. "You know I have a girlfriend, right?"

"Oh. Right. Sorry." She let out a long sigh, rubbing wearily at her forehead. "I didn't mean to, like, jump you."

"It's cool," I said. "It was just kind of . . . like . . . I didn't expect you to do that, is all."

She shook her head, two of her fingers swiping idly at her bottom lip. "I didn't expect me to do that, either, to be honest. Sorry. I didn't mean anything by it."

Something tightened in my chest. "It's okay," I said, even though it wasn't. It wasn't okay at all, now that I actually stopped to think about it. But I went on: "We can pretend it never happened, right?"

"No, we can't," she said, laughing weakly. "I'm not that good at lying to myself."

"Oh," I said, because what the hell else was I supposed to say? "At least don't tell Brandy."

Leah narrowed her eyes. "Right. Brandy. Does that girl know *anything* true about you?"

"What do you—"

"She doesn't know about your weird magical powers. You're planning on lying to her about kissing me."

"*You* kissed *me*," I reminded her.

"Uh, yeah, and you kissed me right back," she said. "So, what else? Do you just lie to her about everything?"

No, not everything. But lying about the reaching thing covered a lot of territory, considering how many times I'd stolen from Brandy.

"I love her," I said. "I don't lie about that."

She nodded. "I love someone else, too," she said, moving close to me again. Too close. "And that's the one thing I *do* lie about."

Jesse. Yeah. Until her admission a few minutes ago, she'd tried claiming they were just friends.

Her eyes flicked over to the letter again, sitting there on the desk, spilling secrets. Her hand touched my sleeve, then crept up to rest on my shoulder. Her face was so close to mine. Her eyes were dark, and her lips were full and perfect and there was that little mole right above the left corner. The one I'd failed to steal.

"Leah?" I said, my throat suddenly dry. "I told you. I have a girlfriend."

"Watch me care," she said.

She kissed me again. And again, I kissed her back. This time, we didn't stop.

△ BEFORE △

Brandy's dad lived in Brooklyn, and her mom lived up in Washington Heights. While she mostly lived with her dad, she spent alternate weekends with her mom. Or, at least, that was what her dad thought. In reality she spent maybe one weekend every two months at her mom's place (I'm still not sure how she'd made that happen), and the rest of the supposed Mom Weekends, she spent at Theo's. And on Theo Weekends, she could stay out all night, without either of her parents trying to chase her down.

These were Brandy's favorite weekends. And even though they invariably ended with BrandyAndTheo going home to-gether and probably doing stuff that I really didn't want to think too hard about (Theo lived in an old brownstone so huge that his parents probably didn't even notice his girl-friend practically lived there), they were kind of my favorite weekends, too.

This particular Saturday night, Theo, Brandy, Brandy's friend Lauren, and I had hit up two clubs and one of those shitty midtown pubs that never asked for ID. Then? Pizza. We always ended our nights with pizza.

Eventually Lauren went home, and Theo went to the bathroom, leaving me alone, temporarily, with the remains of a large pepperoni pie, and the girl of my dreams. Her eye makeup was smeared all over, and her blond ponytail was more than a little bit askew. She looked completely happy, and completely gorgeous.

"You've got glitter on you," she said, touching her left cheek with two fingers.

I touched the same spot on my own cheek; sure enough, my fingers came away sparkly. I shrugged. "Well, so do you."

Brandy smiled. "Yeah, but mine's intentional. What'd you do, rub cheeks with Laur?"

I frowned. Not at what she'd said, but at the way she'd said it: kind of suggestive, kind of hopeful.

"Because that'd be so cute," she went on. "The two of you. Aw."

"Uh, no it wouldn't," I said. And then, because that had come out meaner than I'd intended, I added, "She's not into me anyway."

Brandy laughed, leaning back in her pleather seat. "Hello, are you blind? She's *completely* into you. She has been for months. Why do you think I keep inviting her out with us?"

Well, I'd thought it was because they were best friends, and that was what best friends did. Invite each other out. Occasionally it'd also occurred to me that it was to keep me from feeling like a third wheel. But I hadn't seen this one coming.

"Oh," I said stupidly.

"Yeah," said Brandy. "And because I am sick of waiting for you to notice, and because I am an excellent wingman,

I'm gonna give you a piece of advice: Ask her out already."

I remember intending to say *But I'm not into her* or *I don't feel like we'd be good together* or something like that. Something nice and vague and not incriminating.

Instead, what came out was, "But I'm into *you,* not her." Maybe because it was like five in the morning. Too late for anything but blunt honesty, I guess.

Brandy's mouth made an O.

"Um, forget I said that. It's late. I'm tired." I rubbed my hands over my eyes, probably getting glitter all over the place.

She was silent for a moment. Then she said, her voice all low, "You know, I used to think about that. You and me."

"You . . . wait, really?"

She nodded. "I thought about asking you out."

My stomach folded in on itself. "Why didn't you?"

"Why didn't *you?*" she said.

Because I didn't want to risk her saying no. That was the real answer. But that would've made me look like a spineless coward, so I just said, "I dunno."

"Same," she said. "And then Theo just . . . got there first. I figured I'd give it a shot. And. Well. He's nice."

"I'm nicer," I said.

"Ha." Brandy fiddled with the straw in her soda cup, not quite looking at me. "Well, I'll give you a call if things don't work out with Theo. How's that?"

"You should give me a call anyway." I remember not being sure, even then, whether or not I was joking.

Brandy's face, however, was dead serious. "I'm not a cheater, Aspen. And I'm not breaking up with him for you. Got that?"

Theo came back from the bathroom then, and dug into his third slice of pizza. I watched as Brandy put her hand on his back, a small and silent gesture of togetherness. She caught my eyes, and I nodded.

Yeah. I got it.

CHAPTER ELEVEN

I mean, Leah and I did stop making out *eventually*, but it wasn't for a good long while, and it wasn't until we heard the distinct sound of footsteps, perilously close to where we stood. Then Leah patted my shoulder in this weirdly businesslike way, snatched Heather's letter off the desk, and ran out of the room.

By the time I'd regained enough composure to follow her back out into the store, Leah was digging her purse out from under the register. Harry was lurking nearby, watching her.

"You're sure everything's okay?" he was saying. "Is it something to do with Jesse? Is he *ever* planning on coming back to work?"

Leah shook her head. "He hasn't decided yet. But no, it's not about him. I just need to . . . there's some stuff, is all." She straightened up, looked right at me, and jerked her head toward the door.

As I followed her outside, obedient as a puppy, I felt Harry's eyes on me. Maybe making assumptions. Maybe assumptions that were right.

"Where are we going?" I asked Leah—right before I noticed where she was heading: away from the commercial part of town, toward the residential one. "We're not going to your house, are we?"

She rolled her eyes. "We're going to Jesse's place, not mine." And she kept walking.

"Whoa," I said, holding my hands up as I took a step back. "If you wanna tell him you kissed me, that's your business. But I so don't want to be there for that conversation."

"Oh my god," she muttered, pinching the bridge of her nose between two fingers. "This is not about the kissing. This is about *me* wanting *you* to tell *Jesse* why he's suddenly blind. Remember? That whole thing where you stole his sight?"

"It wasn't me, though! I already swore—"

"I know," she said impatiently. "But didn't you read Heather's letter? She said she offered something to the Cliff. The color of her hair. Then she said *the Cliff wasn't interested*. It ignored what she offered, and it went for something bigger instead. What did you say you stole from Jesse? His competitive streak?"

I bit my lip. I'd also seen the similarity, when I'd read Heather's letter the first time. Apparently it was too much to hope that Leah wouldn't see it, too.

"And the Cliff went for something bigger instead," I said, resigned. "Again. That doesn't mean it was my fault."

Leah glared. "You're still coming with me. Jesse can't spend the rest of his life not knowing that his sight was stolen from him."

And then she turned and walked away. I jogged to catch up. "Leah, come on. Leah!" I said, grabbing her arm when she didn't turn around. "I'm not telling him anything. Neither are you. You were friends with Heather, right? So you know how important it is to keep this stuff a secret. I can't just go around telling everyone—"

"Why not?" she said, infuriatingly calm.

"Because . . . just *because*. It's one of those things you don't go around telling people."

Leah just looked at me.

"Besides," I added, "it's not like telling him would help him. I can't exactly fix him, you know. Once something's been stolen, it can't be reversed."

"Unless you took someone *else's* sight and gave it to Jesse," said Leah. "Heather said that was an option. You know—right before she refused to do it for Rachel."

"You read the letter, though," I said. "You can't use that loophole if it's something the Cliff took. Heather tried. So did her mom. Jesse's eyesight wouldn't be any different."

"You could at least try, though." But she sighed, all deflated, like she already knew it was a lost cause.

So I didn't reply.

"Hey, Aspen?" asked Leah, after another moment of

quiet. "What happens if you stop stealing stuff for the Cliff?"

I shrugged. "It collapses. There's a big avalanche, and the whole town gets crushed. Rocks fall, everyone dies."

She frowned. "That's what Heather used to say. But it doesn't make sense. The Cliff isn't that big, and it's far enough away that . . . I mean, geology, right? Even if an avalanche happened, it wouldn't reach the town. It probably wouldn't even reach your house."

"My grandma's house," I said. "And yeah, that's what I thought, too. But I figure, hey, it's magic. It's a magic cliff. It can do what it wants, I guess."

Worrying at her lip with her teeth, Leah pulled Heather's letter from where she'd stowed it in her purse. Unfolding it, she pointed to something at the bottom of the front page.

And trust me, the Cliff can NOT be allowed to collapse. I didn't find out the real reason why until after we stopped being friends, but just . . . trust me.

"The real reason," she said. "They told you the same thing they told Heather when she was just a little kid. But she found out later that it wasn't the truth."

My skin prickled, even though it wasn't anywhere near cold. If it wasn't really true about the Cliff falling and burying the town of Three Peaks, then what was it?

I didn't know.

But that didn't mean I'd *never* known. What if someone had told me, and the knowledge had been stolen away? Somehow, that seemed even worse.

I had to call my dad.

As soon as I thought it, my phone rang, making me jump like eight feet in the air. But it wasn't my dad calling. It was Brandy.

I swiped the screen to pick up. "Hey, you."

Beside me, Leah pointedly rolled her eyes. I ignored her.

"Hey, where are you?" asked Brandy. "I mean, no rush or whatever, but Theo's itching to get up to the lake. *Coooorey* is meeting us there today."

My neck tensed at the thought of the lake. A boat. Murky water. The uneasy feeling of not being on solid ground. . . .

Stupid bounceback.

"I'm not sure," I began . . . then glanced at Leah. Leah, who wanted answers—and who wanted me to fix her friend—and who'd just kissed me, for god's sake.

"Aspen?" said Brandy.

"Right, yeah!" I said, making my voice sound as urgent as possible. "I'll be there as soon as I can!"

"The girlfriend?" asked Leah, when I hung up.

"Yeah. I gotta go. Sorry."

"But what about all this—"

"Gotta go!" I said again, backing down the sidewalk. "Bye!"

And I turned and ran.

Only once I was around the corner, out of Leah's sight line, did I slow down. I looked back a few times to make sure she wasn't following me. Because this? This was *my* mystery. My family. Not hers. No matter how close she'd been with

Heather, and no matter what had happened to her sister, this whole situation just wasn't her problem.

But it was definitely a problem.

What was the connection between the things offered to the Cliff and the things taken? There had to be a connection. But . . . hair color and healthy lungs? A competitive streak and the ability to see? It just seemed so random.

Or maybe there wasn't a connection at all. Maybe the Cliff just took whatever the hell it wanted. Which was scary to think about for any number of reasons.

I walked faster. The sooner I got back to the house, the sooner I'd have Brandy to distract me.

"Honey, I'm home!" I called out, kicking my shoes off as I shut the front door behind me.

The sound of laughter came from the living room, followed by Brandy's voice: "In here!"

I rounded the corner, and there they were: Theo on one side of the couch, Brandy on the other. Except she was facing him, and her legs were stretched out over the length of the couch. Her feet were in his lap. He was massaging one of them.

"Hey," I said, looking back and forth between them. "Um."

"Something up?" said Brandy, as Theo dug his thumb into the bottom of her arch. I watched, transfixed. I'd never touched her there. I'd never thought to. "You don't look so great."

"No. I mean yeah. I mean no! I'm good."

Brandy grinned. "Because if it's your feet, I'm sure Theo could do you next."

"In his dreams," said Theo, without even looking up. Brandy laughed.

My neck hurt. My stomach twisted. How did this keep happening? I'd been so careful about keeping their feelings for each other platonic. So careful. Despite all the little seeds of affection I'd stripped away from them, time after time, here they were, sitting there with her feet in his lap.

"So where'd you go?" asked Brandy.

"Nowhere important," I replied, moving over to stand behind her, massaging her shoulders lightly with my hands.

"Cool," she said, and tipped her face up. "Spider-Man kiss?"

I leaned down, and she leaned up. It was pretty strange, kissing upside down like that, and before long she was giggling against my lips. So I pulled away and went back to massaging her shoulders instead.

"You know, this is the perfect day," she said. "Two massages at once, from my two favorite boys. . . ."

Okay. That was it. Taking care not to let my annoyance show on my face, I reached into the fabric of her shirt again and stripped away, in one swift yank, the pleasure she felt at getting her feet rubbed.

"Ow!" she cried, jerking her left foot out of Theo's hands.

"Sorry," he said, looking sort of alarmed. "Too hard?"

"Yeah," she said, sitting upright again. I lost hold of her shoulders in the process, but it was a small price to pay for the end of Theo's goddamn foot massage. "It's . . . just, I dunno, too much all of a sudden. But hey, shouldn't we get going? You said you wanted to meet Corey."

A small smile tugged at Theo's lips. "Yup. We should head. Aspen, you need to change or whatever?"

The lake. Boats. I'd almost forgotten.

"Okay, now you *really* don't look so great." Brandy stood up and put her palm against my cheek. It was so warm. She looked so worried. "Maybe you should stay home today. Get some rest. Drink some water, for once."

And leave her alone with Theo? For all I knew, Theo'd end up having a threesome with Corey *and* Brandy out in the middle of the lake. "No, just give me a second to—"

"Hey, man, stay here." Theo had gotten up, too, and now he looked concerned. Not devious. Not like he was trying to get me out of the way so he could steal Brandy back. Just concerned. "It's summer vacay. Sucks to get sick in the summer. So just chill, and chug some DayQuil or something, and we'll see you later."

I could trust Theo, couldn't I? More than that, I could trust Brandy. She wasn't the kind of person who'd start cheating just because she had more-than-friends-type feelings for someone else.

Unlike you, said a snide little voice in my head, which I silently told to shut up.

Out loud, I said, "Sure. Yeah, that's probably a good idea. Tell Corey hi for me, I guess."

"Will do," said Theo. And then they were gone.

I hadn't heard Grandma or Aunt Holly when I'd come in just now, but I poked around just to make sure. The house was empty. I couldn't put this off any longer. I had to call my dad.

He picked up on the second ring.

"Aspen!" he said, voice all warm. "I was wondering when I'd hear from you! How's upstate?"

"Fine," I said.

"And Holly?"

"Still . . . sad," I replied. Really it was more like drunk and mean and depressed, but he didn't have to know that stuff. Besides, that would lead to a whole different conversation than the one I actually wanted to have.

"Hey, Dad?"

"What's up?"

I sat down on the couch, where Theo had just been. Braced my free hand against the cushions. "Have you ever stolen memories from me?"

Another pause, longer this time. And then Dad's cautious voice: "What makes you think I would do something like that? We have a rule—"

"Just answer the question. Memories. Have you stolen them?"

Dad swallowed audibly. "Only when I thought it necessary. When it was for your own good."

"After Heather's funeral, right?" I said. "Grandma said I thought her death was suspicious, and I tried figuring out what really happened. I don't remember any of that. And

Mom!" I said, remembering very suddenly, very vividly, a phone conversation we'd had right after she'd left. "Mom said I cried. I don't remember crying. What the *hell*, Dad?"

"I took the edge off your sadness," said Dad, so gently that it made my skin crawl. "You've never been good at dealing with grief. No, that's an understatement. Even your counselor said that boys your age usually process things much faster—that we might start looking at more effective options—"

"My *counselor*?" My hand was shaking now, which made the phone unsteady. "When did I have a counselor?"

Dad was quiet.

"What about the Cliff?"

"What do you mean?"

"The Cliff, and what happens when it falls. What *really* happens, not the bullshit about it crushing Three Peaks. Did I know that? Did you make me forget?"

"It used to give you nightmares," said Dad, sounding a little desperate by now. "I didn't know how else to make them stop."

"Nightmares. Come on. It can't be that bad."

"It definitely sounded bad to you when you were eight. I told Holly you were too young to know the details. But she went ahead and told you anyway."

"Told me what?"

"Aspen, it . . . it isn't the town," said Dad.

I frowned into the darkness of the living room. "What isn't?"

"The Cliff. If it falls, it won't be the town that gets crushed. It'll be us."

I shook my head. "What do you mean? Us who?"

"Our family," he said. "All of Willow's descendants. If we let the Cliff die, it takes us with it."

"All of Willow's . . . Wait. So. Like, just you and me and Aunt Holly?"

"And everyone else related to us," said Dad. "Aspen, when your aunt told you the truth, you were terrified. You'd grown up thinking you were safe from the Cliff so long as you stayed far away from Three Peaks. Then Holly told you the truth—against my wishes, I'll remind you—and you had such bad nightmares. You barely slept. You started acting out in school. Your teachers—"

"So, wait, hold on," I said, squeezing my eyes shut. "You stole memories from me because some stupid-ass teacher couldn't deal with me? And some stupid-ass counselor?"

"She said boys your age—"

"Oh, my *age*. Great. So, what, I'm too old to be sad? Is that it?"

"*Jeremy*," he said firmly, which shut me right up. "You're missing the point. You've always been this way. The same thing happened when my mother passed. Your grandmother. You were six, and you were inconsolable. You became obsessed with her death, you wouldn't stop crying, and it interfered with—"

"Wait. Wait." The air around me seemed to grow colder. "Did you just say my grandmother?"

"Yes . . . ?"

"She died. When I was six."

"Well . . . yes. Don't you remember? We went up to Three Peaks and scattered her ashes in the woods by the May Day field, just as we did with Heather."

I had to be hallucinating this. Or dreaming, maybe. I had to be. That was the only rational explanation. I pinched myself, just in case. Nope.

"We're talking about your mom? Aunt Holly's mom? My *paternal* grandmother?" Obviously we were; Mom's mother had died four years before I was born.

"Yes, of course."

"Then who the hell is Willow?"

". . . What?"

"She's . . . not my grandmother."

"Aspen. No. Of course she isn't. Your grandmother's name was Ivy. You know that."

Ivy. The room was spinning. Or I was spinning. Or my brain was spinning, or something. I shut my eyes again. Because no, I didn't know that. *Ivy.*

"Okay," I said. "So who told you I'd be better off not remembering my grandmother at all? Another counselor?"

"What? What are you talking about? Aspen . . ."

"Why'd you steal my memory of her?"

"I didn't!" Dad yelled. Then calmed down almost immediately. "I didn't. And I can't think why you'd have forgotten. You loved her."

I hadn't forgotten. When you forget something, you can

be reminded. A name, or an event, will ring a bell somewhere deep in your memory. But the name Ivy meant nothing.

Except . . . no. That wasn't true. I *had* heard that name before, and recently. From the guy in the bookstore where Leah worked. Ivy and Lily, he'd said—right before he'd added that he'd never met anyone named Willow. I'd meant to ask Grandma about that, and then it had slipped my mind.

"You still there, son?" said Dad. "I really don't know what happened, but we can figure this out, okay? I'll talk to your aunt, and—"

I hung up.

△ BEFORE △

"You stole it, didn't you."

My nine-year-old ears perked up, like they always did, at the word *stole*. Coming from most people, it meant something super mundane—but coming from Mom, it could easily go either way.

I crept out of bed, eased my door open, and sidled down the hallway toward the light of the living room, where my parents were still awake. I hid just around the corner, just past the point where they'd be able to spot me. My dad was speaking now, but too softly for me to hear him.

Then my mom again: "Andy, you can't keep doing things like that for him."

(Andy, for the record, was not my dad's original name. He'd legally changed it when he'd turned eighteen. I couldn't blame him; I mean, who would want to be saddled with a name like Dandelion for his entire life? Apparently it'd been his idea, too, to give me a normal first name, and use my middle name to carry on the Quick family tradition.)

"I was just trying to defuse the situation," replied Dad, barely loud enough for me to hear. "That dog was *huge*."

"Yes, it was," said Mom. "But that's beside the point."

"No, that *is* the point!" Dad said. "It was huge, and it was lunging at him. I swear it was part wolf or something."

I didn't know why Mom and Dad were fighting, but I did remember the dog. I'd come face-to-face with him on the way back from the grocery store with my parents, and as soon as he'd seen me, he'd started jumping and barking, all teeth and snarl and hungry eyes.

"I'm so sorry," his owner had said, gripping the dog's leash with both hands as she tried to calm him down. "He's a rescue, and he—down, boy! He just gets excited—he doesn't mean any harm. *Down*, Benny!"

I remember thinking that of course he meant me harm. He could obviously eat me in one bite, and that was exactly what he intended to do. Every inch of me was trying to run away, but for some reason I couldn't make my feet move. I was too scared.

Then Dad had put a comforting hand on my shoulder, turned to the woman with the leash, and asked, "May I?"

The woman had nodded, and Dad had gone over and started petting the dog. Jumping and barking instantly became sniffing and licking, and the dog suddenly wasn't a would-be killer anymore, but a friendly pet desperate for some attention. I inched closer and closer, until finally I was close enough to pet him, too.

He was a husky. His name was Benton, and his eyes were two different colors, and his fur was so, so soft.

"Still not the point," Mom was saying. "You can't just magic things better every time there's an issue."

"Come on, Annie, you saw how scared he was—"

"Fear is a part of life," said Mom. "It sucks, but that's the way it is. And if you're always there to play Mr. Fix-It every time he's scared of something, he'll never learn to deal with his fear on his own. Is that what you want?"

Fear. The dog. Dad magicking things better. Well, that explained why Benton the husky had suddenly become so friendly—because Dad had taken away his meanness. Why did Mom think that was a bad thing?

"Of course it's not," said Dad with a sigh.

That was when I coughed. Or sneezed, or something like that. I don't remember exactly. What I do remember was Mom darting around the corner and catching me.

"Your bedtime was half an hour ago, you know," she said.

I looked back and forth between her and Dad. Decided there was no point in telling them what I'd heard.

"I'm thirsty," I said. "I just wanted water."

So Mom got me a cup of water and sent me back to my room, where I started thinking about Geoffrey, our tiny corgi who'd died almost a year ago. I still missed him a lot—but more than that, I missed having a pet. I fell asleep wondering how soon I should start asking my parents for a husky of my own.

CHAPTER TWELVE

Dad called back a few times, but I didn't pick up. Eventually he stopped trying, and just texted me instead:

You ok?

I replied—**Yeah**—and then went into the kitchen to make myself some coffee. This was way too much to process on only one cup.

About twenty minutes later, I discovered that it was also too much to process on two cups. So I took a nap instead. Some time later, my phone woke me up. It was Aunt Holly.

"Hello?" I said, my voice coming out scratchy. My eyes were dry from not taking my contacts out. My clothes felt gross. My neck hurt for no good reason, like usual.

"Aspen, there's a fault that needs repairing. Ma says it's urgent."

Ma. Why did Aunt Holly call her that? Who the hell was Willow? I should have asked. I shouldn't have hung up so quickly. I should have pumped my dad for information, but my brain had just been too fried.

Anyway, it was too late now. There was a fault in the Cliff, and I had a job to do.

"Be right there," I said, reaching for my eye drops.

"Good," said Aunt Holly, and hung up.

I trudged downstairs, willing myself to wake up. Aunt Holly and Grandma—Willow—were waiting for me by the door.

It felt weird, walking down to the May Day tree in daylight. A little more mundane. A little less magical. Especially the part where Grandma instructed Aunt Holly, just as we stepped out of the woods and into the May Day field, to play lookout. Because while we never really ran the risk of people coming across us at night, midday was a whole different matter. People had picnics on this field. Hell, *I'd* had a picnic on this field.

Luckily for us, it was empty, at least for now. As Aunt Holly planted herself between the tree and the road, I followed Grandma over to the tree and watched as her eyes began to rove over the offerings underneath.

Your grandmother's name was Ivy. You know that.

"One object. A gift, not a throwaway. Something meaningful." She moved counterclockwise around the tree until she spotted something. Pointing, she said, "That. Fetch it, would you?"

It was a thick bracelet—a cuff, really—made of leather straps, all woven together into a pattern that looked like a really complicated braid. It looked kind of familiar, but I couldn't place it. Whatever, though. It didn't really matter.

Once we were back inside and ready to go, Grandma nodded at me to go first.

"My name is my self," I said, feeding my aspen leaf into the fire, "and I give them both freely."

The holly leaf, the willow leaf, and the oak leaf all followed. The fire turned blue-green-turquoise, and the Cliffstone underneath the logs glowed as it heated up. Grandma nodded toward the bracelet, and I picked it up and closed my eyes and reached inside.

God, it was weird doing this with sunlight sneaking in behind the curtains.

"Something small and sharp," said Grandma. "Something that might never be missed."

I concentrated. There was a brightness that colored the bracelet's memory of its owner. A female owner, I could tell right away. The bracelet had been a gift from someone she'd loved. A family member? No—a boyfriend. A boyfriend she'd loved fiercely, passionately, then suddenly not at all. They were just friends now.

Suspicion surfaced; I reached further. I looked for a face to go with the story.

And there it was. Brandy. I remembered her, now, asking me about the town's May Day tradition. Leaving something under the tree, despite my protests. Refusing to tell me what it was.

My eyes flew open as I withdrew my will from the bracelet.

"What?" said Aunt Holly, clearly annoyed.

"This is Brandy's," I said. "We can't steal from her."

Grandma tilted her head just so. "Why not?"

"She's my girlfriend. That's why not." Grandma looked unmoved, so I went on: "Plus she doesn't even live here. She just thought it was a quaint townie tradition. She didn't even put it under the tree on May Day."

"Oh, Aspen." Grandma reached out and touched my cheek. Her hand was shaky. A tremor, she'd said. Just a product of old age.

Still, I pulled away.

"What's wrong?" she asked.

"N-nothing," I said, because I wasn't totally sure *why* her touch had freaked me out. "Just . . ."

"Just your grandma's old-lady hands," she said, shaking her head and flexing her fingers and letting out a little sigh. "Never get old, Aspen. Anyway, you were saying? About these new scruples you have with regard to stealing from your girlfriend?"

Ah. Right. The woman who wasn't my grandmother knew what I'd done to win Brandy's affection. Or at least, she knew enough that her question hit its mark.

"Family comes first, Aspen," she said softly, as Aunt Holly looked on with furrowed brow. "Never forget that. Family comes first, and being a member of this family means doing as the Cliff commands. We are the only ones who can prevent its falling. So if the Cliff demands this energy in particular, this is the energy we shall give it."

If it falls, it won't be the town that gets crushed. It'll be us.

"Do you understand?" asked Grandma.

I understood that there were things she wasn't telling me. I understood that as soon as this ritual was over, I was going to ask what I needed to ask.

"Yes," I said. "I do."

And I felt my way into the bracelet, searching for something small. Small and sharp. And there it was: a single memory, inextricably tied to the thing that contained it. The moment Theo had given Brandy this bracelet. Bought it for her on a whim at a street fair, after she made a casual remark about liking it. She put it on immediately, on her right hand—and then she switched it to her left, because it was exactly the right size to cover up this cluster of freckles that she'd never liked much—

Ah-ha. Perfect. Wrapping my will around that tiny little cluster, I drew it out, ever so carefully, and pushed it into the fire. Aunt Holly sent it to the Cliff. And then, after a few long moments, Grandma nodded and said we were finished.

"You did well, Aspen," she said.

I looked at her. Studied her hard. She resembled Aunt Holly, was the thing. And my dad. They all had the same rounded chin, which I'd inherited, and the same blue eyes, which I hadn't. I'd assumed for so long that she was my dad's mother. My grandmother. I called her Grandma, for god's sake. And she'd never corrected me.

"I talked to my dad earlier," I said.

"Oh?" she said. Over by the fireplace, Aunt Holly paused.

"You were right. He stole my memories. A bunch of them, actually."

Aunt Holly looked sharply at me. "The rule, though."

"Guess he doesn't care," I replied. "But there was one thing he didn't remember stealing. It's . . . well, it's you, Grandma. Willow. It's—I mean—I mean, who *are* you?"

"I don't follow," she said softly. Aunt Holly was stock-still.

I felt so young all of a sudden. A little kid, standing in front of adults who didn't understand him, saying, *You aren't my gramma.*

"My grandmother's name was Ivy," I said. "She died when I was six. My dad stole my sadness about her death, or something like that—but it's more than that. I don't remember her dying. I don't remember her living, even." I took a deep breath. Here was the truth. "I thought you were my grandmother."

Willow gaped at me. Aunt Holly's eyes darted from me to her, then back again. The room, for several long moments, was painfully quiet.

To my surprise, it was Aunt Holly who spoke first. "God. I'll kill him."

"What?" I said.

"Your stupid father," said Aunt Holly. "My stupid brother. Andy doesn't know when to stop. Never has. He always reaches too far, takes too much. The number of times he's screwed up the triad . . ."

"Reaches too far?" I repeated, totally lost.

Aunt Holly's eyes were blazing by now. It was actually kind of cool to see her this pissed off at someone who wasn't me. "I'll bet you anything he tried taking away—what, your sadness, was it?—and didn't know when to stop. Or *how* to stop, the idiot. I'll call him and give him a piece of my mind—"

"No," I said. "Don't. Not now. I don't want to start a fight. I just want to know what's going on, okay?" Turning back to Willow, I said, "I've been calling you Grandma since like forever. Why didn't you correct me?"

"Aspen, love," she said. "Everyone has things that they call me. Holly calls me Ma; her daughter, rest her soul, called me by my given name. You call me Grandma. The fact is, there simply isn't a term for how you and I are related."

My stomach flipped. I sat down on the couch, because I had to. "So how *are* we related?"

She paused. "You really, truly don't remember?"

I shook my head.

"In that case . . ." Willow leaned forward in her chair. "Jeremy Aspen Quick. May I tell you a story?"

My full name, and a question phrased so formally that it sent a shiver skittering up my back. "Okay," I said. "Sure. Story. Yes."

Willow smiled wide, leaned back in her chair, and began to speak:

"A long time ago, I lived south and east of here, in a

lovely town on the coast of what had recently become the Province of Massachusetts Bay."

"Recently?" I said, as the shiver grew stronger. "When did you—"

"Please don't interrupt me, Aspen." She rubbed her forehead and sighed, as if thinking hard. "It was . . . 1690? 1691, perhaps. I really ought to make sure of the dates, one of these days. But as I was saying, I lived on the coast. I was married to a wonderful man, and I'd borne him two children. Ash and Rose, we called them, after two things my husband and I both found beautiful. The story begins when my children were nearly your age, Aspen. A few short months after my husband caught a fever and passed away."

My head should have been spinning. This should have sounded ridiculous. I should have been begging for the *real* truth this time. But I felt oddly calm.

"Rumors of black magic were in the air," Grandma continued. "Witchcraft, you understand. Now, what you ought to know is that my husband had magic. Not witchy magic—not the kind the accusations were about—but a certain affinity with the earth. An ability to influence certain natural phenomena. And he'd passed those abilities on to our children. Rose was a talented girl, quite self-assured, more than able to keep her powers hidden from prying eyes. But Ash had yet to learn full control over his magic. It was only a matter of time before he slipped up in front of the wrong person—so I made up my mind to flee. I didn't want to see my own son hanged in all that madness.

"So I sold my house for a wagon and supplies, and we started to move west, setting up camp in new places nearly every night, learning the ways of the land. Building fires. Hunting for our dinner. . . .

"My children were out hunting the night it happened. I'd stayed with the wagon and built the fire, and I was waiting for them to return when a great rumbling shook the earth. The Cliff, you see. We'd camped in the shadow of the Cliff. And that night, it fell, crushing me beneath a mountain of falling rock. That was how they found me, when they returned."

This time, I couldn't stop myself from interrupting: "Crushing you? You mean you *died?*"

She regarded me, unblinking. "That is exactly what I mean."

"But . . ."

"Let her finish," said Aunt Holly quietly.

Zombie great-great-grandma, I thought, and pressed my mouth shut.

"It was my children who brought me back," said Grandma Willow. "The night I died, they built a fire atop the rocks that had crushed me. They burned an ash leaf and a rose petal: symbols of their willingness to give of themselves to bring me back. The next morning, both the Cliff and I were perfectly intact again. In the spot where I'd died, instead of a pile of rock, there was an oak sapling."

"The May Day tree?" I guessed. She nodded. "But . . . it's nowhere near the Cliff now."

"It's been *moved* since then, obviously," said Aunt Holly.

Willow silenced her with a look. "We had it moved, several years later. The tree attracts people to it, encouraging them to give of themselves in the same way that my children did—in older times, some even looked on it as a sort of holy place. But its nearness to the Cliff frightened people away. Only once we transplanted the tree did our sparse little community start to become a town."

"Wait, you mean Three Peaks exists *because* of the May Day tree?" I said.

Willow shrugged. "There certainly isn't a better reason for a settlement to have begun here as early as it did. But people came, and some of them stayed." She gave me a not-quite-smile. "A good thing, too. We'd have been horribly lonely otherwise."

"Couldn't you have moved somewhere else? If you were lonely, I mean?"

"That was the original plan," said Willow. "Going west, as I said before. We tried to move on the very next day. The Cliff stopped us. Or, more accurately, it stopped *me*. As soon as it felt that I'd wandered too far from the valley, I felt its voice in my head. Its hunger. I felt a fault in the stone that could only be repaired by means of my children's magic.

"Because, you see, that was the bargain that the Cliff had struck. It granted a wish for my children, and in return, it gave them the means of keeping it alive. Insofar as it perceives itself as *alive*, of course."

"You mean the reaching," I said. "That's where it comes from? The Cliff gave your kids the power to steal stuff?"

Willow nodded solemnly. "It did indeed. And so it's been, ever since. I am tasked with hearing the Cliff's voice. My descendants are tasked with carrying out the Cliff's commands. My children, my children's children, and so on."

Her smile faltered a little, and she adjusted herself in the chair.

"I won't pretend it isn't a nasty business, this thing we do. Stealing from people, feeding the Cliff with their energy. But it's necessary." She cast a fond look over at Holly. "For the sake of preserving our family, it's necessary."

Nasty business. That was interesting. I'd never heard her say anything negative about the ritual before. But that was hardly the point of the story she'd just told me.

"So you're immortal?" I said. "Is that why you have us steal people's memories of you?"

She nodded. "I'm so sorry. I honestly thought you knew the reason. Or, rather, *remembered* the reason. I didn't mean to deceive you."

"And . . . you died. You actually *died*?"

Willow let her eyes flutter closed, her lashes casting odd shadows against the wrinkles in her cheeks. "I felt my bones break. I felt my chest cave in. It wasn't a pleasant thing, dying."

Shivers threatened to overtake me again, but I pushed them aside. "But, so . . . what are you? A zombie?"

She met my eyes again, leaning forward in her chair, all

earnest. "I'm your family, Aspen. That's all that really matters."

That was when Aunt Holly finally spoke up again. "We're both your family. And being part of a family means we have obligations to each other. You understand that, right?"

I nodded. "Don't steal from each other. Yeah, obviously."

"No. I mean yes, of course, but not only that." Aunt Holly looked pained, like every word was costing her something. "We . . . we have a question for you."

"Holly," said Willow sharply. "This is hardly the time."

"It's as good a time as any," Aunt Holly shot back. "Aspen, would you consider . . . that is . . . Heather was . . ."

Her voice began to wobble. My stomach began to churn.

"What Holly is trying to say," Willow cut in, "is that the triad ritual needs a third person. A permanent one, not just a series of relatives kind enough to fly in for a week or two. We need someone who can stay. Someone who understands the ritual's importance—"

"Someone who's actually got control over his magic," said Aunt Holly. "Unlike, for example, your father. Or, god forbid, Calla, with her damned ego."

"You'd be able to have your friends up to visit anytime you like," said Willow. "We've already shown you that they'd be more than welcome."

My friends. Theo. Brandy. *Brandy*. We'd only just started dating. If I moved up to Three Peaks for good, we'd hardly ever be able to see each other.

"You don't have to decide now," said Willow gently.

"And you don't have to say yes. We'd prefer it if you did, of course, but please know that this is an invitation, not a demand."

Aunt Holly's lips were pressed together so hard that they'd gone white—but she nodded. My stomach roiled, and my neck was all kinds of tense, because the thing was, after that phone call with my dad? I kind of wanted to say yes, just so I wouldn't have to keep living with him.

But I had to wait. I had to let my anger at him cool off. I couldn't just make a rash decision about something like this.

"I'll think about it," I said.

Willow smiled. "That's good enough for me."

△ BEFORE △

The time with Geoffrey. It made sense now. Geoffrey, the corgi we'd had when I was little, had been really fond of snatching our food right off the dinner table. Until, one day, he wasn't.

One day, he just started eating his kibble and paying no attention whatsoever to what the humans were eating.

Even at eight years old, it didn't take me long to put two and two together. Dad had stolen Geoffrey's desire for people-food.

When I asked Dad if I was right, he nodded and said, "There's no sense in having a pet who misbehaves if you can do something about it, right?"

Curiously, right around the same time, Geoffrey stopped jumping onto our beds and chewing up our shoes. I asked Dad if he'd meant to take away those things, too. If he'd taken away every single bad-dog thing that Geoffrey kept wanting to do.

"Hm," said Dad. "Now that you mention it, my shoes *have* looked less slobbery lately. . . ."

"But that was on purpose, right?" I said, feeling slightly alarmed without knowing why.

"Not exactly . . ." But Dad's worried face quickly gave

way to a winning smile. "But it's a nice side effect, isn't it?"

I remember wondering how side effects could be a thing. I remember wondering if my own reaching had side effects, too.

It had never occurred to me that Dad might just be really terrible at using his magic.

CHAPTER THIRTEEN

I needed air. I needed space, and that space needed to be away from this house, because I had to *think*. So I called Brandy and asked if they were still at the lake. I had no intention of getting into a boat with them today, or ever again, but at least I could chill out on the beach. Maybe get drunk. Whatever. Anything that didn't involve Willow and Aunt Holly being right there, watching me, waiting for my answer.

But Brandy said they'd left the lake almost an hour ago. They'd gone back to Corey's place to play video games—and there'd be beer if I wanted it because, apparently, Corey's parents were never, ever home.

"You feeling up for coming out, though?" she asked. "You really looked bad this morning."

"I think I was just tired," I said. "But I took a nap, so hey."

"Hey hey," she replied. "Well, totally come over. It's

number twelve, Cherry Street. Yellow house. You'll recognize it from the party."

I probably could have asked to borrow Aunt Holly's car, which would've gotten me there faster—but it was only maybe a twenty-minute walk. And walking was good for thinking.

Still, when I got to Corey's place, I was no closer to a rational decision than I'd been when I'd left.

They'd left the front door unlocked for me, so I let myself in and followed the sound of voices through the darkened living room, then up the stairs to the second floor. Four people were inside the nearest bedroom, staring intently at a large flat-screen TV, on which four Mario Kart characters were racing around a track.

"Don't you *dare* take that—you asshole!" yelled a familiar-looking guy, jerking a game controller violently to one side. He and Theo and Corey were sitting side-by-side-by-side on the bed, like a line of gamer ducklings.

"You so deserved that," said Brandy, who was sprawled in a beanbag chair and holding another controller. I glanced at the screen, expecting to see her usual Kart character, Princess Peach, in first place. Brandy was awesome at this game, so it only stood to reason.

But no, this time Peach was last. Had someone else claimed the character before Brandy got to her?

"Hey," I said, stepping into the room. Not too far, though, so as not to block their view of Corey's TV. Thanks to Brandy, I knew what happened when you stepped between gamers and their screens. It wasn't pretty.

"Ooh, Aspen, hey," said Brandy, eyes still glued to the television.

"Who are you playing?" I asked.

I expected her to say Yoshi, since Yoshi was currently in first place—but Brandy replied stiffly, "Peach. Duh. I'm always Peach."

I frowned at the screen. Peach's kart wasn't doing very well. "So how come—"

"Shh, you're distracting me," she said, glaring at the screen as Peach approached a tricky-looking ramp thing. "Ooh wait, hold on hold on I got this I got this—*dammit.* Aaaand I'm dead."

Tossing her controller dramatically to the floor, she leaned back and closed her eyes.

"Level's not over yet, Brandy," said Corey.

"Yeah, but I am," said Brandy. "You can grab the desk chair if you want."

This last was directed at me. I sat and watched as Corey and Theo and the other guy finished the level they'd been playing.

Only once it was over—and Yoshi, played by Corey, had won—did Corey introduce the other guy.

"Aspen, this is Kendrick," she said. "Kendrick, Aspen."

"Oh, right!" said Kendrick. "From the party. You're the one who passed out on the deck."

Corey laughed, and so did Kendrick, and I immediately remembered where I'd seen him before. He'd been hanging around the drink coolers at the party, bugging Leah to refill his cup.

"Yeah, that was me," I said. "Sorry about that. Again."

"S'all good," said Corey. "At least you didn't puke, like certain people I could mention." She said this last with a pointed look at Kendrick, who waggled his eyebrows.

"Want to play?" asked Brandy, nodding at the controller she'd tossed on the floor. She'd folded her arms across her chest, tucking her hands under her biceps like she was trying to keep them warm. "You can take over for me, if you want. I'm sick of losing."

Theo craned his neck a little to peer at her. "Yeah, what's up with that, anyway? You usually kick our asses at this."

Brandy stuck out her tongue. "My hands have apparently committed mutiny."

"So you want in, Aspen?" asked Corey, leaning over to retrieve Brandy's controller.

"Not yet," I said. "You guys play a few rounds. I want to assess the competition so I know exactly how to beat you when I join in."

"You wish," muttered Corey. Within a few seconds, the three of them had chosen a new level and were playing again.

"Mutiny, huh?" I asked, moving the desk chair a little closer to Brandy. "What's wrong? You sick?"

"I don't think so," said Brandy. "I mean, I don't *feel* sick. My hands are just . . . I dunno. They just sort of started shaking. Like out of nowhere. That's why we left the lake early—because I fumbled a canoe paddle. I thought maybe it was just because it was a little cold on the water, and it'd go away once I got inside, but . . ."

I frowned. "Maybe you're getting a fever?"

"Feel my forehead," she said. So I did. Her skin felt totally normal.

"Hm," I said.

"Right? Now feel this."

She unfolded her arms and held out a hand. I took it—and she was right. She was shaking. Even when I clasped her hand firmly between both of mine, I could feel it vibrating against my skin. My breath caught in my throat as the sensation forced a memory—a very recent memory—right to the surface of my mind.

Willow's hand. A tremor. *Never get old,* she'd said.

But Brandy wasn't getting old. She was only seventeen, and I was pretty sure teenagers didn't just develop tremors out of nowhere. So what the hell was going on?

"When did this start?" I asked.

"At the lake, like I said."

"Right, yeah, but what time? Do you know?"

"I dunno. A few hours ago? Oh! No, that's right, it was three thirty when we returned the canoe."

Three thirty. Half an hour after Aunt Holly's phone call had woken me up.

My palms went slick.

"Maybe you're right, though," she said, sneaking a quick

glance at the three Mario Kart players. "Maybe I'm getting sick. Maybe I should see a doctor."

I curled my fingers into fists, digging my nails into my palms. Heather had seen doctors, too. They hadn't been able to do anything. How bad would this get? Brandy wouldn't die, right?

Well, of course she wouldn't. This wasn't lungs that had straight-up stopped working. This was just a little shakiness. Tremors were normal. People got them all the time . . . didn't they?

The uncertainty propelled my hand forward, until it was gripping the blanket that covered Brandy. Sweet, amazing, sexy Brandy, who absolutely didn't deserve this. I reached into it, poked around long enough to confirm that it was definitely Corey's, and then started searching for her hands. Her healthy hands, which didn't shake, and—

And then I remembered. You couldn't replace things that the Cliff had stolen. Heather had said so in her letter.

Whatever. Screw that. I reached anyway, found the steadiness in Corey's hands, and gave it to Brandy. A careful, precise reaching job, just like I always did . . . except it didn't work.

I waited; maybe it would take some time to kick in. Seconds passed. Then minutes. But Corey's hands remained steady as ever, and Brandy's kept shaking in her lap.

That was that, then. I couldn't fix Brandy. She was finally mine, and now she was broken, and I couldn't even do anything about it.

"Hey, you okay?" asked Brandy, reaching out to ruffle my hair a little.

I made myself smile. "Yeah, no, totally. I'm fine."

Does that girl know anything true about you?

I'd dismissed the question when Leah had asked it, but now I couldn't help wondering if maybe Leah had a point. It wasn't fair that stuff like that could happen to Brandy, and she wouldn't have any idea why.

But I'd never told anyone my secret—and besides, what good would it do her if she knew?

But then again, shouldn't couples be honest with each other? If Brandy and I were going to stay together—and I had every intention of staying together—I'd have to tell her eventually. Like Dad had told Mom. And Mom herself had told me once that she wished Dad had said something sooner in their relationship. . . .

But, once more with feeling: *What good would it do?*

Then, the phone call happened.

Brandy and I were making out like crazy on my bed, door shut, clothes starting to come off as I tried to ignore her shaking hands, when her phone rang. It was the chorus of "Piano Man," which meant her dad was calling.

She groaned as she extricated herself from my sheets. "Sorry. I have to get this."

"No problem."

As Brandy crossed the room and found her purse, I flopped back onto my pillow and willed my breath to slow down.

"Hey!" said Brandy, in her best no-I-definitely-wasn't-just-about-to-get-laid-what-are-you-talking-about voice. Then she fell silent, nodding slightly as she listened to whatever her dad was telling her. She rolled her eyes at me, then did a yap-yap-yap motion with her hand, which made me smile. Then she stopped, and her face started to fall, and she sank back down onto the bed. The nodding stopped, too.

"Dad, come on," was the next thing she said. "Just because one guy was . . . Yeah, I'm listening. Sorry."

She shot me a look. My neck tensed right up. I had a feeling I knew what was happening.

A few moments later, Brandy sighed into the phone. "Toronto? We're nowhere near Toronto. . . . Yes, I know New York borders Canada. But we're *nowhere near*—oh my god, yes, I hear you."

I sat up and rubbed her back. I never saw Brandy more anxious than when she was talking to her dad.

Finally, she shut her eyes. "Okay, I'll check the bus schedule. I'll let you know tomorrow." A pause. "No, I said tomorrow. It's late, Dad. I'm not packed, and anyway, nobody would be able to drive me to the bus stop tonight."

Oh, god, seriously?

"Fine," she said. "Yeah, fine. Love you, too. Bye."

She hung up. Looked at me silently, visibly seething.

"Toronto?" I said.

"Someone got shot," Brandy said. "A gang thing."

"In Toronto."

"Uh-huh."

"Toronto, which is like five hours away. Maybe six."

"Yyyyyup."

"And he's making you go home?"

Her answer was a grimace, only slightly exaggerated. "Honestly, I'm surprised this didn't happen sooner. And I can't say no when he gets like this. You know I can't."

I did know. How many times had she trudged out of various classrooms during the school year, ready to spend the rest of the day at home because her paranoid dad had decided she wasn't safe without him? Stupid me, assuming this vacation would turn out any different.

But then, everything clicked into place. The answers to the questions that had been circling my mind ever since the Mario Kart tournament.

"Hey. Brandy. What if he *didn't* get like this?"

"Oh, sure," she said with a roll of her eyes. "Because I really want to suggest therapy for a fourth time. God, I am so done with that conversation. I just have to wait till graduation when I can move out and—"

"You really think he's gonna get better after you move out?" I asked. "I guarantee it'll be exactly the opposite. No, listen, I'm talking about . . . fixing him. Permanently."

She narrowed her eyes. "You sound like you're planning on killing him or something. Which, for the record, please don't do that."

I laughed. "No, no, I mean . . . Okay. Um. Brandy?" This was it. I was finally going to stop lying to her. This was *it.* "There's something I need to tell you."

240

"Ohhh, I knew it," she said. "You're pregnant, aren't you."

"Har-har. No, I'm serious. This is . . . I've never told anyone this before."

This time she didn't reply with a joke. She just tilted her head and stayed quiet, waiting for me to go on.

"See, when I said I could fix him, I meant—god, how do I even say this?—I meant taking away his paranoia. Just reaching into him, finding it, and taking it out."

She blinked a few times. Frowned. "Isn't that what therapy does?"

"Over time, probably, sure," I said. "But I'm talking about instantly. Insta-cure!"

Brandy rolled her shoulders: an unsubtle hint that I should get my hand off her back. "I'm not sure what you mean, Aspen."

Of course she didn't. I was explaining this really badly.

"I can take things away from people. That's . . . it. That's the thing."

But Brandy was still frowning. "Like what kind of things?"

"Any kind of things. Thoughts. Memories. Physical stuff."

"So you're like . . . what, a wizard?" Brandy looked very, very unimpressed.

"Ha. No. Look, I can prove it."

God, this was making me nervous. Even more nervous than when Leah had shown up in my room, all rain-soaked and wild-eyed, knowing all my family's secrets. I mean, where was I even supposed to begin?

"Your burn scar!" I said. "Remember the burn scar you had on your arm? Ninth grade. You said it was from your hair curler. You told me you didn't like it, so I took it away for you."

She made a noise of disgust. "That *healed,* Aspen. That wasn't you."

"No, it was me," I said. "Here, hold out your arm."

Brandy hesitated, but eventually did it. I turned her hand over so it was palm down, then pointed to a small clump of freckles near her wrist. The same freckles I'd tried, and apparently failed, to steal for the triad ritual this afternoon. "Watch those," I said.

Then I touched her shoulder. I reached through the fabric of her T-shirt, into her mind, into all the things that made up the girl sitting beside me.

The freckles were near the surface, tangled up in the confusion of what I'd just told her, and her irritation with her dad, and her sadness at having to leave two weeks earlier than she'd planned, and her annoyance at not being able to steady her hands. It was a small enough thing, though, that I pulled it away with ease. I dropped my hand, and I let the freckles go.

Her wrist was empty.

Brandy stared at it. And then at me. And then at her arm again. She touched it gingerly, like she was afraid it would feel different.

"Told you," I said, grinning and giddy now that the telling part was over.

"You . . ." She shook her head slowly. "Did you really . . . ?"

"Yeah!" I said. "See? This is good! I can fix everything. With your dad, I mean. I can take away his paranoia, and he won't think you're dead every five minutes, and you can stay here with—"

"No," Brandy said softly. She'd started shaking her head a couple seconds ago, but this was the first time she'd spoken. "No, no, you can't."

"Why not?"

"Because you can't! Okay? That's my dad you're talking about. You can't just turn him into some . . . some alien body-snatcher version of himself."

I completely did not understand why that was a bad thing. "He'd be totally the same. Just without the part that drives you—"

"You'd be stealing his *personality*," she said. "His *thoughts*. The stuff that makes him who he is. You can't just change stuff like that."

"I mean, it's not like I haven't done it before," I said. "I'm really good at it. He wouldn't even know anything was missing."

Brandy narrowed her eyes. "You've . . . done it before."

"Well, yeah." My neck tightened. This was not the reaction I'd hoped she would have. "Look, I'm just trying to be honest, okay?"

Brandy paused. Stared right into my eyes, right past

them, like she could see the blood and bone and gray matter that they were hiding.

"Have you stolen thoughts from *me*?"

I hesitated. I'd stolen feelings, for sure. Doubts and suspicions and other things. But did those technically count as thoughts?

On the other hand, I'd meant what I'd said: I was trying to be honest. And honesty meant not avoiding the question because of a technicality.

So I said, "Kind of."

"Do tell."

"Well, there was this night you started getting jealous of Corey, because, I dunno, she's Theo's new girlfriend and you were his old one, so I took your jealousy away—"

"Are. You. Serious."

"Well, I mean, it was making you sad," I said. "Don't you think I wish I could've made *myself* not be jealous, every time I saw you and Theo making out? I tried, actually. But I can't steal stuff from myself. That's why I . . . uh."

Brandy was very, very still. "That's why you what?"

Shit. I'd come so close to slipping and telling her the one thing I knew I had to keep secret. "Um. I mean, that's why I stole some stuff that made you sad."

"*Some* stuff," she repeated, very softly. "So that wasn't the only time."

"Uh. No."

"Go ahead, then. Give me the list."

I froze. Suddenly I couldn't think of anything else that

I'd stolen from her, because my entire brain was full of the thing I wasn't telling her.

Before I could make my mouth form words, though, Brandy's expression morphed from disgusted into dangerous. "Wait. Aspen. Why did we start dating?"

I felt my heart speed up. "Well, because you hit on me at that party."

"You didn't, like . . . like *make me* hit on you, did you?"

"No! God, no." That, at least, was one hundred percent true. "That would be gross. I'd never do something like that." Then I made myself stop, because I was fast approaching protesting-too-much territory.

Brandy nodded. "But that night . . . I remember thinking it was fast. I even said so, in the car. I'd just broken up with Theo, and there I was, all ready to get it on with you, and I thought it was weird. Nobody gets over a breakup that fast. Just, nobody, ever." My neck tensed up as I realized what she was about to ask. "Did you make that happen?"

I could have lied. I *should* have lied, maybe. But the look on her face told me she already knew the truth. So I nodded. "You and Theo both. You guys were devastated after you . . . after the breakup. So I . . . you know. I fixed it."

"You fixed it," she said. I nodded. God, my neck was killing me. "Okay. Did you make us break up, too?"

"No, you did that yourself. I just—"

Shit. Shit shit *shiiiiiiiiiit*.

I made myself continue: "I just, uh, watched it happen."

Could that have been a worse cover-up? No, no it could not. Brandy's chest heaved as she took a deep breath. "Watched it happen. That wasn't what you were going to say."

No. It wasn't. I rubbed furiously at my neck.

"So you didn't make us break up," she said. "Then what? You stole something that *led* to me breaking up with him?"

I couldn't say no. I couldn't lie to her. Her lips went thin and oh my god this was it she was going to leave me. Unless I fixed it. I could reach into her right now and take away her anger, and hope that there was understanding buried beneath it.

Reach, I told myself. *Do it.*

I couldn't move.

"What did you steal from me?" She was standing now, staring me down.

"The, um. The love you had for him." My mouth was so dry. It made my voice sound grimy. "For Theo, I mean. That's, um. That's what I stole."

"Really," she said softly.

I nodded. "You guys fought all the time. It's not like it would've worked out in the long run, so—"

"In other words, you *made me* fall in love with you."

"No!" I said. "No, no. I just . . . took your love for Theo away, so you'd have *room* to fall for me instead. I told you, I would never—"

"In other words, I'm incapable of deciding for myself who I should be with. You were holding the strings the whole time. None of those decisions were actually mine."

"I'm not saying that."

"No, no, totally not," she said, crossing her arms protectively over her chest. "Except that is *literally* what you *just said*."

"Brandy."

She looked at me with clear eyes. Shook her head slowly. "I always thought you were different from the other guys," she said after a moment. "All the other guys I've dated, all the other guys at school."

"I am," I said.

"Yeah. You definitely are. Just not in the way I thought." She was edging away from me now, edging toward the door. She bent down and picked up her purse.

"I'm gonna go pack," she said. "I'm leaving in the morning, and I do not want to see you again before I go. Oh, and here's some free advice, okay? Never date anyone again. Ever."

"Brandy, just wait a second—"

But she didn't wait. She stormed out of my room, out into the hall, toward the east wing. I followed her, saying her name over and over until finally, she rounded on me.

"Stop it, okay?" she said. "Just stop it. Don't you dare follow me another step."

So as she went into her room and slammed the door, I just stood there and watched.

Because the thing was, I didn't have to follow her in order to stop her. She'd left her phone on my bed. All I had to do was reach into it and take away her desire to leave. Or maybe all her negative feelings about the secret I'd just told her.

Or I could take away her memory of this whole conversation. We'd be better off that way, wouldn't we? Happy. Like before.

I picked up the phone.

Does that girl know anything true about you?

Brandy knew the truth about me now, and she'd decided, with eyes wide open and all the facts at her disposal, that she didn't want me. If I didn't erase her memory, Brandy and I were over for good.

But if I did, I'd have to live with knowing that I'd done to Brandy exactly what my father had done to me.

I sat there with the phone in my hands until, a few minutes later, she knocked on the door. She held out a shaky hand. I gave her the phone. And just like that, it was too late to change my mind.

△ BEFORE △

Disco balls overhead. The smell of sweat underlining the cloying sugary perfume of punch and cookies and cake. Some truly heinous pop song blaring from the speakers. Everyone dressed in their awkward teenaged best. It was more carnival than prom, with distractions enough to get lost in—but I wasn't lost. I knew exactly where I was (leaning on the wall, not too far from the soda table, next to this shrimpy kid named Omar), and I knew exactly where Brandy was (dancing with Theo), and that was all that really mattered.

"She's just so hot," said Omar, beside me.

"Yeah," I agreed—and then realized he probably wasn't talking about Brandy. "Wait, who?"

"Tanuja," he said, nodding toward a girl I vaguely knew from English class. She was standing with a group of her friends, wearing a silvery sleeveless dress.

"So go ask her to dance," I said.

Omar grimaced. "She'll say no."

"What if she doesn't?"

"She will."

Tanuja was single, as far as I knew. And I remember thinking that if Brandy were single, I'd've asked her to dance before the music even started. Basically, I would've killed to be where Omar was.

I put a hand on his skinny shoulder, reached into him, and looked for his shyness. It wasn't hard to find; it had woven itself like a fungus through his entire personality, which meant it would've taken far too long to steal away. So I bypassed that and went for the quick fix instead: I took away his certainty that Tanuja would turn him down.

Then I leaned down and said, "Dude, just ask. You'll regret it forever if you don't."

Omar straightened up a little, took a deep breath, and marched over to Tanuja and her friends. Moments later, I saw him leading her onto the dance floor.

Moments after that, I spotted Brandy again. She wore a midnight-blue dress that swished against her calves, tiny straps highlighting the ridges of her shoulder blades. She'd pinned her hair up with sparkly things, leaving a few tendrils loose to drift down her back. She was moving toward me. She was smiling.

"May I have this dance, good sir?" she said.

The music was just changing: fast to slow. It was that song "Every Breath You Take." The one that sounds like a love song until you realize it's kind of stalkery, and then you feel gross for having thought it was romantic.

Brandy was holding out her hand. Smooth pale skin, nails painted pink, Theo's corsage on her wrist.

"Where's your date?" I asked, more out of politeness than anything else.

"Stuffing himself with cake," she replied. "He's sick of dancing. And between you and me, he's kind of terrible at it. So how about it?"

I was hardly going to say no a second time. So we danced, Brandy and me, swaying slowly to a song that had probably been popular like four hundred years ago. My hands on her back. Hers around my neck. Me, pretending for four minutes that I'd come as Brandy's date, not as part of her giant group of friends.

When the slow song ended and a faster one began, Brandy leaned up and kissed me on the cheek. I almost stopped being able to breathe.

I love you, I wanted to say.

"You're great," was what I said instead, which, ugh.

Brandy just laughed. I would remember that laugh for the rest of my life. That laugh, and "Every Breath You Take." Because if Brandy wasn't ever going to be mine, at least I'd always have those four minutes of pretending.

CHAPTER FOURTEEN

They were gone by the time I woke up the next morning. Both of them. I didn't know what Brandy had told Theo, but he didn't pick up his phone when I tried to call him and ask. *It's because he's driving,* I told myself.

Yeah. It was that. It was not because Brandy had told him everything and he'd reacted badly and decided never to speak to me again.

As I made my way through breakfast—through coffee and eggs and Grandma asking after my friends and Aunt Holly looking on with narrowed eyes—I wondered why I wasn't freaking out more. But I didn't feel like freaking out. I didn't feel much of anything. Just sort of shell-shocked. Sort of numb. And I stayed that way for most of the day.

Eventually, Grandma asked if I was all right, which meant she could tell I wasn't. And since I had zero desire to spill my guts about my girlfriend—ex-girlfriend, now—

to my zombie one-million-times-great-grandmother, I left the house.

I didn't realize I was heading for the May Day field until I actually arrived there. I thought about walking the rest of the way into town, maybe getting food. But I didn't want to do those things. I just wanted to sit there and play stupid games on my phone and wait for the numbness to fade.

My phone rang, jostling me right out of my Bejeweled-induced brain haze. But it wasn't Brandy, like I'd hoped it would be. Or Theo.

It was my mom.

I rejected the call, like I always did—but for some reason I couldn't look away from her name on my screen.

She'd left my dad, then taken all her stuff so he couldn't reach into her anymore. Dad could have brought her back, and he didn't.

Brandy had stormed out of my room, disgusted with the newfound knowledge of what I could do. What I *had* done. I could have brought her back, and I didn't.

All that time, I'd never understood.

Before I could second-guess myself, I pulled up Dad's number.

"Aspen, I'm so glad you called," he said, after picking up on the first ring. He talked fast, like he wanted to get everything out before I hung up on him again: "I spoke to Holly. I get why you're upset. I didn't mean to take so much from you. I honestly had no idea that you didn't remember my mother at *all*, and—"

"Dad," I said. He fell silent. "You remember when I asked you to bring Mom back?"

"More like demanded," he said. "But yes. Of course I do."

"And you said no?"

He paused. "Aspen, son, I'm not going to change my mind."

"No, no, it's not that." I flopped back on the grass, staring up into the green of the May Day tree. "It's . . . I mean, it was because . . . like, you wouldn't have been able to live with it, right? Being married to someone when you knew that if you hadn't used magic, she wouldn't want you anymore?"

"That's part of it," he said slowly.

"What's the other part?"

"The other part is . . . god, I'm bad at explaining this."

"Try," I said.

Another pause. I could hear him taking long, deep breaths.

"The short version is, it's wrong."

I frowned, waiting for him to elaborate. He went on: "When you take away someone's thoughts, or feelings, or . . . or impulses or whatever, you're taking away part of who they are. I fell in love with your mother for exactly who she was. I'd never change that."

"Even if it meant losing her?" I said.

"Yeah," he said quietly. "Even then."

"You've changed things about me, though. Sadness about stuff. Memories, even. Is that it, or did you ever take other things?"

"The memories were an accident," he said. "I'm so, so sorry about that. I really am."

"That doesn't answer my question," I said.

Dad sighed. "Not a *lot* of other things. But yes. Fear, for one. I took away your fear a couple of times."

Something curdled in my stomach. "Fear of what?"

"Oh, god, I barely even remember now," he said. "Let's see. Oh! You remember when you wanted to try out for Little League, but you were afraid of the ball?"

"I was?"

"You were." Dad chuckled. "You were absolutely convinced that the ball would hit you in the eye and somehow that would lead to your untimely death. Useless, baseless fear—so I took it away and, lo and behold, you made the team, just like I knew you would."

Holy shit, I totally remembered that. But I hadn't known Dad was the reason I'd been less afraid on the second day of tryouts . . .

"And your obsession with huskies, remember?" he went on. "It all started with this one dog. You met him on the street, and he was barking up a storm. You were terrified— at least at first."

"Wait, wait, no," I said, because I remembered the dog, too. I'd been so small, and the dog had been so big, and it had turned from mean to friendly in two seconds flat, because Dad had . . . "Wait, but didn't you reach into the *dog*? Take away his meanness or something?"

"The dog?" said Dad. "No, of course not. I took away your fear."

So the dog had never been mean. I'd just been afraid, was all. I was so stupid for not seeing it sooner.

"And there was one time in midtown—"

"Okay, okay, stop, I get it," I said. "But . . . okay, if you did all that, doesn't that mean—you know, like you said—you took away who I am? Or who I was?"

And then, of course, the question beneath the question: *Who would I have been if you hadn't taken those things away from me?* I couldn't bring myself to say that out loud, though. It was too big. Too much.

"Son, I was doing you a favor. God, the number of times I've wished I could steal my own feelings . . . just erase them . . . but I don't have anyone to do that for me. Holly refuses to break that goddamn rule, and it isn't right for a father to ask his son for something like that. But don't you think I would've erased everything I felt that time I got laid off? Or the things I felt after your mom left, if I could? You're so lucky, Aspen. You have no idea."

A horrible thought occurred to me.

"Did you erase what *I* felt after Mom left?"

Yet another pause. Long enough that I knew what the answer was.

"You've never been good at dealing with grief, son," he said brusquely. "You were better off not being sad."

What did he mean, *not being sad*? I'd totally been sad . . . hadn't I? I thought back to the weeks after Mom had left, trying to find a specific moment that I could point out . . . but it wasn't sadness that I found in those memories. It wasn't sadness that had made me ignore Mom's phone calls, or yell at her the one time I'd picked up.

"You took away my sadness," I said. "But you didn't take away my anger?"

"Of course not," said Dad. "Anger's a natural reaction for a boy your age."

"So anger's okay," I said slowly, "but sadness isn't."

"Son, it's not about what's *okay*—"

"Then what? It's about what's easier for you to deal with?"

A pause. Another goddamn pause.

"Aspen." Dad sighed. "Son. It was about what's easier for *you* to deal with. No father enjoys seeing his son in pain. But most don't have the means to ease that pain. I do have the means, so obviously I used it. What other choice did I have? I'm your *father*. I had to help you."

"And by 'easing my pain,' you mean 'taking stuff away from me without even asking first.'"

Dad's voice got quiet then. "I was only trying to help you."

"No you weren't," I said. "You were making me pick sides. Mom left, and you made it so I didn't even want to *talk* to her, and meanwhile you were all like, 'Oh, let's have some father-son bonding time with Scotch and movies and whatever!' and I was like, 'Sweet, cool, awesome!' because

I couldn't feel anything except angry at Mom, because *you made me that way*. Didn't you."

There was no response.

Well, that answered that question. The branches and the sky loomed above me. I closed my eyes.

"Don't steal from me anymore," I told him firmly. "Even if you think you're 'helping' or whatever. We have that rule for a reason: No stealing from family. You were the one who taught me that rule, for god's sake."

"But you're my son, and I—"

"I'm *her* son, too," I said. "Or at least I was. Until you took her away from me."

"But—"

"No buts! Okay?" Breathe. Calm. Breathe. Calm. "I don't want you messing with my head anymore. Ever. I mean *ever*, unless I explicitly ask you to. Okay?"

Yet another pause. This one seemed to go on forever.

Finally, I couldn't stand it any longer. "Promise me you won't steal from me anymore."

"Of course." He sounded kind of defeated. Kind of hurt. "If that's what you really want, then of course I promise."

I thought about making him swear not to touch my stuff. But I didn't need to turn into Mom about this, taking our furniture because it was partially hers. He'd promised, and I believed him, and that was that.

"Okay," I said. "Thanks."

"Can I, um, ask where this is coming from? Did something happen up there?"

Yes, something had happened. I'd called to tell him about Brandy, about how she'd left and how I hadn't stopped her and how I understood about Mom. But now . . . there were so many other things in my head. Sadness. Shame. Other things that I couldn't even name yet. And I didn't want my dad to steal them away from me before I could figure out what they were. Sure, he'd promised, but still. Old habits, right?

"No," I said. "Nothing happened."

"Are you sure?"

"Well . . ." I closed my eyes, pressing the phone closer to my ear. "They asked me to move up here, actually. To help with the ritual in Heather's place."

". . . Ah. Yes, I thought they might."

"I'm thinking about doing it."

Dad was silent.

"You think I should?" I asked.

"I think," he said carefully, "that you're a young man who knows his own mind. I think you'll give this your full consideration, and I think . . . well, I think whatever decision you make will be the right one."

The right one. How could I possibly make the right decision, if I was missing parts of myself?

No, that was a dumb thing to think. Dumb and dramatic. Dad was right. All I had to do was take some time and think about this.

"Yeah," I said. "You're probably right."

⚠

259

I thought about calling Mom. But after what I'd just learned, I had no idea what to say to her. So I set my phone aside, settled into the grass, and tried to think.

The sun moved overhead, and eventually the bright blue of daytime gave way to faint streaks of pink and purple over the mountains. Over the Cliff.

Then, soft footsteps. Shoes whispering against grass, moving toward me.

"Hey." Leah nudged my shoulder as she sat down next to me. I'd texted her right after hanging up with my dad, and she'd agreed to meet me as soon as her shift at the bookstore was over. "Communing with nature?"

"Yeah, not exactly," I said, shooting her a small smile. "Mostly I was wondering how different it would look."

"Different?"

"If the Cliff fell."

"Ah," she said.

Shrugging, I angled myself away from the Cliff, so I could see Leah's face instead.

"It's my family, you know," I said. "Not the town. That's what Heather meant in her letter. If the Cliff falls, it kills our family. Everyone who ever descended from Willow. Um. Did she tell you about Willow?"

"Immortal matriarch of the Quick family?" Leah smirked. "Yeah, she told me."

"She asked me to move up here."

Her face tightened. "To replace Heather."

I nodded.

"Gonna do it?" she asked.

"I dunno," I said. "Probably. Ugh, I dunno. Should I?"

Her lips quirked into something that wasn't quite a smile. "Is that why you texted me? To ask for advice?"

"No, no. Well. Yes? I don't know who else to ask, is the thing."

"How about your girlfriend?" she said. "Oh wait. Right. You're still lying to her."

"Actually, no, I'm not."

Leah's eyebrows shot up. "Oh yeah?"

"She left this morning," I said flatly. "Apparently I'm a horrible, gross person who shouldn't ever date anyone again, just because I—"

My throat felt tight.

"Aspen?" said Leah. "Just because what?"

"Because . . . god. She was right, wasn't she. I did make her fall in love with me." Leah's eyes went wide. "I mean, not exactly, but it adds up to the same thing, doesn't it? I changed her. I changed who she was as a person."

"Wait, hold on," said Leah, making a calm-down gesture with one hand. "You made her fall in love with you? And you *told her about it*?"

"Well, yeah," I replied. "You said—"

"I know what I said! But holy shit, Aspen, there's such a thing as too much truth, you know?"

The question barely registered. My whole life was falling apart at the seams. Everything I knew about myself was crumbling like an avalanche.

"I'm just as bad as my dad." My voice sounded tinny and far away.

"Your dad?" she said.

I nodded. "We have a family rule. No stealing from each other. No matter what. But he stole stuff from me anyway. He stole my sadness away when Heather died, and when my mom left. He stole sadness, and he stole fear, but he left everything else, and everything else is just me being pissed off a lot, but apparently that's *fine,* anger's just *natural,* but how is it still natural if he steals *some* stuff and leaves *other* stuff just because I'm 'bad at dealing with grief' or whatever?"

"Bad at dealing with grief," Leah echoed, her voice low. "As opposed to what? It's not exactly something you can get *good* at."

"I don't know," I said, leaning forward, covering my face with my hands. "Apparently some counselor told him I was too sad for a boy my age. Something. I don't know."

"So, what, boys can't be sad?" Leah said. "And your dad wants you to be some robotic manly-man who doesn't feel feelings? Is that it?"

"Ha. No. Or yes? God, I don't know. But would I have done all that to Brandy if none of the stuff with my dad had happened? Because, I mean, what else did he steal? Maybe I *am* a robot. Maybe I can't empathize with actual human people."

"What, did he steal your empathy, too?" asked Leah.

I thought about that. "Well, no . . . at least, I don't think so. But he took a bunch of other stuff. I don't feel all the things a person is supposed to feel. Isn't that where empathy comes from?"

She crinkled her nose a little. "Maybe? I guess? I dunno. Seems to me you could be as empathetic as anyone else, if you bothered trying. Maybe it'd take a little more effort for you than for the rest of us, but . . ." She spread her hands wide, leaving the rest of the sentence unsaid.

"Great," I said. "Awesome. So my dad's the one who stole all that shit from me, but it's still my own fault that I'm such a . . ."

"Such a what?" asked Leah.

That was a very good question. What was I? What would I have been if not for all the things my dad had taken—or if I'd known about those things, and bothered making the effort to compensate for them? Hell, what would I have been if I'd never had this power in the first place?

"A screwup," I said. "Leah, I really screwed up."

She offered me a little smile. "Maybe you did. But you love that girl, right? Brandy. Love makes people do stupid things."

Was it even love that I felt for her, though? Or was it just some kind of stupid obsession?

"I don't even know anymore," I said. "But it wasn't just her. I steal stuff from everyone. Like, okay, Theo used to get pissed at me because I got better grades in math than he did. So what did I do? I took his jealousy away, then I stole some other kid's algebra skills and gave them to Theo."

"What other kid?"

I blinked. "What do you mean?"

"Who'd you steal the math thing from?"

I thought about that for a second. "Um. Not actually sure," I admitted. "But see, that's the point! And Brandy's friend Lauren—she used to have this crush on me. But I wasn't interested, and I didn't want it to be awkward, so I took it away. And we had this neighbor who kept these herbs on the fire escape between our apartments, and they smelled weird, so I took away his memory of having to take care of them, so they died, and—" I stopped. Breathed. "See what I mean? I'm such a horrible person."

It felt like the truest thing I'd ever said.

"Oh sure, and that makes you so special," said Leah, her voice suddenly edged with weariness. "You're clueless as shit and no mistake, but *everyone* hurts other people, Aspen. All the time. That's what people *do*. Even without weird supernatural powers."

Suddenly incensed, I said, "Brandy's brain is all changed around, and that guy Jesse is blind, and—"

"And your cousin spent the last few years of her tragically short life totally friendless. Whose fault is that? Mine."

"How is that the same thing?" I demanded. "It's not even in the same *universe*. Me, I've been stealing stuff from people my entire life, and now that it's finally sinking in how shitty that is, what do I do? Do I stop? No, actually, I'm thinking about moving up here so I can do it *more*. So don't even *try* to tell me your stupid . . . *friendship angst* is even *close*. . . ."

"Friendship angst," she repeated softly, climbing to her feet. "Yeah. Okay, sure. Sorry, you were right. You are the most horrible person in the whole wide world, so my tiny little lady-feelings should just get out of the way so you and your giant man-feelings can have more room to brood about how your daddy ruined your life."

"Stop it," I said, squinching my eyes shut. "That's not what I meant."

"Noooo, no, no, of course it isn't."

"Look, Leah, you don't even know me, okay? So just stop it."

"Are you kidding? I totally know you." Hands on her hips, she regarded me with a gaze that was a little too keen. "You're the guy who thinks nothing is ever his fault. The guy who gets dumped and then tries to blame his dad for it. You'll graduate from college and immediately write a memoir about how hard it is to be a twenty-something in the modern age. Women will never be able to understand you, so you'll never understand them right back, and you'll become an alcoholic by the time you're forty, and you'll start voting Republican by the time you're fifty."

She paused, like she was waiting for me to contradict her. But really, what the hell was I supposed to say to that? Especially when there was a tiny part of me that thought, if I wasn't careful, she'd probably end up being right.

"Leah," I said, moving toward her.

She moved away again, giving me a mirthless smile.

"I'll see you later, Aspen. Call me at the store when you

want to buy your first Jonathan Franzen book."

"Stop. Leah." I darted after her, but she turned away and started walking faster. I walked faster, too. She was the only friend I had. The only person, aside from my own relatives, who knew my secret and didn't think it was gross. "Leah, wait. I'm sorry. Just stop."

She stopped. But she didn't turn around, and she didn't say anything. Which meant it was up to me to speak first.

"Tell me about Heather," I said.

There was a pause, and Leah shook her head.

"I'm serious," I said. "You wanted to talk about Heather. So talk."

She turned to face me again. The not-quite-smile had faded from her face, leaving exhaustion in its wake. Exhaustion and no small measure of distrust.

"You don't want to hear about that," she said.

"Yeah, I do," I said, finding that I actually meant it. "Here, sit down."

I sat cross-legged in the grass and, after only a moment of hesitation, she did the same.

"You know Sherlock Holmes?" she asked.

"Uh, yeah, doesn't everyone?"

But then I remembered Heather's letter. The way she'd addressed it: *For Sherlock's Eyes Only.* The fact that she'd signed it as Dr. W.

"We used to dress up, Heather and me," she said. "I was Sherlock. She was my Dr. Watson. We were, like . . . ten. Well, it started when we were ten, anyway. I'd put on that deerstalker hat and carry a pipe, and she'd wear a stetho-scope and walk with a stick, and we'd solve mysteries to-gether."

"A stick?" I asked, confused.

"Yeah. Like a cane? Because Watson was injured in the war?" She raised an eyebrow like, *hello, everyone knows that.*

"Oh, okay, sure," I said. "So . . . you solved real myster-ies?"

"Some. Mostly we made up our own. But there were a few real ones—like the Case of the Weird Green Goo in the Bathroom."

"Ew," I said.

"Yeah, it was completely gross. We bottled up a sample of it, and Rachel got us into the high school chemistry lab so we could run tests. Except we never solved the case, be-cause Professor Moriarty caught us in the act."

"Professor Moriarty . . . ?"

She grinned, and for a second I could see an echo of the ten-year-old she'd been. "The janitor at the high school. He got us in trouble, therefore he was our archnemesis. Hence, Moriarty."

"I see," I said, realizing that I'd started grinning, too.

"We read all the old stories together," she said. "The Arthur Conan Doyle stuff. We watched every movie and TV version we could get our hands on—and believe me, there are a lot. Five million Holmeses, five million Watsons. Awesome ones, shitty ones. Subtitled ones. . . ." She took a deep breath, her face sobering. "So, then Heather stole my sister's voice—"

"By accident," I said.

"I know that *now*," snapped Leah. "But yes. Heather stole it by accident, and I stopped talking to her. I stopped having anything to do with her. Including the Holmes stuff. I gave away all my books and DVDs, and I started hanging out with Sadie and Jesse and a few other people instead.

"But Heather didn't find new friends. Not real-life ones, I mean. She found a ton of them online, though. All these people I'd never heard of kept popping up on her Facebook wall, and *all* of them were talking Holmes with her. I'd click on their profiles, and they'd be from, like, Europe and India and California and stuff. Never anywhere close."

"You stalked her on Facebook?" I said. "Even though you didn't like her anymore?"

Leah shot me another look. "Of course I did. But the point is that she kept up with it. All the TV shows and movies and fan fiction and whatever, and once in a while she'd . . . you know . . . shoot me an email, or stick a note in my locker, or even come up to me in the hallway. 'Hey, you'd like this thing on the BBC,' or 'Hey, you should read this fanfic,' or 'Hey, do you still have the hat?' Stuff like that.

"And I tried to be nice about it, at first. Just sort of smile and say no and then ignore her. But she just kept *going*. Like, for *years*, to the point where I couldn't see why she didn't just get over it already. I thought she was pathetic and whiny and clingy, so . . . I got mean about it. Really, really mean."

"Mean how?" I asked.

She reached down and started fiddling with the hem of her jeans. "Just . . . stuff I said. I'd call her a baby and tell her to grow up. It was always Sadie who said the really bad stuff. Started rumors about her, made fun of her for being a nerd and a loner and whatever. That was all Sadie. But I didn't stop her. I just sort of stood there and listened and watched Heather get sadder and sadder, because I figured, hey, it doesn't matter if nobody in real life likes her, right? She has all those internet people."

"People she'd never have to meet," I murmured, curling my fingers protectively into my palms as I thought of Aunt Holly. Heather's mom didn't have any friends, either, as far as I could tell.

"What?" said Leah.

"Internet friends," I said. "They were all far enough away that they probably wouldn't end up here on May Day, putting stuff under the tree with everyone else. She wouldn't run the risk of having to steal from them somewhere down the line."

Leah looked so stricken that, for a second, I thought she might start crying again. "I never thought of that."

I shrugged. Maybe, if I decided to stay up here, it was just as well that I sucked at being a friend.

"You remember that one thing she said in her letter? About not being a parasite?"

"Yeah . . . ?"

She smiled tightly. "I called her that. Just a few months ago."

I winced. "Ouch."

"In the middle of the hallway at school. In front of . . . well, everyone, really." She paused, biting idly at her bottom lip, looking off into the distance with soft eyes. I watched her jaw work. "She was trying to talk to me about this TV show, I guess, and I told her to go away, and she wouldn't, and I *snapped*. I started yelling. Calling her names. Leech, parasite, all kinds of horrible stuff. God. The look on her face. But she just stood there and waited till I was done, and then . . ." Leah gave me a weird, strained smile. "Then she asked me if saying all that stuff made me feel better. She asked if I could finally forgive her now, and she said she still wanted to be friends again. I mean, can you imagine?"

I thought about all the messages Mom had left me: *I love you* and *I miss you* and *Come visit,* no matter how much I'd ignored her.

"Yeah," I said. "I can imagine."

"And I felt bad, obviously," said Leah. "So I took her aside and . . . and that's when I tried to make a deal. If she could give Rachel her voice back, and make Jesse fall in love with me, we could be friends again. She said no. That was that. And now she's . . ." Leah cut herself off, biting her lip and looking down at the grass.

"Yeah," I said.

"Yeah what?"

"Yeah, that's pretty bad."

She crooked a smile. "See? Look at us. The two most horrible people in the world, sitting under a tree together. We're a supervillain team in the making."

Without any warning, I found myself smiling back. This was, against all odds, kind of making me feel better. Not about what my dad had done, but about . . . well, I wasn't sure yet, really. But with Leah here beside me, cracking bleak jokes, everything seemed just a little less awful.

I sighed, leaning back on the grass. Leah lay down beside me.

"What I still don't get," she said, "is why they covered up Heather's death."

"Oh," I said. "Something about living off the grid? A combination of stealing people's memories and straight-up lying—and there's tax evasion in there, too, I'm pretty sure."

Leah frowned. "Yeah, I know about all that. It's to protect Willow, right?"

"I think so."

"So, okay, they cover up her death on a big-picture level or whatever, fine. But why hide it from *me*? Her mother knew that I knew about the reaching and the ritual for the Cliff."

"She did? For real?" Aunt Holly really didn't seem like the type to put up with that kind of thing. But then again, these days, Aunt Holly didn't seem like the type to do much of anything except drink and scowl at people.

Leah nodded. "Why didn't she tell me?" There was fury

in her eyes now. "Heather was my best friend, and she's been dead since *February*. I had a right to know."

"Yeah," I said uncertainly. "Maybe you did."

Leah stood up and brushed off her jeans. "Come on," she said.

"Wait, come on where?"

"I'm giving you a ride home," she said, smiling grimly. "I want to have a chat with Heather's mom."

△ BEFORE △

"How come your mom makes that face all the time?"

We were in my family's apartment when Heather asked me that. She'd just come back from a tour of some art school—one of the many art schools she'd never end up transferring into when freshman year rolled around—and my parents weren't home from work yet.

"What face?"

"You know." Heather stretched her features into a squinty-eyed grimace. "That one. She makes that face and she says to be careful. Be careful about what?"

Oh, now I knew which face she was talking about. "About stealing," I said. "She's afraid I can steal stuff by accident, just by touching things."

"Oh my god, that's so dumb," said Heather. "It doesn't work like that. Duh."

"Well, *I* know that. But it's not like she can reach, right? She's just watching out for me."

I remember wondering at my sudden urge to defend my mom. Usually her cautiousness around my abilities drove me nuts. But there was something about the way Heather was talking. All contemptuous, like we were somehow better than my mom, instead of just different.

"That's so dumb," she repeated. "She really needs to get over it."

I agreed with her, at least a little bit. But right then, mostly I still just felt defensive.

Which was why I told her that she should shut up, because she didn't even know what it was like to have two parents. She'd never even met her dad. She'd told me so, back when we were little.

Heather looked stricken for half a second, but the expression soon turned right back into a smirk. "That's because my mom had the right idea," she said smugly. "Why bother marrying someone who can't do magic? We're better off just the two of us."

I didn't speak to Heather for the rest of the day.

The next morning, she made pancakes for just her and me—an apology in food instead of words. And just like that, we were cool again. But for the rest of their visit, I couldn't help wondering if, just maybe, Heather was right about my mom.

CHAPTER FIFTEEN

"Aunt Holly?" I called, throwing the front door open.

Almost immediately, she came running. Well, walking fast, at least. There was a glass of amber liquid in her left hand, and she was taking obvious care not to spill it.

"We were wondering where you'd gone," she said—and then looked behind me. Her eyes hardened. "You. Get out."

"No," said Leah, stepping forward. She lifted her chin just a little, and her dark eyes were full of fire, and in that moment I had absolutely no doubt that if she wanted to, she could totally take Aunt Holly in a fight.

Aunt Holly swallowed, like she was thinking the exact same thing. "No?" she echoed, like she didn't quite understand the word.

"No," said Leah again. "I want to talk to you. About Heather. I want—"

"Get *out*!" said Aunt Holly, her face contorting as soon as she heard Heather's name. "You do *not* come into my house uninvited and talk to me about my own daughter. You, of all people, after what you . . . you . . ."

She was shaking with rage, and the glass was starting to slip from her fingers. I darted forward and, before she realized what I was doing, snatched the glass away.

"She's not uninvited, Aunt Holly," I said calmly. "I invited her."

"This isn't your house, Aspen," she said, eyeing me—and her Scotch glass—as I moved out of her reach.

But Leah jumped in again before I could reply. "Listen, Mrs. Quick, I just want to talk to you. Okay?"

"Miss," said Aunt Holly.

Leah blinked, clearly thrown.

Aunt Holly smirked a little. "Not 'Mrs.' Heather's father and I were never married, so don't address me like I'm someone's wife. Got that? It's Miss Quick or Holly."

So, she'd had maybe one or two drinks already. Drunk enough not to care what she was saying, but still sober enough to say it without slurring.

"Um, okay," said Leah.

"And why the *hell* should I talk to you about my daughter?" Aunt Holly went on, creeping closer to Leah, her eyes bright. "After everything you did. You were her only friend, you know that? You broke her heart. She was never the same after you dropped her. And you never even told her why."

"Heather knew why," said Leah softly. "It was because she stole my sister's voice for one of your ritual things."

Aunt Holly's mouth fell open, but Leah went on: "It was an accident, and she tried to tell me so, but I refused to believe her. I was so shitty to her, and I know I should have let it go. Made friends with her again, said I was sorry."

"You . . ." But Aunt Holly trailed off, apparently at a loss for words. In the silence that followed, Willow stepped out of the living room and into the foyer.

"No swearing in the house, please," she said.

Leah, ignoring Willow completely, kept talking: "Now I'll never get to apologize. I'll probably regret that for the rest of my life." Leah took a deep breath. "But I want to know something. Why didn't you tell me that she died?"

But before Aunt Holly could answer, Willow said, "Why do *you* know about the ritual? Holly, I thought your daughter removed her knowledge of what we do."

"I . . . I thought so too. She told me she had."

"Removed my . . . ?" Leah shook her head, a little laugh escaping her. "No, my *knowledge of what you do* is plenty intact, thanks."

Willow sighed. "Aspen, if you wouldn't mind? We can't have people roaming about, knowing this family's secrets."

"Yeah, Aspen. Go for it. Steal from me." There was a glint in Leah's eyes, but I couldn't tell whether it meant she was angry or just amused. She knew exactly what would happen if I tried to steal from her.

"Guys, she isn't gonna tell anyone," I said. "She's known for years and never told anyone."

Willow tilted her head a little, giving me a small, devious smile. "Aspen. Come now. Why the sudden reluctance? It isn't as though you haven't stolen anything from her before."

"You did *what*?" said Leah, looking at me in horror. "What the hell did you take from me?"

"Nothing!" I said, which was technically true. But I couldn't explain in front of my family. Not without giving Heather's secret away. "I'll explain later, okay?"

Leah hissed a breath out between her clenched teeth. Shook her head. "I swear to god. You people."

"Hey," I said, incensed. "*You people*? Come on. I didn't even know you then."

"Aspen, it doesn't matter if you didn't know me!" she practically shouted. "You know me now. You had plenty of time to say something."

"Get out," said Aunt Holly, for the third time.

"No," said Leah. "Not until you explain to me why you didn't tell me—why—we were best friends for so long, and I never got to . . . if I'd known she was *sick,* I could've . . ."

Ah, so that was her real reason for being here. She didn't really want an explanation for the cover-up. She'd wanted to tell Heather she was sorry, and she was angry about it being too late.

Willow rubbed her temples. "Aspen, for the love of all things holy, please remove this girl's memory and escort her from the house."

"I'll do it myself," said Aunt Holly, her voice almost a growl as she lurched toward Leah.

I caught her arm before she could make contact. "Aunt Holly, come on."

Leah, though, was already edging toward the door. "No, you know what? Never mind. You were right. I shouldn't have come here. You're all just . . . just . . ."

But I never got to find out what we were, because Leah spun around and walked out the front door. It was a moment before I gathered my wits enough to go after her. "Leah! Wait up!" I called from the front stoop. She was already well on her way down the driveway, and she didn't look ready to stop, so I ran after her.

"Leah," I said, reaching for her arm.

But she shrugged me off, a gesture so violent that it made my neck tense up in sympathy. "Don't you dare follow me."

"Come on—"

That was when she rounded on me. Eyes full of fury, hands clenched into fists, chest heaving with some volatile cocktail of emotions that I couldn't even begin to identify.

"Get away from me," she said. "And stay away, you got that? Look, I know you only want to be my friend because, whatever, you can't steal from me so I guess you feel *safe* or something. But even if you can't screw *me* up, you already screwed up one of my best friends—one of the most important people in my entire life. I'm done with this stupid family. I'm just done."

I opened my mouth to reply, but nothing came out.

Leah turned around again and walked away. She got

into her mom's car, revved the engine probably a little more than necessary, and drove away.

I stared after her. Was that really it? Was she really gone?

"I'm going after her," said Aunt Holly, who'd apparently followed me out onto the driveway.

"Good," said Willow, standing on my other side. "I can't stand the thought of that girl knowing—"

"And I'm not stealing anything from her, okay, Ma? So drop it."

Willow blinked rapidly, looking kind of stunned.

"Then what are you gonna do?" I asked.

"Talk to her," said Aunt Holly curtly. "As much as I hate it, that girl was right. She was the only real friend my Heather had in this godforsaken town. She deserves . . . Heather would want . . . Aspen, you're sober, aren't you?"

"Yeah," I said, and offered her my sleeve. "Go for it."

Aunt Holly's fingers touched my shirt for only a few seconds. Just long enough to steal some of my sobriety so she'd be okay to drive. Then she slipped her sandals on, grabbed her car keys, and left.

"Do you like that girl?" said Willow, making me jump. "Leah Ramsey-Wolfe?"

"I mean . . . sure? Kind of? But she's, um. Well, you heard. She's totally not into me."

Willow nodded, touching my elbow in a way that I guessed was supposed to be understanding. Or something. "Brandy left when you told her the truth about yourself. Didn't she."

"How'd you know that?" I asked.

She smiled sadly. "I've seen it happen far too many times over the years. I know the signs. The averted eyes. The refusal of breakfast before she left. My Holly reached into her and confirmed it. Then took the memory away, of course—"

"She did what?" I said, my whole body snapping to attention. That was the whole reason I hadn't stopped her from breaking up with me—because I knew how much it sucked to have memories stolen, and I hadn't wanted that to happen to Brandy.

Willow looked alarmed. "She removed Brandy's memory. We can't very well have people wandering about, knowing our secrets, can we?"

"But . . ."

"Holly was very careful, if that's what you're worried about. She made sure not to take anything else by mistake."

I nodded. That was something, I guess. "Then she's not going to remember why she broke up with me," I said.

Willow shrugged. "I expect she'll fill in the blanks with her own version of events. The human mind is remarkably elastic in that respect."

Right. Like how Dad had stolen my memory of my real grandmother, and I'd filled in the blank by assuming Willow was my grandmother instead.

I sighed.

"But," she said, "you should know how sorry I am. She was a charming girl."

"Charming," I said. "Yeah."

"Aspen? What's the matter?"

281

"It's just . . . I stole so much from her. I took away all the negative things she thought about me, and all the new feelings that kept popping up for Theo, and I . . . I didn't even think it was a bad thing to do, you know?"

She laughed. "You have a talent that few people have. It's only natural that you should want to use it."

Only natural.

Like it was *only natural* that a boy my age should be pissed off, but not at all sad, about his mom leaving.

"I guess," I said uncertainly . . . and that was when my entire brain skidded to a halt.

Willow's hand. Still touching the bare skin of my elbow. Yesterday she'd been shaking—and now, she felt totally normal.

Oh.

Oh, shit.

"Grandm—uh, Willow?"

She gave me a smile. "You can continue calling me Grandma if you like. It's up to you."

"Um," I said. "The other night. You said you had . . . you know. A tremor in your hands. But now . . ."

I nodded down at her hand on my elbow, and she pulled it away. "It comes and goes," she said.

The suspicion in my gut bloomed, slowly, into something larger and uglier.

"How?" I made myself ask. "How, exactly, does it come and go?"

"I'm sure I have no idea. It isn't as though I can compare

notes with other women my age." She looked at me with clear eyes. "Why do you ask?"

"Because of Brandy," I said. "We stole from her to fix the Cliff yesterday."

She thought for a moment. "Yes, that odd bracelet. What about her?"

"She's . . . she was shaking," I said. "She said it started when they were at the lake. And I can't fix her."

Willow raised an eyebrow.

I went on: "Was yesterday when your tremor stopped?"

A moment passed, and Willow nodded. Slowly, her gaze never leaving my face, she nodded.

"It's for you," I said, clutching at the back of my neck, which had suddenly gone tense as hell. "All the extra stuff. It's not for the Cliff. It's for *you*."

"Extra stuff," she echoed, sounding weirdly impassive. "Such as?"

"Yesterday, all I took away from Brandy was a couple of freckles. That was seriously all I took. But the Cliff stole something else. And—and your eyes!" I said, pointing.

"My eyes?"

"When I got here, right up until the first time we did the ritual, your eyes were all—I mean, I saw you read with a magnifying glass once, for heaven's sake."

She nodded. "I remember that."

"And after the ritual," I said, "Leah's friend Jesse went *blind*. That night. The first ritual I did. That was when your eyesight got better. And then there's—"

Heather. Then there was Heather. And I almost said so, except that was when I realized what was really happening here. I was telling Willow all this stuff, and she was listening, and she was nodding . . . and she was *smiling*. Just like she'd smiled after I'd completed my very first triad ritual when I was ten years old.

She looked like she was proud of me.

"Oh," I said. "You knew."

Willow smiled kindly, her eyes twinkling as she pressed one warm palm against my cheek. "Aspen, dearest. Of course I knew. And look at you, clever thing, figuring it out so fast. Even Holly, bless her, still hasn't figured it out."

"Well, obviously," I said. "If she'd figured it out, she would know that you're the real reason Heather died."

"I'm . . . sorry?" said Willow, the kindness draining from her eyes. "Maybe I misheard, but it sounded very much like you just accused me of murder."

"No, god, not—not *murder* exactly, but—but her lungs—she—"

"Deep breath," said Willow. I took a deep breath, because she was wearing the kind of look where disobedience wasn't an option. "Now explain yourself."

So I did. I explained about Heather creating the bounce-back to protect Leah, and how it had backfired when the Cliff stole from Heather, presumably to patch up Willow's broken-down lungs. "Am I right?" I said, when I was done. "You couldn't breathe right, and then you could? Right around the time Heather died?"

Willow nodded slowly, looking so stricken that I honestly believed she hadn't known. "Poor girl," she whispered. "Poor foolish girl."

"Foolish?" I said, indignant. "She's *dead*."

Willow smiled tightly. "Death, unfortunately, doesn't make fools any less foolish."

My whole body went tense, and my hand clutched at my neck. That was probably the most callous thing I'd ever heard anyone say.

"I guess," I said slowly. "It's just . . . I mean, don't you feel, I dunno, guilty?"

"Her death wasn't my doing. It was the Cliff."

"Sure, but it was still *for you*," I countered.

"Indeed it was," she said. "And believe me, if I could have chosen anyone but Heather, I would have. I value my family above everything, Aspen. You know that."

I nodded. I did know that. But she seemed awfully composed for a woman who'd just learned that her several-zillion-times-great-granddaughter would still be alive if not for her.

"You seem troubled," said Willow.

I snorted. Troubled. Yeah.

Then she said, "What's that you're doing?"

"Huh?"

"You're massaging your neck," she said, mimicking the gesture. "Do you know how many times I've seen you do that since you arrived here?"

I paused, thinking. "I dunno. A lot, probably?"

"Why do you do it?"

Well, by now it was as much habit as anything else. But the reason the habit had started . . .

"Old injury," I said. "I was in a car crash when I was . . . ten? Eleven? Just a little one. But I got really bad whiplash."

"You poor thing," she said quietly.

I shrugged. "It's not horrible. Acts up once in a while, but whatever."

"Ten or eleven," she mused, tapping her bottom lip with one finger. "Why didn't your father heal you?"

"Oh, he did," I said. "It hurt like a b—um—it hurt a *lot,* at first. But he reached in and took all the pain away until it healed."

She narrowed her eyes, considering. "But it never fully healed, did it. He took away the symptoms of your injury, but not the injury itself. You were left with a neck, which, and I quote, *acts up* once in a while."

I shifted my weight a little. I'd never given much thought to that. "Well, right. But . . ."

"But nothing. Come with me." She turned and headed away from the driveway, toward the woods.

"Where are we going?" I asked, jogging a little to keep up with her brisk pace.

"To the May Day tree."

Through the woods we went, Willow nimbly dodging rocks and roots, me following doggedly in her footsteps, until we got to the field. Immediately I was struck by a sense of . . . not déjà-vu. Nothing as heady as that. Just a sense of circling. Of always ending up back at the same place.

It didn't feel good.

"Well? Are you coming?"

Willow's voice made me jump, and I realized that I'd stopped at the edge of the field, while she'd almost reached the tree already. I ran to catch up.

We stood right at the spot where Leah and I had sat together, just a short time ago. Willow's sharp eyes scanned the pile of stuff that surrounded the trunk. Finally, after a long moment, she said, "Pick something."

"Me?" I said. "Aren't you supposed to tell me what to look for?"

She smiled. "This isn't part of a ritual, Aspen. This is just for you. Pick something. Anything."

My stomach curdled. I knew, somewhere deep inside, what was about to happen—what she was going to tell me to do—but I couldn't acknowledge it. Not yet. It was too huge. So, for now, I did what I was told. I went for the first thing that caught my eye: a bright blue hardcover book. It said *The Hardy Boys* on it.

"Is this okay?" I asked.

She nodded. "Bring it here."

I did, and she took a moment to examine it. "Hm."

"Hm?"

She looked up at me. "Reach inside. See if the owner of this book has a neck that's free of injury."

Finally, I let understanding seep in. I was supposed to fix myself.

I was supposed to fix myself by, essentially, passing my injury along to someone else.

I swallowed. "I don't think I should do this."

Willow gave a little laugh—the kind of laugh that made me realize just how weak my protest had sounded. "Oh, Aspen," she said.

"Oh Aspen what?" I resisted the urge to cross my arms over my chest. "I just found out that my cousin died because you keep healing yourself, and now you want me to do the exact same thing?"

"Hardly the same thing," said Willow, her voice so calm that it made me want to break something. "I have to rely on the Cliff to heal the parts of myself that are broken—but I can't control whom it chooses to steal from. You, though. You have control over what you take, *and* whom you take it from."

That was true.

"Besides," she continued, "your injury is such a small thing. You've lived with it for years. Maybe it's someone else's turn to carry your burden."

I found myself nodding. "Plus it's not like it's a real disability or anything, right?" I said. "It's just annoying."

"Even if it were a real disability," she said, "people learn to live with those all the time. Take your eyes, for example. I know you wear those contractual lenses—"

"Contact lenses," I corrected her with a grin.

"Ah, yes. Those. Don't you think that if you're going to shoulder a responsibility like keeping the Cliff standing, you ought to be able to see properly to do it?"

I frowned. I could see just fine, as long as I had my contacts or my glasses. Still, my eyes would probably get worse as I got older. . . .

She moved closer to me, touching the edge of the book that I held. "You can replace yourself over time, Aspen, just as I do. But you can do it on your own terms. You can choose whom to steal from, and whom to protect."

Replace myself. I could heal all the injuries I had now, and the ones I might have in the future. I could keep my body from breaking down when I got old. I could . . .

But the idea still took a few more moments to compute, and when I spoke again, my voice came out quiet. Almost scared.

"Are you saying I could live forever?"

Willow tilted her head, just a little. Just so. Her eyes glinted. "What I'm saying," she said, "is that you ought to start by reaching into that book and replacing your neck injury with something better."

My entire body was close to trembling now. My skin itched, like it was suddenly too big, or maybe too small. I felt drunk and high and totally sober, all at the same time.

I reached.

This time, I only lingered on the surface long enough to make sure that the owner of this book wasn't someone I knew. Once I was sure, I bypassed everything else—all the surface emotions and superficial personality traits that I usually noticed when I reached into people for the first time. I didn't want to see those. I just thought *Neck,* and there it was, instantly. A perfectly healthy neck.

Moving cautiously, I wrapped my will around the health and strength of that particular curve of his spine. I took a small piece away, leaving enough behind that he'd still be able to, you know, hold his head up . . . and I pulled.

I pulled it out, and I absorbed it into myself.

And then, for the first time in who even knew how long, my neck

Felt

Fine.

It was like there'd been an anvil sitting on top of my head for years that I hadn't even noticed until, suddenly, it wasn't there. My head was balloon-light. Almost dizzy. I felt like I was about to cry.

"Oh my god," I whispered.

"Feel better?" asked Willow.

I feathered my fingers over the base of my skull, then downward. "I . . . I didn't even know I *could* feel this much better. Like, I can't even describe this. I . . ."

"No need, my dear boy," she said, smiling kindly. "If anyone understands, it's me. Now let's get back to the house before we lose the light completely, shall we?"

When we got back, Willow led me up to the second floor and pulled down the attic stairs. "Holly usually disposes of the objects we've used in the ritual, but as she's not here, would you mind? Just leave that book in whatever box still has room."

I'd been up to the attic before. Heather had brought me up when we were both much smaller, to show me how many things she'd used in her rituals. How many people she'd stolen from. At the time, I'd thought that it looked like a serial killer's stash of trophies or something, but she'd assured me that it was a family legacy thing, which made it all right. Now, though, as I stared at the piles upon piles of cardboard boxes full of other people's trinkets, my first impression was rapidly returning, and all I wanted to do was get out of there as fast as I could.

So I opened the box closest to the stairs, intending to drop the Hardy Boys book inside—but there, at the top of the pile, was *The Hound of the Baskervilles*—the book that had once been Leah's.

I didn't throw away the Hardy Boys book. Instead, I plucked *The Hound of the Baskervilles* from its box and brought both books with me into Heather's room.

And as I tried to fall asleep later that night, I ran my fingers back and forth over the spine of the Hardy Boys book, wondering about the guy I'd just stolen from. Trying to put my curiosity aside so I could go to sleep.

But after a little while, I found myself thinking about what Leah Ramsey-Wolfe had said earlier, under the May Day tree:

Seems to me you could be as empathetic as anyone else, if you bothered trying.

This was what she meant. This, right here, was the difference between trying to be empathetic and not. Between being a robot and being a person. I could reach into the Hardy Boys book and meet the person I'd stolen from—or I could set it aside and tell myself that it wasn't my problem, just like I'd always done before.

I reached into the book. This time I went slowly enough to see all the things I'd missed the first time around.

It wasn't a guy I'd stolen from, first of all. It was a woman. Young—actually, only a few years older than me. She was studying math at a state school not far away, and she came back to Three Peaks every few weeks to visit her family. She loved dogs, hated cats, and had a secret fondness for peanut butter ice cream. Secret, because she was a health nut. Health nut, because she was a gymnast.

Oh.

I lingered on that for a moment. Then a moment more.

She was a gymnast, this girl. And I'd given her a neck injury.

△ BEFORE △

I don't remember exactly what my mother's face looked like, that night. All I remember is that she didn't look proud of tiny little fourth-grade me. That fact stood out because everyone else looked so proud that they could've floated away. My dad. Aunt Holly. Grandma. Even Heather, more or less. Not my mom, though.

"First try!" said Grandma, clapping my dad on the shoulder as Aunt Holly put out the fire in the fireplace. "You certainly couldn't do that, could you, Andy?"

"I think it took about ten tries for me," said Dad, shaking his head. "But that's the hope, isn't it? For your kids to be better than you."

I remember Mom's face darkening. I remember how she didn't say anything, even though she looked like she wanted to.

"Isn't that great, Heather?" said Aunt Holly. "Aspen can help us with the triad ritual now."

"Uh-huh," said Heather, who'd already schooled her face into an expression of practiced apathy. "I'm still better at it. Can I ride my bike now?"

"It's dark out, sweetie," said Aunt Holly. "We can ride bikes tomorrow before we leave, okay?"

Heather *hmph*ed, crossing her arms and scowling at me, like it was my fault that the sun had already set. I knew she was really mad at me for taking her spot in that night's ritual, so I gave her the toothiest grin I could muster. She just scowled harder.

"Mom, tell Aspen he can't sleep in my bed while I'm gone."

(They were going on vacation to Niagara Falls the next day. My dad and I had come up to help with the ritual for the week that they'd be gone. My mom had come along so she could take me back down to the city, in the event that Grandma decided I wasn't ready to do the triad just yet.)

"I don't want to sleep in your stupid bed," I said. "I don't want to get girl cooties."

"Aspen, be nice," said Mom softly. It was the first thing she'd said since the fire had changed colors.

"Yeah, Aspen," mimicked Heather, her voice all high, "be nice to me."

"That's enough," said Aunt Holly wearily. "Heather, let's go finish packing, okay?"

"But my bed—"

"They'll be sleeping in the guest rooms. Come on, let's go upstairs. We've got a big trip tomorrow."

Heather stuck her tongue out at me as Aunt Holly ushered her from the room, but I just grinned at her again.

"Well, that's a relief," said Grandma, sinking into her chair and smiling up at my parents and me. "I would've been in a bind if young Aspen here hadn't managed it. But aren't we lucky! He's quite the talent."

"He certainly is," said Dad.

"What did you take?" asked Mom. It took me a second to realize the question was directed at me.

"For the ritual?" I asked. She nodded. "Oh. It was a guy who was afraid of snakes. I made him not be afraid anymore."

"Fear's a powerful thing," said Grandma, nodding. "Good energy. He did so well."

"See, Annie?" said Dad. "The Cliff's still standing, *and* our Aspen just improved someone's life. Everyone wins."

It didn't occur to me till later, but he sounded kind of desperate then, like he really, really wanted her to agree with him.

Mom stood up from her spot on the couch, keys jangling in her hand. "Aspen, are you sure you don't want to come back home with me?"

"You're going now?" I said. "I thought you were gonna stay till tomorrow."

Mom hesitated. "Tomorrow's Sunday. There'll be all sorts of traffic. This late, I could probably make it back to the city in just a few hours. You can still come with me if you want."

I was in a place where fire could turn blue and the things I stole could be visible, where people praised me for a talent nobody else even knew I had.

"No way," I said. "I want to stay up here forever."

CHAPTER SIXTEEN

The first time I woke up that night, it was to the sound of the front door closing. Aunt Holly was back. I ran downstairs to meet her.

"Did you talk to Leah?" I asked.

"Mm," she said, not meeting my eyes. It sounded more like yes than no.

"What did she say?"

Aunt Holly's lips twitched, and she put a hand on the banister as if to steady herself. "She said . . . a lot of things."

"Well, what did *you* say?"

She sighed, finally meeting my eyes. "That I forgave her. And she showed me the letter you found."

It took me a second to work out what she meant. "Heather's letter?"

"Why didn't you show it to me?" Her voice cracked on the last word.

"I didn't think—I mean, it was Leah's, so I figured—"

"My little girl died to save her friend," said Aunt Holly. "She was a hero. A martyr, even if she never meant to be. I had a right to know."

Except she still didn't know. Not really. She had no idea the Cliff was siphoning off the healthy parts of other people in order to keep Willow alive.

I found myself nodding. She did have a right to know the truth of how Heather had died. The *whole* truth. And I was the only person in the world who could tell her, because I was the only person in the world who knew.

"Aunt Holly . . ."

But before I could figure out how to continue, she said, "Don't ever have children, Aspen. Now that you know what kind of blood runs in our family . . . don't pass it on. None of us should be allowed to pass it on."

I frowned, thinking of the gymnast I'd stolen from. "Then who would keep the Cliff standing?"

"Nobody," she said.

"No, but seriously . . ."

"This has gone on for too long. The triad ritual, our family being tied up in all this madness. Far, far too long."

"It's better than dying," I said.

She shook her head. "Better? Cooped up in this house, alone, no friends except coworkers you don't even like, only family to understand who you really are and what you're capable of? I'm not so sure sometimes."

"You're not alone," I began, and then paused. "I mean, you don't *have* to be alone. You could have friends, if you wanted."

Aunt Holly thinned her lips.

"*I* have friends," I said.

"Of course you do," she said. "A girlfriend who abandoned you as soon as you told her the truth about yourself, and that boy who left with her."

My cheeks heated up. "Well, I've got Leah."

Aunt Holly gave me a long look, then said again, very softly, "Of course you do."

"Seriously, if you think the Cliff thing should stop, then why do you keep doing it?"

There was a pause. Aunt Holly smiled, kind of hollow.

"Because if I stopped, she'd only replace me," she said. "We're all replaceable. Even my baby girl. My poor, poor girl."

Before I could reply, Aunt Holly was gone. Through the kitchen and into her bedroom. After a moment, I heard the faint sound of a bottle clinking against a glass. I fled upstairs, where my phone was waiting, and I sent a text to Leah:

I have something to give you. Come over tomorrow?

She didn't reply.

The second time I woke up, it wasn't because of the door. It was because of my phone, buzzing on the nightstand beside my head. A text from Leah. Finally.

I opened it.

Why? You want to cry on me for hours, too?

Aunt Holly had *cried*? Oh, great.

No no no no no, I typed back. I just want to give you something. You free tomorrow afternoon?

Leah: No.

Me: ???

Leah: No I am not free.

Me: I can come by the store if you're working.

Leah: Pls don't.

Me: ???????

Leah: Please do not come by the store.

Me: Ok what's going on

Leah: I thought I was pretty clear about that. I'm done with you people. End of story.

Me: Leah, come on.

Leah: Unless you figured out a way to give Jesse his sight back.

Me: …

Leah: ……

Me: You know I can't do that. It's not possible.

Leah: Do us both a favor, ok? Lose my number.

I didn't text her back after that. Nor did I delete her number. For all I knew, she was just annoyed, and she'd get over it eventually, and then we'd be fine again.

But maybe we wouldn't. Leah had friend-dumped Heather when she wouldn't use her powers the way Leah had wanted her to, and she hadn't bothered feeling bad about it until she learned that Heather was dead. I was not dead. She had no reason to feel bad about dumping me.

I put my phone back down, next to the two items I'd set aside for Leah: *The Hound of the Baskervilles,* and Jesse's one-armed Batman.

Jesse. The boy Leah wanted me to help. The price she wanted me to pay for her friendship.

And the thing was, I wanted to pay it. The only thing stopping me from reaching into some complete stranger and stealing their sight for Jesse was the fact that I *couldn't.* Sure, I'd feel guilty if I did it—but hell, I'd known I would feel guilty about passing my neck injury to someone else, and I'd done it anyway, because . . .

Well, because I'd chosen to do it. No matter how much Willow tried to justify it, and no matter how much I tried to blame my dad, I was the one who'd actually done it. Only me. Just like I'd chosen to steal, over and over again, from Brandy.

And from Theo. And from other kids at school. And from more strangers than I could even remember.

If I really kept going down this path—down the path that Willow had forged, that my father had shaped, that I'd never questioned—how many more people would suffer?

I could *stop* stealing, of course. I could run away from Three Peaks and back to Brooklyn and swear never to steal from anyone again—but Willow and Holly would find someone new for the triad ritual, just like Aunt Holly had said. Maybe my aunt Calla. Maybe someone else. But either way, nothing would be different. Not really.

Something—something bigger than only me—had to change.

But what?

The third time I woke up, it was because I'd been dreaming. In my mind's eye I'd seen the entire triad ritual, start to finish. The trek, the tree, the gifts, the leaves, the fire.

And the stone inside the fire.

The little piece of rock that belonged to the Cliff.

Throwing the covers aside, I made my way over to the bedroom door, opening it slowly so it wouldn't creak. I couldn't risk waking anyone up.

I went downstairs, the full moon lighting my way.

Without a fire crackling inside it, the living room's fireplace looked weirdly ordinary. Kind of small. In need of some repair, which I'd never noticed before. I knelt in front of it, my knees protesting against the hard floor, and looked for the thing that would save us: the single stone from the Cliff, half hidden among the logs.

The Cliff wasn't just a pile of rocks. It was a sentient being. It felt hunger, it preferred certain energies over others, it bargained, and it threatened. Hell, it'd actually given our family *magical powers* so we could keep it alive.

And if it was a sentient thing, that meant I could reach into it.

Pushing the charred logs aside, I touched the rock and looked for a way in. It was a second before I found it—

and when I did, it felt different from the way into people or animals. It was . . . narrower? And sort of twisty.

Still. In I went. Only to find a jumble of things that didn't point to the Cliff at all. A memory of fire, and of the feeling of rain on leaves, the sense of standing alone alone alone, the anticipation of people watching, and the memory of Willow, of Aunt Holly, of Heather, of Aunt Calla . . . of me.

It *used* to belong to the Cliff. Of course. That meant it didn't anymore. This stone belonged to the ritual now. It held so many memories and feelings and peculiarities— from the tree, from the fireplace, from my family—that it would be impossible to untangle the Cliff from all the rest.

I withdrew my will from the stone, replaced the logs I'd moved, and sat back on my heels, brushing soot from my hands.

If I was really going to do this, and if the stone really didn't belong to the Cliff anymore, then there was nothing in this room—nothing in this house—that would help me. If I was really going to do this, I had to go to the source.

I had to go up to the Cliff itself.

Aunt Holly kept her car keys on a hook by the door. I grabbed them, slipped my shoes on, and ran out to start the car. The engine seemed about forty times louder than usual, but there was nothing I could do about that. Even if I woke someone up, at least I'd have a hell of a head start.

I took the route that we'd taken on the Fourth of July, and pulled into the same empty field where everyone had parked that night: the place where the more-or-less-even ground started sloping more purposefully upward, and the woods became too dense to drive through. I'd have to walk the rest of the way, but that was okay. I had my phone, and my phone had a flashlight.

The path got steeper as I walked, and it was really freaking cold. So I tried to climb faster, skirting around boulders, winding my way around thick tree trunks like a pro—but when I nearly tripped in a small gully, I slowed down again. I was panting. Yeah, hiking was Theo's turf, not mine. I had to be more careful.

Finally, after a painfully long time, I reached the top. The place where the upward slope gave way to the flattish expanse of grass where we'd watched the fireworks. I could see the exact point where the grass ended, where one more step would mean a fatal fall.

Kneeling down, I pressed my palms into the grass. I closed my eyes and felt the shape of each blade. I moved my hands, searching, searching, until . . . there it was: a way in. Narrow and jagged and winding and so far from human that it kind of scared me. But still.

A way in.

But following the path felt like trying to carve a tunnel through solid rock. My heart raced, and I could feel the muscles in my neck and my stomach and my thighs and my forearms tightening so much that I was sure they'd snap at any moment. But I had to make this work. There was no other option.

I pushed harder, feeling it in my fingernails and my eye-balls and my bones, wondering if I'd actually burst apart before I managed to get through—

And then, it happened.

The rock gave way, and I was inside.

I let out a long, ragged breath.

It didn't feel the same as being inside the mind of another person. Not that I'd really expected it to be, but still. Where people, and even animals, were made of layers upon layers of thoughts and traits and neuroses and memories and infinite amounts of other things, the Cliff was . . . surprisingly simple.

In fact, once I cleared my mind enough to really look, I could make out only three distinct things.

First, there was the round, hollow feeling of hunger. That was no surprise.

Second, there was the sharp pinprick of a memory. A young man and a young woman, both around my age, hunched over a fire they'd built.

Ash and Rose. Willow's children. I knew them by what they clutched in their hands—a rose petal in hers, an ash leaf in his—and I knew them because I *knew*. Because the Cliff knew.

They were crouched atop one large rock, amidst a giant pile of rubble that extended a short way into the valley. There was bargaining, and there was desperation, and there was magic.

Threaded through the larger memory was a series of

smaller, more staccato memories that weren't quite images, and weren't quite feelings, but somewhere in between. A sense of being born. Of many small pieces coalescing into a whole. An instantaneous transition from not-being into being.

My breath caught as I realized what I was seeing.

Pieces becoming a whole. Not-being into being. Before Willow's children had built that fire and brought their mother back to life, the Cliff had just been another quirk of geology. A tumble of rocks and dirt and whatever else you found in these mountains. But now it was a unified entity, far more than the sum of its parts.

Rose and Ash hadn't awoken the Cliff. Because it hadn't been sleeping. You can't sleep if you aren't sentient. Willow's children were the ones who'd *made it sentient.*

Then there was the third thing I saw: a thin, barely visible spiderweb, connecting the Cliff to the May Day tree—and to Willow's bloodline.

This was the thing that allowed Willow to feel when the Cliff needed feeding. This was also the thing that would allow the Cliff to kill us all—all her descendants—if it fell.

I closed my eyes and breathed, making sure my hands were steady. I hooked my will around all those little tendrils of connection, taking care that each piece was accounted for—that the cut would be clean.

This was it. The last moment that my family would have to serve this thing that existed only to feed its own hunger. This was the moment we would all be saved.

I mean, I was a goddamn superhero, basically.

I took a deep breath, and I got ready to steal the link away, and—

"Aspen."

The suddenness of the voice made me jump, pulling me out of the Cliff's consciousness, as my hands flailed around to keep me from losing my balance.

Willow.

She didn't look angry. She didn't come toward me. She just stood there in a pastel bathrobe and Crocs, and she looked at me, and she smiled.

"How's your neck feeling?" she asked.

"Um. Fine? But how'd you know where I—"

"Aspen, my love. I'm not stupid. Where else would you be?"

I closed my eyes, blowing out a long breath.

"I was just—"

"There's no need to explain." Now she was moving toward me. Not running, like she wanted to stop me, and not creeping, like she had to be cautious. Just walking. Like this was a normal night, and we were both normal people doing normal things. "I know what you were doing."

I stood up. At least this way I could be taller than her.

She drew closer, the pale moonlight falling softly onto her face. Her kind, grandmotherly face.

"Aspen," she said, all smile and warmth and understanding. "You think you're the first of us to have doubts?"

I stared at her. Was that a rhetorical question? I couldn't tell.

Just in case it wasn't, I replied, "Well, the ritual's still going strong. So maybe yeah. Maybe I am."

"Solid logic," she said. "But you're wrong. You're far from the first. You aren't even the first Quick to try severing our tie with the Cliff."

I wasn't?

"Then how come it's still standing?" I asked.

"Because," she said, "while you're far from the first to have the idea, you might just be the first of my descendants strong enough to make it happen."

My descendants. A reminder that I belonged to her. That my powers, my magic, my *life* wouldn't exist if not for her.

"You have a remarkable power, Aspen," she continued. "I've truly never felt anything like it. Such strength. Such precision. However, you do realize, don't you, that that connection is the only thing keeping me alive?"

I frowned. "I thought it was just keeping you immortal. Like you'd still be alive, right? Just . . . normal. We'd all be normal."

She raised an eyebrow. "Is that really what you want? Normalcy?"

"Yes!" I said. "God, yes."

For the first time, her expression grew cold. "And what about the rest of us? This is about far more than just you, Aspen."

"That's kind of the point," I said. "I thought—"

"You thought you'd just upend our entire way of life without even asking anyone first?" she said, moving steadily toward me. "Think of your aunt Holly, Aspen. The ritual is the only thing left in her life that gives her purpose."

"No, the ritual is the only thing tying her to *this town*," I said. "The town where her daughter died. You don't think she'd be happier if she could leave?"

"Perhaps," said Willow. "But what about everyone else? I had two children, Aspen. They both had children of their own, and they had children of *their* own. There are hundreds of us, all over the world! Will all of them be happier once you take their powers away?"

"How the hell should I know?" I said. "I've never even met most of them."

"My point exactly. And as for me . . ." She trailed off meaningfully.

"You, what?" I said. "You'll die somewhere down the line? Like a normal person? Because, oh, boo-hoo, right? Because nobody else has ever had to deal with getting old and dying? People's bodies break down. That's just what happens. Suck it up and deal with it."

She shook her head. "Things like that are so easy to talk about when you haven't lived them. How old are you, Aspen? Sixteen?"

I frowned, feeling indignant. "Seventeen."

"Seventeen, then," she said. "An infant. How foolish of me to think you'd care a whit for immortality. People your age already think they're immortal."

"I do not," I said—then immediately shut up, because I

sounded like a whiny little kid. I was proving her point.

She tilted her head. "Even so. Do you really think it will be as easy as that? You steal away the Cliff's means of survival, and you cause it to fall, and I'm free to grow old like a regular person?"

"Well . . . yeah."

"Sweetheart," she said, coming closer to me. "The Cliff has been keeping me alive for centuries. Fixing me, sometimes before I even know I'm broken. And why? Because it trusts me to return the favor. It trusts me to protect it. What do you think it'll do to me, if I betray that trust?"

When I'd reached into the Cliff, I'd seen nothing about trust and betrayal. Those were human concepts. Too human for the Cliff to understand.

"Nothing," I said firmly. "It won't do anything at all."

Her eyes narrowed. "Says the boy who doesn't have the Cliff's voice in his head. If the Cliff falls, Aspen, it will take me with it."

"You're lying," I said. "You don't know it'll do that."

A mirthless smile. "You don't know that it won't."

Maybe not. But there was one way I could find out.

I lunged for her, catching the hem of her robe in my hands—but only for a moment, before she jerked it away.

"Don't you dare," she said, circling away from me. "Don't you *dare* reach into me, Aspen Quick. You know the rules—"

"Yeah, I do," I said, following her, step for step. "No reaching. No stealing. No lying. But you've been lying to me since the day I met you, so I don't think I'm gonna feel really bad about breaking the other rules."

I lunged again. Again she jumped back, just out of my reach.

"I didn't know!" she said. "How could I have known that your incompetent father had muddled your memories so badly? I thought you already knew the truth about me!"

"Not the whole truth," I said. "You never told anyone about the Cliff keeping you immortal. Listen, if you don't let me reach into you, I'll just keep assuming that you're lying."

She considered me.

I considered her.

And that was when I heard it: a crunch, soft and sharp, like footsteps on twigs. And then a voice.

"You found him."

Aunt Holly. Her skin was pink with exertion, and she was clutching at her chest like she was about to pass out. She glared at Willow. "I told you—I can't run—as fast as you—"

"Few people can run as fast as me," said Willow, smiling placidly.

"You *ran* here?" I said. I mean, she wasn't out of breath at all. Had the Cliff stolen someone's speed for her? Or was this her healthy lungs—*Heather's* healthy lungs—at work?

"Indeed I did," said Willow. "Since you stole Holly's car, we were left with no other option. Don't you know that stealing from family is against the rule?"

A little smile played around her lips. She was joking. She thought this was a *joke*.

"What are you—what are you doing—up here?" said Aunt Holly, who was slowly beginning to catch her breath.

"Oh!" said Willow, still calm as ever. "He was just about to decide whether killing his own grandmother was a worthy price to pay for the alleviation of his guilty conscience."

"You're *what*?" said Aunt Holly, gaping at me.

"Tearing down the connection between our family and the Cliff," I replied, more to Willow than to Aunt Holly. "Tearing down the whole screwed-up system that lets us keep thinking we're better than everyone else, just because we can do some shitty magic that other people can't." Willow wasn't smiling anymore. I added, "Also, you're not my grandmother."

"But I'm still your family." Her voice was dangerously soft. "And family comes before everything."

I shook my head. "Not when we're the kind of family that screws up other people's lives just so we can have it easy."

"Unimportant people," said Willow, waving a dismissive hand.

"Was Heather unimportant?" I asked.

Willow fell silent. My question hung heavy in the cool night air.

"Heather?" said Aunt Holly. "Aspen, what do you mean?"

"You saw her letter," I said. "The one she wrote to Leah. She tried to protect Leah by stealing from herself instead, for the ritual—"

"Aspen there's no need to get into all that," said Willow, looking almost fearful.

Ignoring her, I went on: "But the Cliff took more from her than what she offered it. It took her lungs. She tried to protect Leah, and the Cliff killed her for it. And do you know why?"

"Why?" asked Aunt Holly, barely audible.

"To keep *her* alive." I pointed at Willow. "She keeps the Cliff alive by doing the triad ritual, and the Cliff returns the favor by skimming extra stuff off the people we steal from. Leah's sister's voice. Her friend Jesse's eyesight." Deep breath. "Heather's ability to breathe. The Cliff took that stuff and gave it all to Willow."

"But . . . but my Heather . . ." Aunt Holly's hands were claws. Her face was a mask of pain. She turned toward Willow. "You knew this?"

"Our family does what it has to, in order to survive," said Willow, her face hardening. "Your daughter chose her friend over her family. She forged her own path."

"You . . . you . . ."

Aunt Holly didn't finish. Maybe she couldn't.

Willow turned back toward me. "Let our family continue to survive, Aspen. That's all I'm asking of you."

"You aren't talking about our family," I said. "Our family's gonna be fine. And I think you'll be fine, too. I think you'll live for a long time, and I think you just don't want to. I think you're afraid of getting old for real."

"And I think you'll be sorry," Willow replied, "when you don't have me anymore. When the Cliff takes me, and you're back to being surrounded by people who will never understand you. People who will *never* appreciate how unique you are. Your girlfriend, who fled the moment she learned the truth. Your poor mother, who never stopped distrusting the most special, most unique part of you. . . ."

But if I severed the connection, my magic would be gone. I'd be normal.

"Yeeeeah," I said. "Yeah, I don't think I'll be sorry at all."

I crouched down again, pressing my palms into the grass. But before I could begin to force my way into the Cliff again, Willow sprang forward.

"Aspen!" she said.

My name came out half formed, though—cut off before it could even take its full shape. Because Aunt Holly had grabbed Willow, jerking her backward, holding her in place with elbows hooked under Willow's shoulders and hands clasped behind Willow's neck.

It was the single most ridiculous-looking headlock I'd ever seen in my life, all flailing arms and flyaway hair and bubblegum-pink nightgown peeking out from under her robe.

"Aspen, do it fast!" said Aunt Holly. "She's really strong!"

"Don't you dare, Aspen!" Willow cried. "Holly, let me *go*. . . ."

Ignoring her protests, I dug my fingers into the grass. I found the spot . . . and I reached.

It took me less than a minute to reach back in, to find all those little tendrils of connection between the Cliff and my family, and to wrap my will around them.

I took a deep breath.

And I pulled.

I'd expected it to be difficult—at least as difficult as getting into the Cliff in the first place—but it wasn't. Maybe because the connection wasn't tangled up in thousands of other things, like it would have been for a human being. Whatever the reason, it came away easily.

I withdrew my will from the Cliff and opened my eyes, still holding the connection firmly in my mind. It sat there, a pulsing mass of instinct and energy and possibility . . .

. . . and then I let it go.

Just like that, we were free.

The reaching hangover was different from anything I'd felt before. Usually I simply didn't want to move, but this time I felt like I literally *couldn't* move. I was myself, but I was also immense and immobile and ancient. I'd seen things—I *knew* things—but I couldn't translate that knowledge into logic.

Despite all that, one thought—one thought that was purely my own—managed to shine through the confusion:

I couldn't believe it had been that easy.

The thought made me feel giddy and lightheaded and

human—enough that the hangover began to fade in earnest. I sat back on my heels, and I looked at the two women who'd fallen silent just a few yards away from me.

Willow wasn't flailing or shouting anymore. She'd gone slack-jawed and limp, like she knew it was done, and knew there was no going back.

"Aspen." She said my name like a funeral prayer.

"Did you do it?" asked Aunt Holly.

But before I could answer, I heard something. A faint sound, like rumbling, deep and dark. And getting louder.

"Shit," I said. "Shit, shit, shit. We have to get out of here."

Willow hung her head, and a tiny sob escaped her.

"The Cliff?" said Aunt Holly.

Now I could feel it, too. A tiny earthquake, blooming right under our feet.

"It's falling," I said. "It's falling *right now*. Run. Run!"

Aunt Holly unhooked her arms from around Willow, and took off. She disappeared into the trees, and she didn't look back once, probably because she trusted that we were right behind.

And I *would* have been right behind, except . . .

Except Willow wasn't moving.

She was just staring into the void beyond the edge of the Cliff.

I grabbed her hand. But her fingers were slack.

"Willow?" I said. "We have to go. We really, really, *really* have to go."

A *crack* resonated through the air, and I knew what it

was, deep in my bones. A rock, maybe a big one, breaking off. *Crack. Crack.* Then something crumbling.

The ground was shaking under my feet. The edge of the Cliff would start disappearing soon. My heart clanged against my rib cage.

Willow still wouldn't move.

"For god's sake, come on!" I gripped her hand tighter, and I pulled.

But she pulled away, stronger than me, and turned to look me right in the eyes. Then she smiled and said softly, "I wasn't lying, Aspen. I can't live if the Cliff falls."

Then she turned and ran—so fast that one of her ugly shoes slipped off, Cinderella-style, and landed in the grass. She ran toward the night, toward the blackness beyond the edge of the Cliff.

And she kept running until, soundless, she fell.

△ AFTER △

By the time I made it back through the woods and down to the car, the *crack crack* of the Cliff falling had grown into a roar.

Aunt Holly was down there already, pulling on the handle of the car door like she could unlock it by sheer force of will.

"Oh, thank god," she said, when she saw me tearing toward her. "You still have my keys, and—"

Her gaze landed on the blue Croc dangling from my fingers.

"Where's Ma?"

I shook my head and dug in my pocket. Threw her the keys. "It's still falling, and I don't think we're far enough away to be safe. Let's go."

She unlocked the car and jumped in behind the wheel, and I took the passenger seat. She started the engine, and off we went: away from the Cliff, away from the rumbling and the quaking and Willow running and running and not stopping . . .

The winding mountain lane began to even out, and soon we were driving down an empty four-lane road. We were not in Three Peaks anymore. Aunt Holly pulled over.

She rested her forehead on the steering wheel, eyes closed, breath heavy.

"Did she fall, or did she jump?" Aunt Holly asked quietly. There was a weary accusation in her tone:

Or did you push her?

"She jumped." And in my mind's eye, she was still jumping, over and over again, disappearing over the edge, and . . .

I had an idea.

"Hold on," I said. And then I reached into Willow's shoe.

I moved quickly past layers of anger and indignation, of hatred and love, of memories upon memories of children and grandchildren and great-grandchildren and pain and pain and pain and *crushing, crushing pain*—I moved past all that, and I found the two things I sought, and I ripped them away, as fast as I could.

"Done," I said, and threw the shoe into the backseat. I didn't want to look at it anymore.

"You . . . stole something?" she said, straightening up so she could meet my eyes. "From Willow?"

I slumped down, letting the cool leather of the passenger's seat cradle me. I nodded. "I stole her consciousness. And her ability to feel pain."

Confusion creased Aunt Holly's face. For the space of three seconds, I had no idea why. But when Aunt Holly spoke again, it wasn't to ask me why I'd done what I'd done. What she asked was, "How?"

It hit me then. Spread like ice water through the pit of my stomach.

"No, no, shit, no. I shouldn't have been able to—it was supposed to be *gone*," I said, my voice frantic as my heart pounded against my ribs. "Why isn't it gone? The Cliff's the reason we have magic in the first place, isn't it?"

Aunt Holly's lips thinned. She shook her head. "Ma's children inherited their magic from their father. Not the Cliff. The Cliff just shaped it."

Of course. I was such an idiot. I'd heard that part of the story, too. I just hadn't bothered remembering it.

"Then I did all that for nothing," I said. "I . . . I wanted to fix us. Make us normal."

"Isn't that what you just did?" said Aunt Holly. "We don't have to keep the Cliff intact anymore. We don't have a reason to keep stealing."

I swallowed hard. "We also don't have a reason to *stop* stealing. I wanted to make it so we couldn't do it anymore."

Out of the corner of my eye, I saw her face change as she began to understand. I saw my intentions reflected in the line between her eyebrows as they furrowed, in the thin set of her lips, in the way her nostrils flared as she breathed deep.

I saw her see me for what I was. Not a person willing and able to make the choice to stop stealing, but a person who preferred to have the choice taken away from him, so he'd never have to make it again.

"I see," she said at last.

I covered my face with my hands. I'd basically killed my not-quite-grandmother, and nothing had even changed. I could still reach and steal, and so could all the rest of her hundreds of descendants. There was nothing stopping me from being the same selfish asshole I'd been when I'd arrived here.

"How long have you known the truth about Ma?" asked Aunt Holly. "I mean, the truth about . . . how Heather . . . um . . ."

"Only since tonight," I replied, my skin crawling at the memory of Willow taking me out to the tree. "I'd've told you when you came home, but you were a little bit . . . you know."

"Upset at Leah," she supplied.

"Yeah."

There was silence, then. Off in the distance, the very edge of the sky began to turn purple.

"We'll have to tell your father," said Aunt Holly, drumming her index finger on the steering wheel.

"And everyone else," I said.

She wrinkled her nose. "As if they care. Come on. Let's go home."

Right. The rambling mansion, with its turrets and its history and its attic full of strangers' forgotten May Day tokens. And its lack of Willow.

"That place isn't home," I murmured.

Aunt Holly gave me a tight little smile. "I know the feeling."

I offered to be the one to call my dad, but in the end it was Aunt Holly who did it. She told him that she was driving with me down to the city that very afternoon, and that he'd get the full story when we arrived. I packed up my stuff and threw it into Aunt Holly's car. She'd packed a suitcase, too.

I plugged my phone into the car's speakers and cranked up music as loud as Aunt Holly could stand it. That way, we had an excuse not to talk. We'd done plenty of talking before we left Three Peaks, and all I wanted to do now was think. About what I'd tried and failed to do, and about what that meant for my future.

Because if I was really going to try and be a decent person from now on—a person who *didn't* suck the life out of every single friend he ever had—it was going to take a lot more than knocking down a mountain and expecting all my problems to be over. It was going to take effort. Willpower. It was going to mean giving up a lot of shortcuts that I'd always taken for granted.

It was going to mean starting over.

Fortunately, I knew someone who could help me with that.

When we hit the city, Aunt Holly dropped me off at Penn Station, just like we'd planned.

"Are you sure about this?" she asked, as she pulled over. A cab honked at us. She ignored it. "Reaching is a huge part of your life. All our lives. And quitting cold turkey . . . it's not easy. Trust me."

"I still have to try," I said. "Can you pop the trunk?"

She did, and I dragged my suitcase onto the curb. She rolled down the passenger window and leaned over. "Aspen. Before you go, I just wanted to say . . . I think you did a good thing. Okay?"

I clutched at my neck. Not because it hurt. Just out of habit.

"What Willow did was her choice." Aunt Holly's voice was firm, even though her eyes were starting to look watery. "She could have lived. She chose not to. You understand?"

I nodded. I understood that better than Aunt Holly, even. I was the one who'd seen Willow's face in the moment she'd decided to jump. I could *still* see it.

I could still see her falling, too.

"I have to go," I said. "My train's really soon."

Aunt Holly forced a smile. "Take care of yourself, okay? And text me when you get there, just so we know you're safe."

We. My aunt and my dad. I wondered how long she'd stay with him. Or, hey, maybe she'd just move in. We had an extra room, and I couldn't see her wanting to go back to Three Peaks any time soon.

Or she could have my room, maybe.

It wasn't rush hour, so there were no lines for the ticket machines. My suitcase and I headed down the escalator and onto the LIRR train waiting on the tracks.

I didn't call ahead.

The walk from the train station to the house was a short one, and soon enough I found myself lugging my suitcase up the three steps to the porch. I rang the door-bell. I couldn't tell if anyone was home, since the garage was closed and the curtains were drawn and—

The door opened. In the pale hallway light was a face I hadn't seen in nearly six months. I tried for a smile. It didn't quite work.

"Aspen," she whispered.

"Hi, Mom." I hesitated for only a moment, then asked, "Can I come in?"

ACKNOWLEDGMENTS

Thanks to all those who helped me write this book. You know who you are, but in case you don't . . .

To my family: You guys rock. Thanks for rocking.

To Jess Verdi and Corey Haydu: Thanks for your early reads, back when this thing was still an amoeba instead of a book.

To Nikki Vassallo: Thanks for those evil drinks of yours. Apparently they, uh, made an impression.

To Amie Kaufman: Thanks for filling me with Australian wine, dunking me in the hot springs, and then solving the entire middle of my book without even trying.

To Alison Cherry, Michelle Schusterman, Nina Lourie, and Jeri Smith-Ready: Thank you for reading this thing five billion times, for all your notes and suggestions, for all the months of brainstorming and replotting, and for being generally amazing at life.

To everyone at Penguin (especially Claire Evans) and Greenburger (especially Wendi Gu): Thanks for everything you've all done in support of my work.

To Brenda Bowen: Thanks for basically being my publishing therapist. And for the tattoo! That's how author/ agent relationships are supposed to work, right? Totally.

To Kathy Dawson: Thanks for always getting what I'm going for, even when I don't. You are terrifyingly awesome.

To everyone reading this book: Thank you for reading this book!

TURN THE PAGE FOR A PREVIEW OF LINDSAY RIBAR'S ENCHANTING FIRST NOVEL:

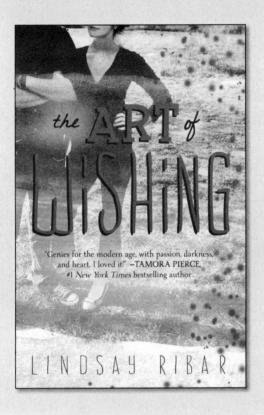

the ART of WISHING

"Genies for the modern age, with passion, darkness, and heart. I loved it!" –TAMORA PIERCE, #1 *New York Times* bestselling author

LINDSAY RIBAR

"Stands head and shoulders above the competition because of its main character Margo . . . a decisive, strong-willed heroine."
—Tor.com

"Rich with romance, magic, and action, this novel will captivate teens."
—*SLJ*

Prologue

The plan was this: I'd get up on that stage, blow them away with the best damn audition they'd ever seen, and walk out knowing the part I wanted was mine.

And when I was called into the auditorium, that was exactly how it happened.

I walked over to the piano and handed my sheet music to George. "You know this one?" I asked him.

He peered quickly at the title. Nodded and said, "Yup." Of course he did. Silly question.

George flexed his fingers, and I strode up the little side staircase and onto the stage. Bright lights flooded my face, but I was used to that. I shielded my eyes so I could focus on the lone figure sitting in the first row: Miss Delisio, math teacher by day and play director by night. I smiled warmly at her. This was the woman who was going to cast me in my dream role.

"Margo McKenna," she said in greeting. "I do love a straight-A trig student with stage presence. How's calculus treating you?"

1

I wrinkled my nose. "Straight A minuses this year. Calc is hard. Who knew?"

Miss Delisio laughed appreciatively. "Why do you think I don't teach it?" she said. "All right, what are you singing for us today?"

"I'm doing 'Last Midnight' from *Into the Woods* by Stephen Sondheim," I recited.

"Great song," she said. "Whenever you're ready."

This was it. I took a moment to steady myself, then nodded to George. On my cue, he started playing. I molded my body into the shape of the song, and the lyrics flowed out of me like I owned them. For those few minutes, I became someone totally different from my real self. Someone worldly and manipulative. Someone with very real power.

I'd chosen "Last Midnight" because of that power. And as the song grew in intensity, and my performance grew to match, and the air in the theater seemed to dance to the rhythm of George's piano and my voice . . . I knew I'd chosen right.

When I finished, a couple of breaths passed before anyone said anything.

"That was lovely, Margo," said Miss Delisio. I couldn't see her face, but I could hear the smile in her voice. "Really, really lovely."

"Yup," said George.

"Thanks," I said breathlessly.

I heard the rustle of a notebook page being flipped. "Stick

around for a little while, okay?" said Miss Delisio. "We'll pair you up and have you read from the script."

"Sounds good," I said. "I'll be in the hallway."

Naomi Sloane, my best friend and Miss Delisio's stage manager, was manning the door that stood between me and the hallway full of nervous students outside. She gave me a thumbs-up as I approached her.

"McKenna, you just nailed that," she said. "Don't tell the masses, but you're the best audition I've seen so far."

I flashed her a coy smile. "I bet you say that to all the girls."

She laughed and held the door open for me, and I floated out into the hallway as she called the next student's name. Sure, I still had to do the reading part of the audition, but that would be a piece of cake. The hard part—the important part—was over. And Naomi was right.

I'd nailed it.

Chapter ONE

Sweeney Todd is a musical about cannibalism. More specifically, it's a musical about a barber named Benjamin Barker,
alias Sweeney Todd, who kills his customers and gives the bodies to his landlady, Mrs. Lovett, so she can turn them into meat
pies and serve them to people. There's a lot more to it than
that—love and obsession and revenge, everything you'd expect
to find in a good musical—but for most people, cannibalism is
the show's biggest selling point.

For me, though, it was all about the music. Nothing in the
entire universe made me happier than sinking my teeth into
a really juicy song and performing it for anyone willing to listen—and of all the musicals I've ever loved, *Sweeney Todd* was
the ultimate source for juicy songs. Especially if you were playing Mrs. Lovett, which was exactly what I planned to do.

A week after the auditions, Miss Delisio announced that she'd
made her casting decisions and the list would be up at the end
of the day. So when the last bell rang, I raced out of my last class
and up to the theater. There was already a throng of drama club

students milling around the door. A piece of light green paper was there, held up with Scotch tape.

I started pushing my way through the crowd, but a hand on my shoulder stopped me before I could get very far. "Congrats, girl!" said Naomi, pulling me into a quick hug. "You got a lead. Told you so, didn't I?"

Naomi had never been interested in acting, but she'd stage-managed our shows ever since freshman year. She was a natural at it, too: level-headed, loud, and popular enough that people actually listened when she told them to do things.

"Really?" I said, returning her grin. "Wait, don't tell me. I want to see for myself."

Call it superstition, but even in a case like this, where I knew beyond a doubt what part I'd gotten, I had to see it in writing before I let it become real. *Margaret McKenna—Mrs. Lovett.* Ever since Miss Delisio had announced that *Sweeney Todd* would be our spring musical, I'd pictured those words in my head, willing them to come true.

I skirted around Naomi and wove through a bunch of guys high-fiving each other, until finally I reached the cast list. It only took a few seconds for me to zero in on my name, about half-way down the green paper. I followed the line that would lead me to the name of my character.

Margaret McKenna—Tobias Ragg.

No way.

The chatter around me dissolved into white noise, and I

blinked a couple times, just to make sure I wasn't imagining things. I traced the line with my finger. No, I'd really been cast as Tobias Ragg. Toby, who only had a couple of songs. Toby, who was young and simple-minded, the exact opposite of the devious and amazing Mrs. Lovett, who I was certain I'd get to be.

Toby, who was a boy.

I mean, sure, I was short and kind of flat-chested, but come on. . . .

"I'm Toby," I said to myself, trying the idea on for size. It didn't fit.

"Yeah," came Naomi's voice from just over my shoulder. Apparently she'd followed me through the crowd. I turned to her, and her congratulatory smile faltered when she saw my face. "Listen, I know you wanted Mrs. Lovett, but Toby's still a really good part. You'll be so awesome."

But her consolation-prize words washed over me, totally devoid of meaning. "Who *is* playing Lovett?" I asked. I hadn't even thought to check. "Wait. Don't tell me."

So she didn't. She just bit her lip and waited for me to find the name. Find it I did. Recognize it, I did not.

"Who the hell is Victoria Willoughbee?"

Naomi went quiet for a moment, her face frozen in an expression that I couldn't read. "You know Vicky," she said at last. "Sophomore? Plays clarinet in the band?" Nothing rang a bell, so I just shook my head. Naomi shrugged. "Well, she's nice."

"But why—"

"Woo-hoo!" came a shout, so close it made me flinch. Just behind me was Simon Lee, looking over my head at the cast list. "I'm Sweeney Effing Todd, suckers! I am the Asian Johnny Depp! I've always said that! Haven't I? Haven't I always said that?"

He punched the air, and a few people yelled out their congratulations and gave him those back-thumping man-hugs. Nobody seemed to begrudge him the lead role, or even the bizarre victory dance he was now doing. Mostly because we all knew he was the most talented boy in the entire school. Not to mention the cutest.

Simon found me in the crowd and gave me one of those lopsided grins that made my chest feel like a tiny hot-air balloon. That was when it hit me.

I wouldn't get to be Simon's costar.

Suddenly, I was absolutely certain I was about to lose it. I had to get out of there. I couldn't let all these people see me cry over a part in a high school musical. Especially not Simon.

"Congratulations," I managed to choke out, and ran like hell toward the girls' bathroom.

I didn't even see the boy coming around the corner until I bumped right into him. My shoulder smacked into his arm with a force that nearly spun me off my feet.

"Sorry!" he said automatically, stepping gingerly out of my way as I looked up in alarm to see who it was. I didn't know him.

But his eyes widened as he looked down at me. "Margo," he said. "Oh. I'm really, *really* sorry."

I gave him a quick once-over—dark hair, light eyes, thin and wiry, cute enough in a nondescript sort of way—but no, I definitely didn't know him. "Sorry about what? Who are you?"

"Nobody," he said quickly, holding his hands up like a white flag. "I'm nobody. Never mind."

I darted past him. Out of the corner of my eye, I saw him turn to watch me go.

The bathroom smelled faintly of weed and cigarettes, and the powers that be had long since stopped scrubbing away the rude graffiti that covered the walls, but at least it was empty. Feeling about nine years old, I locked myself in a stall, drew my knees up to my chin, and shut my eyes.

Miss Delisio always gave the lead roles to seniors. That was how it worked. You paid your underclassman dues in the chorus, or maybe in small roles if you were lucky, and then you got a good part right before you graduated. So why were the rules different for that Vicky Willoughbee girl?

I only allowed myself out of the stall when I'd calmed down enough to form a new plan of action. If I couldn't be Mrs. Lovett, then I would be the sort of person who was totally okay with *not* being Mrs. Lovett. I smiled at myself in the bathroom mirror until it looked real, and then I took a deep breath and headed back toward the theater for the first rehearsal.

Miss Delisio was already sitting primly on the stage when I came in. In addition to being my tenth-grade trig teacher, she'd directed every musical I'd been in since freshman year. I liked her well enough—but sitting next to her, wearing tight jeans, clunky boots, and a black biker jacket, was the real talent: George the Music Ninja.

Even when George was just noodling around on the piano during breaks, it was like listening to some crazy musical genius at work. And that wasn't even counting his other job. When he wasn't musical-directing us, he was the front man of an indie band called Apocalypse Later. He didn't write their music, which probably explained why I wasn't totally sold on their sound, but his vocals and guitar solos were absolutely killer.

"Grab your script and have a seat," Miss Delisio announced in her usual buoyant voice. "We'll start as soon as everyone's here."

One by one, we made our way up to the stage, where there was a pile of scripts, each labeled with the name of an actor and the role they were playing. I watched Miss Delisio closely as I approached, wondering if she would say anything to me. She knew I wanted to be Mrs. Lovett. In fact, last time I spoke to her, she'd stopped just short of outright promising me the role. Would she bother to explain why she'd given it to someone else?

Apparently not. By the time I reached the stage and fished my script from the pile, she and George were engrossed in conversation. I took a deep breath. It didn't matter, I reminded myself. What's done is done. I was okay with it. No, I was more than okay; I was going to kick ass in this role.

Most of the actors with leads had settled in the front row: Callie Zumsky as Johanna, MaLinda Jones as Pirelli, Dan Quimby-Sato as Anthony, Ryan Weiss as Judge Turpin, Jill Spalding as the Beggar Woman. All seniors, of course. But I joined Naomi in the second row instead.

"You okay, McKenna?" whispered Naomi as I sat down beside her.

"Why wouldn't I be?" I whispered back. "Just because Sophomore McWhatserface got Lovett and I didn't?"

Naomi snickered. "You mean Willoughbee," she said, trying and failing to sound disapproving.

I grinned. "That's what I said. Anyway, whatever. I'm over it."

"You don't look over it."

I raised an eyebrow at her. "Perhaps your eyes deceive you."

She looked like she wanted to press the issue, but I was saved by the arrival of Simon, who slid into the empty seat on my other side. "Heya, Toby," he said, grinning.

There was something witty I could say in response to that. I was sure of it. Unfortunately, the best my brain could cough up was: "Actually, it's Margo."

He feigned shock and slapped his forehead with his palm. "Duh. I'm always doing that. Calling people Toby. When will I ever learn?"

Something witty. Something witty. I needed to think of something witty.

But his arm kept brushing against mine as he arranged his stuff on the floor, and that was enough to distract me. I was just about to give up on being witty and blurt out something inane like "Never, I guess," when Miss Delisio began to shush us.

"We've got almost everyone," she said, frowning down at the scripts beside her. "We're just missing Vicky—oh, there she is!"

Her gaze shifted to the back of the auditorium, and everyone twisted around to see who she was looking at. There, at the top of the left aisle, was a girl I was pretty sure I'd never seen before. Clutching a small pile of books to her chest, she hesitated there like she'd been caught in the act of . . . what? Walking into a room?

This was the girl who'd been cast in the role of a lifetime?

"Here you go," said Miss Delisio, holding out a script. Hugging her books closer, Vicky darted down the aisle to collect it. Miss Delisio, beaming, said something I couldn't hear, and Vicky gave her a tight smile in return. Miss Delisio gestured to the front row.

But the front row had already filled up. Vicky hesitated again, and for one relieved moment I was sure she would head toward the back, with the other underclassmen.

Then Simon waved at her. "Saved you a seat over here!" he called, much to my dismay. Vicky slid into the seat on Simon's other side as he gave her his trademark arched-eyebrow smile.

The one that made my heart beat just a little faster when he used it on me. The one that, last spring, had led to an incredibly awesome kiss at the cast party of *Bat Boy: The Musical*. The kiss had never been repeated. In fact, after that night he'd never even brought it up again. But still: awesome.

Vicky, however, seemed oblivious to his flirty look.

"Margo, right?" she whispered to me, across Simon.

"That's me."

"I saw you as Ruthie in *Bat Boy* last year. You were really good."

"Thanks," I said, and smiled at her, exactly like I'd practiced in the bathroom mirror. I was okay with this. I was not allowed to hate Vicky Willoughbee.

Once we were settled, Miss Delisio introduced George, like there was anyone here who didn't know him. He flashed us a grin and settled himself at the piano. We wouldn't be singing today, since we hadn't officially learned the songs yet, but that didn't mean he couldn't underscore us. He began to play the opening bars of the show, and a little shiver flitted up my spine.

With Naomi reading stage directions, we jumped right in. As usual, speaking the lyrics was odd since, without rhythms and melody, lyrics just sound like really weird poetry. But this was the way the first rehearsal always went: just a read-through, so we could all learn the story together. Most of us were used to it. Some people, like Simon, even managed to make it sound kind of good.

Vicky, however, was no Simon. She read all of her lyrics in

an awful monotone, like she couldn't quite figure out what the words meant. And it wasn't just the lyrics, either. The way she read the dialogue was just as bad. It was all I could do not to cover my ears and run screaming out of the theater.

When we finally reached the end of Act One, Miss Delisio called a ten-minute break. I thought about going outside, but when Vicky got up, I decided to stay right where I was. Running into her in the hallway and accidentally punching her in the face were definitely not part of my I'm-okay-with-this plan.

As I skimmed the second half of the script, I saw a student approach Miss Delisio. A student who wasn't in the cast, which was a little unusual. It took me a minute, but I recognized him as the boy from earlier. The one I'd almost mowed down on my way to the bathroom.

He spoke with Miss Delisio and George for a few moments before digging through the pockets of the hoodie he wore, then through the backpack he'd slung over one shoulder. He pulled out what looked like a camera case. I heard the word *yearbook* come out of someone's mouth, and I groaned softly as I realized what was going on. They were starting rehearsal photo shoots this early in the game? Not fair.

When the cast had settled back in their seats and quieted, Miss Delisio took a moment to confirm my fears.

"Guys, this is Oliver Parish." The boy gave a shy little wave to nobody in particular. "He just transferred here in January. He's going to be photographing our rehearsal process for the drama club's section of the yearbook. And maybe, if we're lucky, he'll get enough to put together a slide show for our cast party."

Naomi nudged me and rolled her eyes, which made me grin. I looked at Simon, to see what he thought of this turn of events, but he was busy typing out a text message on his phone. Beside him, though, Vicky was watching Oliver. And she wasn't wearing that timid, deer-in-the-headlights expression from before. She was absolutely beaming.

I looked at the photographer. He smiled back at Vicky, like there was a secret in the room, and they were the only two people who knew it.

The porch lights were already on when I got home that night, and my mom's car sat ominously in the driveway. And the house, as I'd feared, was a mess. There were coats draped over the back of the couch, shoes strewn all around the floor, and four suitcases in the hallway, one of which was open and spilling clothes everywhere. I tried not to think about how I'd cleaned this room just three days ago.

Ziggy was the first to greet me when I opened the door, jumping off her perch on the couch and rubbing herself against my legs. She purred as I bent to scritch her little tabby head. "Did Mommy and Daddy come home?" I whispered to her. "Did they remember to feed you?"

"Margo?" came Mom's voice from the kitchen. "Honey, is that you?"

I rolled my eyes. "No, it's a burglar. I've come to steal all your silverware and jewelry. And your cat," I added, giving Ziggy another scratch.

"As long as you don't steal our daughter," she replied. Emerging from the kitchen with a huge grin on her face and Dad trailing behind her, she gave me a quick hug and a peck on the forehead.

"How was the cruise?" I asked, unzipping my boots and placing them neatly on the shoe rack by the door. I'd deal with my parents' shoes later.

She sighed dramatically. "Absolute heaven. Maybe even better than the last one. I know they say you should wait for summer to visit Alaska, but what's a little cold?"

"Cold schmold," added Dad. "That's what the parkas were for. Not to mention the indoor cabin."

Mom gave him a secretive little smile. "The honeymoon suite, you mean."

"Honeymoon suite, still?" I asked, doing my best to ignore the dewy-eyed looks they were exchanging. "What is this, the third honeymoon you've been on since the wedding?"

Mom thought for a moment. "Fourth, if you count the Grand Canyon trip."

"Which I do," said Dad. "Oh, and we have pictures!" He ran over to the open suitcase and began rifling through it. "Wait till you see these, Margo. Some of the ones your mother took are just, wow."

Ever since the wedding last May, our lives had been one continuous cycle of Mom and Dad planning a trip, Mom and Dad leaving on their trip, a week or two of peace and quiet, Mom and Dad coming back from their trip, and the grand finale, Mom and Dad showing me pictures of their trip. The pictures were always the same, too: Mom pretending to fall over the railing of a cruise ship, Dad wearing another cheesy Hawaiian shirt, stuff like that. Sometimes it felt like they were the teenagers and I was the adult.

"How's school?" asked Mom. "Anything exciting happen while we were gone?"

"Nope," I said quickly. "Same old same old."

I thought about telling her about the cast list fiasco, but this wasn't the time. At best, they'd both go "Aw, that's too bad" and jump right back into honeymoon talk. At worst, they wouldn't even understand why I was so upset. As far as they were concerned, it didn't matter what role I had, as long as their daughter was onstage. These were, after all, the people who'd thrown me a party after I'd played Frightened Theatergoer Number Two in my first-grade musical about Abraham Lincoln.

"Where did I put that camera?" muttered Dad.

"Red suitcase, inside pocket, next to the toothbrushes," replied Mom almost absently, and then turned back to me. "You'll never guess what movie was playing on the plane today. *The Parent Trap.* Can you believe it?"

"Oh, I almost forgot about that!" said Dad, unzipping the red suitcase.

"It was the old Hayley Mills one," said Mom. "The good one, not the remake they did with that awful drug addict girl."

I was about to point out that Lindsay Lohan probably hadn't been a drug addict at the time, but Mom continued, "And we said, take away the twin thing and the summer camp, and that's our Margo! Making us back into one big, happy family."

"It wasn't exactly me," I said, but neither of them seemed to notice.

"Aw, Celia," said Dad. Camera finally in hand, he came back over and enveloped us in a bear hug. Mom hugged back just as hard, so I did too.

If I'd been a character in a musical, this would have been the point where the lights went down on my parents, leaving them slow-dancing in the background like living scenery, as I stepped forward into a lone spotlight for my big solo. It would be a quirky ballad, probably called "I Am Not Hayley Mills" or something like that, and people would applaud when I was done. Maybe they'd even give me a standing ovation.

Of course, people don't usually get standing ovations in their living rooms, but I still toyed with the idea of dashing upstairs, pulling out my guitar, and writing that song. It wasn't worth it, though. I'd tried a million different times to write a million different songs about a million different things, but it was never worth it. My songs always sucked.

MARGO'S STORY CONTINUES IN *THE FOURTH WISH*, THE SEQUEL TO *THE ART OF WISHING*:

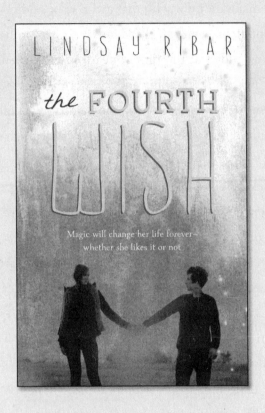

LINDSAY RIBAR

the FOURTH WISH

Magic will change her life forever—
whether she likes it or not

"The truths this novel reveals are
so real . . . quite an achievement."
—*Kirkus Reviews*

"Ribar has delivered fans a fun romantic read with
some deliciously exciting paranormal elements (shape-shifting
anyone?) while casually tackling bisexuality, consent, and
the importance of balancing power with humanity."
—*SLJ*